SAVING ANGEL

DIVISA SERIES BOOK ONE

J. L. WEIL

DARK MAGICK PUBLISHING, LLC

ALSO BY J. L. WEIL

THE DIVISA SERIES

(Full series completed – Teen Paranormal Romance)

Losing Emma: A Divisa novella

Saving Angel

Hunting Angel

Breaking Emma: A Divisa novella

Chasing Angel

Loving Angel

Redeeming Angel

LUMINESCENCE TRILOGY

(Full series completed – Teen Paranormal Romance)

Luminescence

Amethyst Tears

Moondust

Darkmist – A Luminescence novella

RAVEN SERIES

(Full series completed – Teen Paranormal Romance)

White Raven

Black Crow

Soul Symmetry

CHAPTER 1

This sucked.

We had been on the road for three days. Three. Long. Boring. Days.

I missed the Arizona heat. It was like a slap in the face—*crack*. Nothing would ever be the same. Miles and miles stretched between me and everything I'd left behind. I wasn't entirely opposed to the idea of moving; what I was opposed to was where we were moving. My face was pressed to the car window as I watched the sign pass by: Spring Valley, Illinois. A population of 5,558. Correction: 5,560. Unfortunately.

Flashback to a year ago.

I was living in a cozy condo in Tucson. School was school. I had a handful of friends. No boyfriend, and I doubt living in this small town that that status would change. But none of those things gave me nightmares.

It was the memories of my parents screaming at all hours because Dad was drunk again. Shocker. He'd spent the last few years in a drunken stupor, leaving Mom to shoulder all the responsibility. It was the tears I heard her cry when she thought I was tucked in for the night and fast asleep.

But it was one fateful night I knew my life would never be the same. The night my dad became a murderer.

I let out a heavy sigh, bracing myself for the first sight of my new home.

The one-stoplight town was freakishly small—if you could call it that—nothing like Tucson. There were more wheat fields here than residents. I felt so isolated. The closest city was Princeton, a good twenty minutes away. A country girl I was not. They had grain elevators for God's sake. What the hell were grain elevators? I couldn't even Google it.

Savage.

Thank God it had a library, or I might have forced Mom to turn the car around. At least at the library, I might be able to check out movies or video games. As far as I was concerned, it was the only thing this town had going for it.

Pathetic.

Mom put the car into park. "What do you think?"

She didn't really want to know what I thought. "Tell me we're stopping to stretch our legs."

"Angel."

I stared at the large, old, brick farmhouse and repressed the urge to shiver. It looked like nothing but ghosts and spiders had lived in it for the past decade.

What had Mom been thinking?

Apparently, that we were in need of a fresh start, a chance to start over and leave the past behind.

A past I was glad to say *au revoir* to.

But this wasn't the kind of fresh start I had envisioned. I was thinking more along the lines of somewhere exciting, like Miami, Chicago, or Laguna Beach. The kids there always looked happy. Not the middle of nowhere.

The movers had already been here and graciously dropped off our stuff. The house gave me the heebie-jeebies. As I climbed the stairs, I jumped at every creak and groan. I would swear by the Bible this place was alive, haunted, or, in reality, über-old. Sure, it was a ton bigger than the condo we used to live in, but there hadn't been any dead spirits lurking in the corners or cobwebs the size of my head. I shuddered to think about what kind of spiders spun webs like that.

As I regarded the stacked boxes littering my *new* room, the idea of unpacking made me groan. There was so much to do. Maybe I should suggest we stay in a motel ... like two towns over.

Moving blows.

My room wasn't atrocious, but it definitely wasn't the Ritz. It would be fan-freaking-tastic if this place came with unpacking faeries, because I hated the thought of unloading all these boxes as much as I despised being here. Not only had I had to leave everything I'd ever known behind, I was now stuck in some Podunk town in the middle of nowhere.

No freaking joke. I wasn't even sure that Spring Valley was a blip on the map.

I sighed, wishing that at least the Internet had been hooked up. Was that too much to ask after everything? My emails were probably flooded with junk, my Xbox heavily collecting dust, and I was having Call of Duty withdrawals. Not having the Xbox to tool around with was like having my arm or leg cut off.

I was a complete gamer. Mom didn't understand my gaming obsession or the escape it gave me from my real life. Right now, it was all I had to keep me grounded and sane. The move, my friends, my dad ... It was the fascinating worlds, the zombie maps, and the enthralling stories that were my safe haven.

Sitting on the edge of my bare bed, I brushed the dark hair out of my face.

I missed my life before everything changed—that split second when my life shattered.

Before Dad turned into a raging alcoholic.

Before all the heated arguments.

Before the drunken late nights.

Before I lost my life, when everything had been perfect and we'd been happy.

Family vacations to Florida, swimming at the beach, picnicking, and having to swat away the overeager seagulls that tried to steal our food. Mom rolling on the sand laughing or curled up on the couch with Dad … it all seemed like yesterday.

Now, our family was broken. Torn apart. There were no more good-bye kisses before work, no movies on Saturday night. Instead, it was just Mom and me. Well, mostly just me.

My eyes welled up, and I swiped the tears away quickly, refusing to let them roll down my freckle-dusted cheeks. I refused to cry. Crying didn't change the past, and it wouldn't change the fact that I now lived in Hicktown, USA.

Thanks Daddy dearest.

Dad was currently a ward of the Arizona Department of Corrections. How was that for a dysfunctional family? Mine pretty much took the cake.

As soon as the divorce papers had been signed, ink not even dry, I found myself in a mad dash across borders—everything we owned trailing behind us, and some guy, a mere shadow of the man I remembered, locked behind bars.

I knew he was my dad, but after everything, he was as good as dead to me.

Mom wanted to forget his existence. I'd chosen to block most of it from my memory, a little self-induced blackout. My heart ached for the loss of both parents.

Mom was no longer the same either.

Gone was the maternal mother with her whiskey-colored eyes, so opposite of my own dark blue. In her place was a woman given a second chance. She was still Mom but with a carefree youth to her—a single woman for the first time in twenty years. I think she had decided life was too short. Sometimes she was more like my best friend than a mom, always saying something totally inappropriate.

Ever since Dad *disappeared*, she'd been working like a madwoman, doing everything in her power to create a better life for us, including breaking her back with long hours at as many jobs as she could handle in a twenty-four day, which had been too many and another reason for the move.

She was now a second shift employee for the Princeton police department as a dispatcher. Her new schedule included many twelve-plus-hour days, meaning I was going to be spending a lot of time alone. No big deal, except the whole dilemma with the no Internet yet thing. Who in their right mind would want to spend the remainder of their summer vacation closed up in this spooky house with no access to the *real* world?

Hell no. Not me.

I guess I should have thanked my lucky stars that I had bought a slew of new Xbox games before leaving Tucson. Only problem: I didn't know where to start looking.

Opening a box in front of me, I realized there were no faeries coming to help me unpack. I'll admit I was disappointed. How kickass would it be if faeries were real? I was totally down for a little bit of faerie dust here and there. It might make this place smell less like an old, musky barn.

The room was a decent size. I tried to envision my four-poster white bedroom set and, most importantly, where I was going to set up my TV.

Decisions. Decisions.

First order of business: get Internet. This wasn't the blasted Stone Age. *Please, please tell me we get cable in the backwoods.*

Scanning the room, I decided to screw the boxes. There was always tomorrow, and the day after, and the day after that. It wasn't as if they were going anywhere and neither was I.

I raced down the stairs into what was supposed to be a kitchen. It didn't look like much yet with stuff scattered haphazardly.

Mom was sitting on a bar stool, staring at the mess scattered over the house. There wasn't a counter without clutter or a free space on the floor.

I maneuvered my way over the couch, zigzagging through the crap. She was wearing the same facial expression I had moments ago.

"Hey, sweetie, you finish unpacking?" We shared the same dry humor.

"Hilarious," I replied, plopping my bony butt down onto a stool next to her.

If there was one thing Mom had going for her, it was her sense of humor. She was also beautiful. Her body was curvy in all the right places. That was another thing that had changed. She dressed like a Victoria Secret model now. Was it normal to be jealous of your own mother?

The light brown of her shiny hair caught against the lamplight. She had boobs that were envy-worthy, where I had none to speak of. Okay, maybe I didn't have the chest of a twelve-year-old boy, but seriously, an A cup was nothing to boast about.

"Should I order you a pizza before I leave?" She had to work tonight. Our first night in our new home and I was going to be spending it alone. Joy.

"You mean they have pizza here?" The mention of food sent my belly rumbling, reminding me I'd skipped lunch.

"Give it a shot, Angel. It might not be that bad," she said, pulling out her phone.

"It could be worse," I mumbled under my breath.

She gave me the eye, which promptly turned into the sweetest smile this side of the Mississippi when the pizza clerk answered the phone. I bit my nails while I waited for her to finish repeating our address—a disgusting habit I couldn't seem to break.

"What time is your shift?" I asked after she hung up, wondering when she would be home. I wasn't exactly thrilled at being in the haunted house by myself.

"I work from three to three. As soon as I have a day off, we'll get this place in …" she scanned the array of boxes strewn all over the rooms, "… order." She cringed, fishing her fingers through her hair.

Village Pizza wasn't freaking fast, but to pass the time, we managed to dig out a couple plates and glasses. When the doorbell finally rang, I jumped out of my seat not because I was so hungry I thought I might pass out, but because the sound of the bell had a Halloween tone to it. The creepy feelings came back.

Mom beamed at the delivery boy, who was not much older than me, flashing perfect, pearly teeth. "Keep the change."

OMG. Mom is turning into a cougar.

I wanted to crawl under the counter and die, but I was sidetracked by the smells. My mouth literally watered on sight. I put a hand to my stomach to try and quiet the grumbling. "I'm starved." I didn't even bother with a plate. Biting into a heap of cheesy goodness, I sighed. *Yum. Heaven.* "This is amazing," I declared, chomping on a mouthful of pizza paradise. The flavors popped.

She sat beside me with her plate. "It is, isn't it? Chicago style pizza … how did we live without it?"

I was too busy shoving my face to respond. After a moment of her eyeing me thoughtfully, I couldn't stand it anymore. "What?" I asked.

"Are you sure you're okay? I know how hard this has all been on you." Meaning the move, Dad, a new school … the list was growing.

Most parents thought twice about leaving their teenage daughter alone so often. Not mine. She didn't even bat an eye. Did I mention that she wasn't like most moms? And I think it made me love her more for it. With Dad, there had always been trust issues, but with just the two of us, we both realized the importance of trust and relying on each other.

"Mom, I'm fine," I assured her. She didn't look convinced. "Really," I stressed. I didn't want her worrying about me. She had enough of her own stuff to deal with without adding my pile of crap on top.

She let it go … for now, but I think we both knew she wouldn't stop fretting over me. "Are you excited for school? I bet they have some really hot guys here." She dangled the sentence in front of me like a tempting Snickers bar.

I choked on a pepperoni slice, tomato sauce burning up my nose. She couldn't possibly be serious. "I guess," I managed, after taking a swig of pop to ease the burn and wash down the food stuck in my throat. "If you're into hillbillies, overalls, accents thick enough to cut glass, and beer bellies." Confession: I didn't actually know if anyone here had accents, but I didn't see how they wouldn't.

Her eyes sparkled. "You might be surprised. I bet there is a hottie or two."

Goodie gumdrops. My first boyfriend is going to be a farmer.

"Gross, Mom. Stop. If you dig a hole any deeper, I won't be able to pull you out."

"Have you met our neighbors yet?" she asked with a cunning smile, like she had a secret she was dying to spill.

I gave her a strange look, wondering if she was self-medicating. "No. Should I be stalking them or something?" We had only been here a hot minute. Okay, so it was more like five hours, but what did she expect me to do? Knock on their door and ask if they wanted to play?

"I just thought we should be neighborly, that's all. I want us to get off on the right foot here."

That was all, my ass.

Whatever. I had more important things to talk about than my farm lovin' neighbors. "When are we getting Internet?"

She rolled her eyes. "Angel, a few days without your Xbox won't kill you."

I wasn't so sure about that. "Tell me *we're* getting it at least." I was on the verge of whining.

"Yes," she assured me. "They should be out this weekend, on my day off."

Someone up there must love me. I said a silent prayer of thanks.

Rinsing off my plate, I looked over my shoulder. "Any chance I could go shopping? I was thinking of giving my room a makeover. You know, part of the whole starting over thing." I felt guilty as soon as the words left my mouth. She didn't need me rubbing it in and taking advantage of the situation. I almost opened my mouth to tell her to forget it; I didn't *need* to redecorate. What I had was fine.

She smiled at me sadly. "Of course." Digging in her purse, she pulled out a wad of Lincolns and set them on the counter. "Will that be good?"

"Yeah, Mom … thanks." I went over and gave her a hug. Her arms tightened around me.

"Do you remember how to get into town? Oh, and maybe you should get a new outfit or two," she added, eyeing my clothes.

"What?" I said, glancing down at my tattered jeans—just the way I liked them—and my "Trust Me, I'm A Gamer" T-shirt.

She lifted a brow.

"How about I just run around naked?"

She never missed a beat. "You always were at the height of fashion. Just don't expect me to pick up on that trend."

"*Mom!* Fine," I huffed. "And yes, I remember how to get to town. There is only one street in and out anyway. How hard can it be? I'll probably go tomorrow." Someone had to start on these boxes. It was evident *that* someone was going to be me.

She gathered her purse and paused in the doorway. "Angel?"

"Yeah."

"I love you."

My throat constricted. I swallowed hard. "I love you too."

"Call me if you need anything, and don't work yourself too hard. We'll tackle most of these boxes together this weekend. Got it?"

I nodded, watching her walk out the squeaky old door.

Great. Does anything not make a creepy noise in this house?

Relinquishing, I decided that if she could make an effort, so could I. Once upstairs, I started attacking the boxes. Each item I uncovered brought a new spear of yearning for my old life. The family photos I had in cutesy rhinestone frames, the fabric board with memorabilia of my old friends and school—they were all reminders of what I no longer had.

When I finally found the box with my video games, it was like finding an old friend.

Score.

Gathering the empty cardboard boxes, I carted them outside and placed them at the end of the driveway for pickup.

Looking up, the sky was murky and cloudy. *Does the sun ever shine here in this hellhole?* The warmth was nothing like Arizona with its constant sun and dry heat. By nature, I was a sun seeker. The monotonous sky made me miss the blinding brightness of Tucson. I doubted I could get a proper tan here. The people in this town probably looked like ghosts.

Across the road was a wheat field. Something in the distance caught my eye—a flash of amber—but it was hard to decipher.

I shrugged and dusted off my hands, turning to head back inside, and got the fright of my life. There was a girl about my age a few feet in front of me, stopping me in my tracks. She didn't look like any girl I'd ever seen before.

She was extraordinary. Perfect blonde hair, killer body, and sexy dimples highlighting flawless, plump lips. Her smile was bright and friendly. She looked like someone you would see on Hollywood Boulevard, which suddenly made me feel like *I* was the hick.

Just great, I thought. Why hadn't I at least combed my hair this morning? I still had travel hair, which meant it looked like I'd stuck my finger in a light socket.

And to think I thought I was going to stand out like a sore thumb. She would have stood out even in Tucson. Her legs went on forever, but it was her eyes that captivated me the most. They were the craziest turquoise, like shining gems.

Her smile was warm and welcoming. "Hey. I live next door." She indicated the only other house around for miles. The sound of her voice was sweet and innocent. "I'm Lexi. I hope I didn't startle you. I'm forever doing that."

I brushed a hand over my hair, trying to smooth any flyaways. "I didn't hear you. I'm Angel. We just moved in."

Her smile grew as I introduced myself, which I found a little weird. I was pretty sure I hadn't said anything funny. I usually know. "I saw the moving trucks, and I've been waiting for an excuse to stop over and introduce myself. When I saw you come outside, I couldn't resist." She chatted like a chipmunk on speed. "I hope I'm not inconveniencing you. Unpacking can be such a hassle."

"You have no idea," I muttered. I wasn't entirely sure how I was able to keep up, but I liked her enthusiasm. It was a nice change to all the dullness everywhere. This place was so quiet. No cars driving by, no dogs barking, nothing but the occasional cricket.

"I was so happy when I saw you—a girl my age. As you can see, we're kind of lacking on neighbors."

No shit Sherlock.

"It's been so long since someone lived in your house. I'm glad you guys bought it." She was so sincere and eager; I couldn't help but like her. "Do you have plans tomorrow?" she asked.

"Um," I muttered, caught off guard. "I was thinking about going into town and doing some shopping. Clothes and new bedding—I'm redecorating."

"Shopping!" she said as if it was the magic word. "I love shopping. Any chance you want to hang out? I could show you where all the cool stores are." There was a hint of hopefulness in her tone.

It took me only a second to answer. "Yeah, that would be great." Judging by her clothes, she had great taste. Plus, this was me making an effort. If I was going to be stranded here, it would be really nice to have at least one friend.

"Great. I'm so excited. Just come over when you are ready to leave. It was nice to meet you, Angel. I'll let you get back to unpacking."

"Please don't do me any favors."

She laughed, her dimples peeking out on either side of her rosy cheeks. "You're funny."

I started back up the driveway. "I'm glad you came over, Lexi. See you tomorrow."

Maybe Spring Valley wouldn't be such a bust after all. At the very least, Lexi did not have an accent.

Yay for small pleasures.

CHAPTER 2

The next morning, I moseyed onto the white porch of Lexi's house. This time, I made sure I didn't look like trash. I was dressed in a tank top and shorts that made my butt look outstanding. I hadn't bothered with any makeup though. It was too hot today and would melt off my face anyway.

Pressing the doorbell, I took a step back to wait for Lexi. Nervously, I checked the time on my watch, hoping it wasn't too early. Mom was still asleep from after her shift last night. Shuffling my feet over the wood planks, I whirled around at the sound of footsteps behind me and nearly gave myself whiplash.

Heavy footsteps trudged up the steps. Lifting my gaze from a pair of Converse shoes, I found myself staring at a very defined chest. It hugged against a white T-shirt that left no room to guess how many packs this stomach had—at least six by my count. The well-toned body leaned on the porch column, hiking up the hem of his white shirt just a tad. A line of dark curls peeked out and buried into a pair of low jeans, suction cupped in all the right places.

I sucked in a sharp breath.

I'd seen nice bods before, but this was straight out of an Abercrombie

& Fitch poster ad. My eyes traveled up the length of him as I tried not to let the drool fall out of the side of my mouth. I was pretty sure I had stopped breathing too. His jaw line was chiseled to perfection, and his lips made me want to take a bite. They were full, kissable lips—the kind that just begged for attention and, boy, were they getting plenty from me.

I'd never been the swooning type, but I swore when I looked into his eyes, framed by inky thick lashes, I just about fell over. With my luck, I'd topple right over the porch rail any second now. His eyes were a breathtaking stormy gray. They almost didn't seem real, and they burned into mine. His onyx hair was tousled, like he hadn't been to bed yet, and judging by the time of day, I would say he was very well just getting home.

The images that popped into my head just then had me flushing, and none of it was from the heat. I must have died and gone to hell, because it was surely a sin to look that hot.

Holy crapola.

He lifted a brow studded with a silver bar. "Hello?" His voice was deep, dark, and sounded like a wicked dream. I bet he tasted just as sinful. "Can I help you?" he asked, his tone dipping in annoyance.

I hadn't the foggiest idea how long I had stood on his porch, looking like I'd never seen the male species before, but in my defense, boys my age did not look like him. What had Mom said about there being hotties here?

Bull's-eye.

She was dead on.

He crossed his arms over his chest. "Do you like what you see? A picture lasts longer you know." He smirked arrogantly at me.

It was like having a bucket of cold water splashed on my face. I couldn't believe he had the audacity to call out my stunned examination. It was so insulting. Okay, so I totally had made googly eyes at him, but was it necessary to toss it in my face?

I wanted to die.

"I-I was looking for Lexi," I stammered, furthering my mortification. "My name is Angel. I just moved in next door a few days ago." I was rambling, grabbing at anything to redeem my self-confidence that had been shot the nanosecond he stepped on the porch.

"You're kidding me, right? *Angel*. Your name is actually Angel?" he asked, like it was the worst possible name on the planet.

I stiffened. Shooting him daggers of steel, I thought about kicking him in the shin. What a jerk-wad. "Yeah, I'm pretty sure it wasn't my name I stuttered."

He laughed. And as divine as the sound was, it also pissed me off.

"Just. Freaking. Great. I have a neighbor named Angel." He might have laughed, but it was anything but cheerful. It sounded damn right irritated.

"What is wrong with my name?" I demanded, getting more heated by the minute.

"Why are you looking for Lexi?" He completely ignored my question.

It crossed my mind to sock that six pack, yet I was pretty sure it would hurt me more than it would hurt him. And I wanted to hurt him. "Um, we met yesterday. I mentioned that I was going shopping—"

"*Shopping*, that explains it." He cut me off.

He said the word *shopping* with dripping sarcasm. Like her decision to hang out with me had nothing to do with *me* exactly.

"And she asked me to come along," I quickly finished, biting my bottom lip. "Is she here?"

He blinked, running a hand through his unruly, midnight hair. He was one of those guys that looked great even after pulling an all-nighter. "Probably."

Proper etiquette would have been to either let me in or go get Lexi; however, he did neither. He just stood leaning against the wooden pole like he had all day. I, on the other hand, couldn't wait to get away from him.

"Er, any chance you could get her?"

"Not a chance in hell little girl."

My mouth must have dropped to the ground while my eyes widened like saucers. Figures, the hottest guy in Podunk Spring Valley would be the biggest dick. I wanted to stomp on his foot, kick him where the sun don't shine, and leave him groaning on the ground.

"I'm not a little girl. I'm seventeen. And you can burn in hell." Well he deserved it.

His eyes laughed at me, amused by my outburst. "You just might get your wish."

I wasn't anyone's play toy. Just as I was about to turn around and say screw them both, Lexi threw open the front door like a ball of energy. She wiggled her brows at dickhead.

"Angel, you're here." She smiled at me brightly. "I see you met my cousin, Chase." She eyed him narrowly.

"Unfortunately," I muttered.

He grinned like the devil. "Yep, Angel Eyes and I have been getting acquainted."

I snorted. I would like to acquaint my foot up his ass. The gleam in his eyes said he knew exactly what horrible thoughts I was thinking. He was insufferable. How could sweet Lexi be related to douchebag of the year?

"Good. You ready?" she asked me. It was hard to believe that she wasn't suffocating in the thickening tension between us.

I nodded my head, unable to trust my tongue.

Finally, I thought, *freedom from the narcissistic jerk.*

His hand snaked out like a viper, grabbing Lexi's arm. The movement was so fast it blurred my vision. "Where do you think you are going?" His voice had hardened, along with his eyes.

They looked as if they were glowing a little bit. It had to be a trick of the sun. He cast his eyes down at Lexi, hiding them behind a veil of thick eyelashes. I stepped closer, trying to see if it was still there.

"Out," she proclaimed, pulling her arm from his grasp.

"Do you think that is wise?" His deep voice had gone quieter and just as lethal.

"I like her."

He lifted the pierced brow in a habit I was swiftly finding irritating. I was two seconds away from walking off this porch and never stepping foot on their property again.

"We're going shopping, Chase, not on a murderous rampage. Bye," she called over her shoulder, looping her arm through mine. "Let's go."

"See you around, Angel Eyes," he called from the porch, sounding like the smirking prick he was.

I turned my head around, away from Lexi, and did the most mature thing I could think of. I stuck my tongue out at him.

His laugh followed me all the way to the car. Deep. Wicked. Throaty.

Jamming the keys into the engine of my little Fusion, it purred to life.

Lexi fiddled with the straps of her designer handbag. "Sorry about Chase. He can be … difficult. I swear he is pissier than a girl during that time of the month."

Difficult was putting it mildly. I had a few other choice words for him.

"I don't think he likes me much," I admitted, the feeling entirely mutual as far as I was concerned. The less I saw of Chase, the better.

"He's been hurt a lot, so he is super leery of people in general, and he's crabby if he doesn't get enough sleep. You just have to get to know him."

When hell freezes over. It was of little consolation knowing that I had prolonged his lack of slumber—served him right for being such a class act douche.

"Really," she said after the look I gave her, "he's not that bad once you get to know him. I swear. He just looks rough around the edges. I hope he hasn't scared you off. If I know him, he probably wasn't nice." Her eyes were sympathetic and a little sad.

The car was humming along the deserted road. "Don't even worry about it. Like you said, he doesn't know me."

That seemed to pacify her. She smiled, her twin dimples winking. I still couldn't believe how incredibly gorgeous the two of them were. They must have some genetically altered genes or something.

Her long blonde hair was swept off her face in a ponytail, trailing down her back like a waterfall. And again, she was dressed in an extremely cute outfit. Her feet were cloaked in a pair of wedges so *not* appropriate for shopping.

I cringed inside. Just the sight of those shoes made my ankles swell. Not to mention all the calluses they would have given me.

The strip center was, of course, on a street named Main. All country towns have one road in and out of town called Main. It was like a law.

The shops that lined the road were surprisingly normal. Sometimes it was nice to be wrong.

This was one of those times.

I'd had it stuck in my head that when I walked through the stores here, there would be nothing I liked. After all, this was the sticks. Even though Lexi was dressed from Saks Fifth Avenue, I'd still been skeptical, assuming she'd gotten her clothes online or maybe she shopped in the city. So when I walked into the home goods shop, I could have eaten my words … or thoughts.

The shelves were stacked with pretty linens, colorful comforters, designer towels, and so forth. Sure, they had some country style for the bumpkins, but I was positive I could find something suitable.

What a relief.

"So what kind of theme are you going for?" Lexi asked as we strolled down the aisle.

Good question. "I don't know. I guess whatever catches my eye."

She looked at me like I had grown a third eye. "You don't have a design in mind?"

"Nope. I kind of planned on just winging it."

She pursed her lips. "What about a French theme? The Eiffel Tower?" she offered

I shook my head. "Nothing too girly, and I need color. Black and white is too drab."

"How about this one?" She held up a silvery comforter set that was stellar—not my usual style, but something about it appealed to me. There were shades of black and purple woven through the threads.

The color reminded me of *his* eyes. I instantly regretted the thought, angered that it had ruined the comforter for me. The last thing I wanted was a constant reminder of *him* in my bedroom.

I trailed a hand over the material, gnawing my lip. It was pretty and soft.

Damn it. Since when did I let some guy control my life? Not that I knew many guys. Okay none, but that was beside the point. I was getting it, and that was that.

It wasn't until we were checking out that I noticed anything unusual. The store had plenty of business, but as we walked in line, people slowly backed away or switched lanes, like they were deliberately avoiding us.

Odd.

Briefly I wondered if I had stepped in dog shit or something. I sniffed the air, only catching the scent of my peachy body wash and Lexi's expensive perfume. Neither of us stunk.

Then what was the problem?

I looked at their faces. It was almost as if they were subconsciously repelled. It didn't seem intentional, and Lexi wasn't alarmed. But I did notice that mothers gathered their kids closer, and none of them looked us in the eye.

What? Did they fear us? Two teenage girls? Really, what harm could we cause?

Easily, we made our way to the register, and the cashier's bright smile died on her lips at our approach.

Weird.

Then I remembered. I was in Hickville. It didn't have to make sense. Small town … maybe they recognized a newbie.

Great. Now I was a freak.

Mabel, her tag read, took a step back as far as the confined space would allow. "Mornin'," she mumbled with a slight accent.

Ha. They do have accents.

"Hi," I replied over the beep, beep, beep of the scanner as she swiped my items.

"Morning," Lexi said, smiling sweetly.

Mabel ignored her, and Lexi's smile dipped.

Well, that was just plain rude. Maybe Mabel needed a lesson in manners. I bit the inside of my cheek to keep from saying something that was bound to put a label on my head. *Small town,* I reminded myself. *People talk.*

Confused, I looked Mabel in the eyes and was stupefied to see fear and traces of repulsion in her glare. She did not like having to wait on us and looked ready to bolt, if given the chance.

Her glower was aimed at Lexi.

Afterwards, we stepped outside into the gray warmth—again, no sun. Frowning, I realized I was going to lose my awesome tan in no time.

"That was weird," I said to Lexi beside me.

"What?" she asked, like she didn't have a clue, yet I had seen her expression falter.

I gave her an you've-got-to-be-kidding look. "How rude that cashier was ... or people in general. You didn't notice how they treated us like we had some kind of zombie disease?"

Yeah, I totally played too many video games.

She shrugged her porcelain shoulders. "People aren't always the friendliest here."

That went against everything I'd heard about small-town communities.

We weaved in and out of the little shops, and I couldn't shake the feeling that I was being followed. It felt like little beady eyes watched my every move, making the hairs on the back of my neck spike.

I was being paranoid.

Seriously though, Lexi could shop. My feet were numb, and I think I lost a toe somewhere between the chocolate shop and the lingerie store.

While we were perusing, I kept my eye on the people around us. Just like before, they went out of their way to put distance between us. I was starting to feel isolated, and the spooky feeling never left, even as we headed back to my car with packages in tow. Glancing across the street, I spotted a guy staring at me. There wasn't anything strange about him except ... he gave me the heebie-jeebies.

Even with sunglasses covering his eyes, I knew he was looking straight at me.

Lexi stiffened beside me, and I knew she felt it too. "It's getting late; we should probably go."

I couldn't have agreed more.

Safely in my car, Lexi went into full chatter. She talked my ear off until I swore it bled. I wasn't complaining, and I sort of found her exuberance for life refreshing.

"Cute car," she commented as we sped the twenty-minute drive back to my house.

I was finally able to shake the stalker-ish vibe. "Thanks, I think." My car was not boast worthy. The fact that it got me from point A to point B was enough. "So why is your cousin living with you?" I almost hated myself for asking, but the question had been harbored in the back of my mind all day. He was sort of annoyingly imprinted in my mind.

"We're his only living family," she said, a little sadly. "He's been with us since I can remember."

"Oh, I'm sorry. I didn't mean to pry," I apologized, thinking I wasn't all that gung ho about divulging my family history.

"No it's okay … really. But I wouldn't advise asking Chase. It makes him moody." She folded her perfectly manicured hands in her lap.

You don't say. Chase, moody? How could I've missed that?

"Got it, moody. I remember," I replied, letting sarcasm lace my words.

She laughed. "You're funny."

Oookay. "What do your parents do?"

She looked out the window. "It's just my dad. And my brother," she added as an afterthought.

Whoa, there was another one? "You have a brother?" I asked, my voice laced with disbelief.

She nodded her head. "Yep, Travis. He is a year older than me and just graduated last year. Now he bums around. My dad is forever on his case."

"So, you are going to be a senior this year. Me too," I added.

"So is Chase. We're the same age. This is going to be so much fun," she squealed.

Ugh. I groaned inside. We apparently had different ideas of fun. Possibly spending a class period with the unbelievably hot douchebag did not sound fun. Not in the least.

I pasted on a smile for her benefit. "Great," I commented between my clenched lips.

She helped me unload the packages from the trunk of my car. Between the two of us, we had a lot of stuff—mostly hers. There was no way I would have been able to carry it alone, but she lifted the bags like they were feathers. Not even breaking a sweat. And the air was humid.

Mom had already left for her shift so I had the house to myself as usual.

"You have such a great tan. Where did you live before?" she asked as we climbed the stairs to my still disorganized bedroom. I probably should have been embarrassed by the state it was in, but Lexi didn't seem to care. I liked that about her.

"Tucson, Arizona."

"Oooh, you must tell me all about Arizona. I've never been before."

I smiled, plopping the bags in the center of my room. "You would love it. The shopping is out of this world. The weather is always gorgeous and hot. The lightning storms are amazing." My heart squeezed in my chest.

"Wow," she proclaimed. "It must be like a culture shock moving here."

Culture shock was the understatement of the century. This was like living on another planet. "It will definitely take some getting used to, but I'll adjust over time. We're adaptable."

"I've never been anywhere. I have no idea what you must be feeling," she finished, sounding a little wistful.

"Back up. You've never been anywhere outside of Illinois or this area?"

She shook her pretty little blonde head. "Never. My family doesn't like to travel."

Well, damn, that was taking it to an extreme, like the phobia where people can't leave their homes. Agoraphobia I think it is called.

"Do you want help … organizing?" she asked, scanning the chaos that was my room.

"You sure you can handle it?" I teased, scrunching my nose in aversion.

"I got this." She grinned slyly.

And she did. She worked like a cracked out interior designer. I secretly thanked my sore butt that we hadn't stopped to get paint. It was on my to-do list, but after shopping with Lexi, I was worn out.

"You want to hang out tomorrow?" she asked.

We sat back and looked at all that we had accomplished. My room almost looked normal and nothing like the one I'd left behind. Mission accomplished.

The sky outside was getting dark, and I needed to fix something for dinner. I was starving. A part of me wished she would stay, and it was on the tip of my tongue to ask her. Something about this house— all the open space and the darkness—freaked me out.

Better get used to it, I mentally chastised myself.

"Sure," I agreed.

"Great. Oh, and maybe I can get Chase to help."

"You don't have to do that. Seriously, *don't* do that."

She laughed at my discomfort. "See you tomorrow, Angel."

CHAPTER 3

"Angel!" Mom yelled from downstairs.

I doggie-eared my place in my monthly subscription of *Gamer*, a magazine for diehards like me. If I couldn't play video games, I read about them: upcoming releases and reviews. It kept my mind busy. "What?" I hollered in return, placing the magazine on my nightstand.

"There is someone here to see you," she responded equally as loud.

I took the stairs two at a time. "Hey, Lexi. Mom this is Lexi. She lives next door."

"Hi, Lexi. I'm Chloe Morgan."

"It's nice to meet you Ms. Morgan."

Mom waved her hand in the air. "Please, call me Chloe. Anything else makes me sound old."

"You are old," I teased and was rewarded with a mom glare.

"Watch it," Mom warned halfheartedly. "You have two brothers, don't you?" she asked Lexi, winking at me.

I wanted to wilt under the rug. There was nothing worse than your mom trying to set you up and being so obvious about it. It screamed desperate.

And I wasn't desperate.

Lexi grinned brightly. "I have an older brother, Travis, and my cousin, Chase. He lives with us."

"Oh," she replied with too much interest.

I groaned. "Don't you have to leave for work?"

She checked the clock on the microwave. "I have a few more minutes. What do you have planned today?"

Plastering on a smile, I replied sweetly, "The usual. Underage drinking, random sex, and a little shoplifting."

"That sounds nice. Just be sure you're home at a decent hour." She kissed me on the cheek. "Remember, I'm yours all day tomorrow."

How could I forget? It was also the day we finally got the TV and Internet connected. Woot. Woot. "Can't wait."

"Bye, Lexi. I hope to see you around," Mom said.

"Your mom is awesome and gorgeous," Lexi gushed after she left.

I had never thought about her any other way than just Mom. "I guess. So how do you feel about painting?"

She gave me a look like I was speaking Greek. "Why wouldn't you just hire someone to do that?"

Ah, because not everyone has money that grows on trees. "I like doing it. It's like relaxing. I swear it's fun."

She didn't look entirely convinced, but once she found out we were going shopping again, she was totally onboard. "I've never done it before. It might be fun. We're going to paint the walls?" she asked on our way to the hardware store.

I nodded. "Yeah, and an old dresser of mine. It suffered some damage from the move and old age. I figure a coat of paint will give it a fresh look, the walls too. I can't stand white. It's so boring. I take it you're not a DIY kind of girl?"

"D-I-What?" She shrugged. "We usually just buy new stuff. Things don't seem to last long at my house."

Typical.

We pulled into my driveway after picking out paint colors and having them mixed. Painting was a task Mom and I often did together, but with her working so much, I thought I would take on this burden myself with Lexi's help. Lexi did have a great eye for color. She easily matched swatches that would coordinate with the silver of the comforter set.

Immediately, I noticed my dresser and nightstand placed outside the garage. Sitting in my car, I scratched my head. Was I being robbed? If so, they were extremely gracious robbers. I couldn't recall if I'd locked the house.

"How the heck did my stuff get down here?" I wondered out loud.

Lexi glanced over at me, realizing for the first time that something was amok. "Remember when I said that I was going to ask Chase to help?"

"You didn't."

"Uh, I did. Sorry, I didn't mean to upset you. I just thought it would easier on us."

Chase had been in my house. In my room. I think I was either going to hyperventilate or kick his door down. "That was nice of him," I managed after my oh-em-gee moment wore off. He had saved me a huge headache from maneuvering those bulky pieces myself. In all honesty, I probably would have left them in my room.

Grinning, she said, "He has his moments."

"His good deed for the year is done," I said drily.

She laughed. I liked the sound, and for some reason I couldn't explain, I wondered if she laughed often. Something told me she didn't.

We tackled the sanding like two WWF SmackDown wrestlers. There was sawdust flying everywhere—in my hair, stuck on my sticky skin. I was a hot mess, but it was a great stress reliever: sanding the crap out of some wood. I was sure my arms and body were going to protest tomorrow.

We sat back to admire our progress.

"Here." I extended a water bottle to her, wiping the sweat off my brow with the back of my hand. "It's not a beer, but it will do," I joked, remembering the underage drinking comment I'd made earlier to Mom.

"This is fun," she admitted, taking a swig from the water.

"It's kind of relaxing," I agreed. "My dad used to carve wood all the time." The offhanded remark came out before I thought about it, and I instantly regretted it.

"Where is your dad?" she asked.

I felt my face fall, and I stared off into the fields across the road. Did I tell her the truth? I extremely sucked at lying, and I didn't want to lie. "My parents are divorced." That was the truth, just not the whole truth.

"I'm sorry." She laid a hand gently over mine. "That must have been hard on you—moving, a new place, the divorce."

I didn't answer … I couldn't. My throat had closed up.

"You okay? I didn't mean to upset you. It's none of my business," she nervously rambled on.

I shook my head. "It's still hard to talk about."

"I understand, but if you ever do … I'm a great listener." There was something about her that made me want to pour my heart out. We had just met, but I had feeling Lexi was going to turn out to be a good friend.

I nodded, picking up my sandpaper and putting on my brave face.

A few minutes later I heard her say, out of the corner of her mouth, "Don't look now." Her lips upturned.

I never got why people say that. Of course I was going to look. But I wished I hadn't.

Chase. He was strutting across our yards in a sinful swagger.

He looked fine—damn fine. My eyes hurt just looking at him, and my mouth went dry. Forget that I'd just guzzled a bottle of water. The ripped jeans he wore rode low on his hips. His T-shirt looked like he'd just plucked it off the floor, yet it worked with the whole dark tousled hair. He had it going on. Beautiful body. Gorgeous face. Kissable lips. Wicked and dangerous attitude. He lifted his pierced brow at my meticulous inspection. I practically banged him with my eyes.

Don't forget the sucky attitude.

Color morphed into my already flushed cheeks. Fine. I would just ignore him then. Putting more enthusiasm than necessary into sanding, I needed the distraction. I found it nearly impossible to discount his presence.

"What are you doing?" he asked Lexi.

"I told you: painting."

"You said *Angel* was painting, not you." Again, he said my name like it left a bad taste in his mouth.

I could feel his stare at my back, spreading unwanted tingles throughout my body.

I pounded the dresser with the sandpaper, taking my nerves out on the wood grain and doing everything in my power to not look his way. I was finding it increasingly difficult. He was like a magnet. One part of me was pulled to him and the other disgusted.

"Whatever. Thanks for helping out," she said.

I couldn't help myself. I snuck a peek over my shoulder. He was smiling at his cousin, and it lit his entire face. Most of the fierceness and danger had left his expression, softening his already perfect features. The guard he kept masked over his face was gone. I had to smother the moan I swore I almost let loose with a fake cough.

Then his silvery eyes met mine. My world paused, and I stopped breathing. He was that breathtaking. The smile on his full lips turned into a smirk, knowledge lurking behind it, like he knew the kind of effect he had on me or the female population in general.

"What are *you* doing?" he asked, indicating the practically bare dresser.

I snorted. "I think it's pretty obvious, even for someone as small-minded as you."

"Are you always this feisty in the morning?"

I looked up at the sky, seeing it was almost evening. "Um, it's like six o'clock. At night," I pointed out, just in case he wasn't sure which time of day I was referring to.

His glare ran over the dresser. I wasn't claiming to be Martha Stewart, but I had to say, so far we'd done a darn good job. Getting off the glaze was the tricky part, but it was nothing I couldn't handle, just a little elbow grease. I might suck at gardening, cooking, and unpacking, but I was a firm believer in you can do anything if you put your mind to it.

"Do you actually enjoy this?" he asked, like he couldn't figure me out.

Good. Let him wonder.

I shrugged. The last thing I wanted to admit was that it didn't matter if I enjoyed it or not; it saved Mom money, and that was all that counted.

"Chase, stop!" Lexi hissed. "Be nice."

He leaned against the house with his head angled, eyeing me. It was disturbing to say the least. "What? I didn't say anything," he replied, pretending to be innocent.

He didn't have to. It was written all over his face.

Man, did I want to kick him in the balls. He riled me like no one ever had. My blood boiled just on sight.

I took a deep breath and tried to get back into the project before we lost all natural light. His husky voice prevented me from achieving my goal—pretending he didn't exist.

"Is this what you do for fun?" he asked, throwing one leg over the other.

"Among other things," I admitted.

"Like?" he prompted.

"Don't you have somewhere else to be?" I huffed. This was Lexi's cousin, and I really liked her. It would be so nice to know someone the first day at school so I could avoid all the BS of being the new kid. For her sake, maybe I should try to play nice. "Sorry," I retracted. "I think the heat is getting to me."

A piece of hair escaped my tie, and I blew it out of my face.

"You got something in your hair." He moved in front of me faster than humanly possible.

One second he was against the house, the next he was in my face. A breeze ruffled over my skin, making me shiver, even though it was still ninety degrees out. The shiver had nothing to do with the wind and everything to do with his close proximity. He was totally in my personal space.

Didn't he know about the bubble?

His hand moved to brush away the tiny sawdust particles from my hair. I froze. Pieces rained down off my dark hair. His touch was electric. The energy of it traveled to the tips of my toes, and by the look in his fierce eyes, he wasn't all too pleased with me. He yanked his hand away, like he'd been struck by lightning.

Jerk. He was the one who had touched me.

Shoving his hands in his pockets, he backed up, rocking on his heels.

"Thanks," I muttered, avoiding those stormy eyes.

"No problem, Angel Eyes."

"Don't call me that." My eyes flashed with anger. Dots of red hazed behind my lids.

"What? Angel? That *is* your name, isn't it?" He stood his ground, a good foot taller than me. I didn't back down either. His eyes glowered in the darkening sky. They stood out like little neon lights.

"Why do you say it like that?" I demanded and then shook my head. "Never mind, I don't want to know." I refused to let him know how much it bothered me. He didn't deserve that kind of power.

He turned to Lexi. "Lex, we should go. It's getting late."

She put her lip out, pouting. Only Lexi could pout and still look beautiful. "We're not done yet." It was clear she was starving for female attention. Being the only girl in a house full of men could not be healthy, especially with overbearing assholes.

"Lexi, now," he demanded harshly.

It wasn't my place to intervene, but my mouth had other opinions. Plus, he got under my skin. "She can stay if she wants to. She's a big girl."

"This doesn't concern you," he growled. I mean he literally growled, lips curled and everything. His eyes had that eerie glow again, and his voice was deep and menacing.

I took a step back, thinking he was going to bite my head off. "What is your deal?" I argued.

"Chase," Lexi called, stepping between us. She put a hand on his arm. "Please."

I wasn't exactly sure what she was pleading. It only pissed me off more. "You are an asshole."

"I've been called worse."

I swore steam started coming out of my ears.

"Chase, stop. You're being unreasonable. I'm fine." Her turquoise eyes pleaded with him to understand. They had a sad and lonely quality to them.

Who was he to tell her what to do? Didn't she have a parent for that? I had yet to meet her dad, but it made sense to me that he should be doing the parenting. Not her cousin.

"Lex, it's not safe, not this late." His voice had gone gentler and quiet. It was obvious how much he cared for her.

I looked around me, scanning to see what had him so concerned for her safety. Unless there were children of the corn lurking in the fields, it was just the three of us, and he was the scariest by far. He couldn't possibly think *I* would do something to harm her.

I got that he didn't know me well, but I wasn't a mass murderer disguised in a seventeen-year-old's body.

"I got it under control, Chase. I swear. Just a little longer."

He studied her. "Lex, you've got five minutes before I come back out to get you," he rumbled against the darkening night.

I watched him. My eyes transfixed. He looked like a giant cat, roaring and eyes gleaming. He gave me one last look of disgust and walked away.

Unmoving, I stood there until the door shut behind him. "Ass," I muttered under my breath.

"I'm so sorry," she apologized, looking mortified. "He didn't mean anything."

I wanted to thump myself over the head. She was making excuses for his poor behavior. "I think he was pretty clear."

"He's worried and … it's hard for him. Losing his parents, it's made him overprotective. Sometimes it's stifling."

I felt sorry for her. I hadn't the slightest clue what it was like to have a brother or a cousin to look after you, but from what I'd seen, I silently thanked both my parents for never procreating again. No way could I deal with that on a day-to-day basis. "I can see that. I think we're done for the day anyway."

"I should go before he makes good on his word. Still friends?" she asked in a small voice. She sounded almost afraid of my answer.

I nodded. "Of course."

It wasn't her fault her cousin was a raving d-bag. Hot, yes, but that didn't rule out all his other insufferable qualities. I was kind of stuck. We were neighbors, and I wasn't going away any time soon, at least not this year.

CHAPTER 4

It was Saturday. Today, I got my Internet connected, meaning I could finally get on my Xbox Live account. Plus, I got to spend the day with Mom.

Hot damn.

I started the day by waking in my new bedding and hugging the sheets to my chest. I was so excited to finish my project. My room had always been my escape. I needed to have a space that expressed my artistic tastes and me. My cheeks rubbed against the blanket, helpless to falling in love with its softness. The silver was such a striking hue, a color that haunted my dreams.

Chase.

All night the glamour of his gray eyes was there, growling at me, laughing at me, scowling at me. It didn't matter which way. I didn't know why I let him get the best of me. He was just a guy.

Flipping the covers aside, I stared at the chipped ceiling and refused to give Chase another second of my thoughts.

When I padded downstairs, Mom was there talking to some guy in a uniform. Like everything in Spring Valley, he moved at the pace of a snail. Groaning, I cringed to think about how horribly slow my Internet speed was going to be.

Grabbing a bowl of Fruit Loops, I waited for the cable guy to bust his butt. It was quite a wide load. The overall jumpsuit he was wearing did nothing to flatter his odd form, and my mind wandered to an image of Chase. He could make that getup look hot.

I shook the thought of him from my head.

It felt like a lifetime before I was able to power up my Xbox. The speed did suck, but at least it worked. My games were totally going to lag.

I found it utterly stereotypical that girls don't play video games, and I can't tell you the amount of smack I took from players once they found out I was a girl. Such crap. But there was nothing more satisfying than my rank and KD ratio being superior to such egotistical douches, which happened. A lot.

I'm a kickass dork.

An hour later, I hopped on my laptop to check my emails. Deleting more than three-quarters of my messages, there wasn't a single one from any of my friends in Tucson.

I guess I was easily forgotten.

Whatever. I was better off without them.

Slamming my laptop closed with a satisfying snap, I looked out my window.

Stop the presses. The sun was actually shining.

Mom and I had attacked most of the boxes downstairs earlier, and she was currently outside doing some gardening to the flowerbeds. Not having a man around meant all the chores were stuck on us. That was bullshit of the worst kind.

Sighing, I slipped on my shoes, grabbed my iPod, and went out to mow the lawn. We had a deal, Mom and me:

1. You do your own dishes.
2. You do your own laundry.
3. We take turns mowing the lawn.

I might as well get mine out of the way. So I tossed on some grubby clothes and sneakers and made my way into the garage. After a quick wave to Mom, I stuck in my earbuds, cranked the tunes, and kicked the mower over.

No more than five minutes into the backbreaking labor, I noticed the Greek god walking my way. He was leaner than Chase, but that wasn't to say he didn't have a sexy body. The Adonis-like guy pushed the blond hair from out of his eyes—turquoise eyes like Lexi's—and they grinned at me with inquisitiveness. The mower bar slipped from my hands, cutting off the engine. My mouth dropped about ten feet, filling with gnats and grass particles. I swallowed the mess in a stupefied haze.

This must be Lexi's brother—Travis. Sweet Jesus.

"Hey," he mouthed with a lazy grin and dimples just like Lexi's. It was a killer combo—those eyes and dimples. He had a carefree swagger. His mouth started moving again. It was then I realized that the music was still blaring in my ears and I couldn't hear a thing he was saying.

I ripped out my earbuds, dangling them over my shoulders. "Sorry. What did you say?"

"I'm Travis. Lex told me all about you." His voice was smoky and hot.

Nice. Thank you, Lexi.

"I'm Angel."

His eyes sparkled with humor. I seriously didn't get what they found so humorous about my name. It made me want to pull my hair out.

"Is that short for something?" he asked. His tone was like velvet—smooth, gliding over his words.

I nodded. He had that friendly quality that set me at ease, like Lexi did. Nothing like the obscure irritation Chase ignited. I relaxed my shoulders. "Unfortunately. It's short for Angelina. I have no idea what my mom was thinking."

"It's pretty." His voice was dreamy. "Do you play?" he asked, nodding at my *damn campers* T-shirt.

"I do," I replied, waiting for some snarky comment.

"We should play together sometime," he offered.

There was a long pause before I realized he was being sincere. "I would like that," I replied, smiling.

Chase chose that moment to join us, my eyes eating him up as his long strides conquered the space between us. He was truly drool-worthy. My insides flipped. This guy was going to give me an ulcer or something. Looking up, his silver eyes glittered in the sunlight.

"Travis," he barked at his cousin. "Weren't you just leaving?"

"Are you always this bossy?" I retorted smartly.

The glitter turned to fire. "What are you? A new toy everyone wants to play with?"

I ground my teeth. Was it always going to be like this, a raging war of words between us?

Travis laughed. "I like you. But I do have to go. It was nice meeting you, Angelina."

I cooled the heat in my eyes because I liked Travis. "You too," I replied.

Suddenly, I found myself alone with Chase. *Shit.*

Glancing up, I braced myself. He wasn't smiling at me, but he didn't look like he wanted to kill me either. His expression was indif-ferent acceptance. We were kind of stuck in this situation, for at least the next year. Why not try to make the best of it?

"What are you doing?" he asked.

I thought this was a no-brainer. I didn't know; maybe girls in his family didn't do *man* work, but we didn't have a choice. "Er, cutting the lawn, genius."

"Here." He sort of eased me out of the way. "Let me do it. It will go a lot quicker."

"I don't need your help," I protested, trying to push my way back in.

"Look, I'm sorry. This is *me* trying to be nice. Just accept it." That did not sound like much of an apology.

This guy was impossible. Before I could protest anymore, he tore off his shirt and threw it to the ground.

Well, that was one way to shut me up.

His sun-kissed chest was finely chiseled, confirming the six pack I had expected. My fingers itched to touch him, to run my hands over the plane of his stomach. He had me running from hot to cold in a blink, and that drove me freaking nuts.

He lifted his silver-studded brow.

"Knock your socks off," I mumbled, dumbfounded.

Pulling on the cord, the lawn mower jumped to life with a roar. The muscles in his arms bunched as he effortlessly pushed the machine up and down my yard. It wasn't large, and I hated to admit it, but he would probably have it done in half the time. As it was, it took even less than that.

I swore I turned my back for like five minutes to collect myself, and he was finished. The silence of the engine had me snapping my head in his direction. What caught me off balance was the fact that he stood directly in front of me now. His warm palms reached out to steady me, sending shivers down my arms.

The inside of my mouth watered, and I had the craziest images of licking the beads of sweat from his chest, the two of us together—hot and sweaty. I bit the inside of my cheek, bringing myself back to earth.

He took a step forward. I took a step back, and so forth. Eventually, there was nowhere left to go as my back hit a tree trunk. His eyes singed into mine with a wild intensity, and the air spiked a hundred degrees.

"You look a little hot there, Angel Eyes," he said with a twinkle in those silver eyes.

"What?" I stumbled, words failing me. My back dug into the bark. He made my mind go blank. I could feel the outline of his body, his breath fanning my out of whack senses.

"I said you look warm. Are you feeling okay?"

I blinked. The mist took a minute to clear from my brain. "Yeah, I'm fine. How did you do that so fast?"

He shrugged and took a step back, putting some much needed space between us. "It was nothing."

"It *was* impossible," I argued, trying to wrap my mind around it.

Of their own accord, my eyes journeyed the length of him now that he wasn't on top of me. They stopped only when they came across a circular mark with swirls in the center peeking from just above his waistband. His jeans sat low on his hips, and the symbol was easy to see on the left side.

Before I even thought about it, my hand reached out to trace the mark. "What's that? You have a tattoo?" I asked, not entirely surprised.

His breath hissed as my fingers just skimmed over his skin, tracing the bold lines. I jumped, jerking my hand back like I had just been burned. In utter embarrassment, my cheeks bloomed an awful shade of red. What had possessed me to touch him? *There* of all places?

I was going to hurl.

"It's nothing," he grumbled, picking up his discarded shirt from the grass. He pulled it on, hiding the mark from my inspection.

Glaring at him contemptuously, I responded, "That didn't look like nothing."

"Drop it, okay." His voice and eyes had turned to steel.

My stomach dropped at his snapping tone. Anger replaced my embarrassment, and steam could have smoked from my ears. "Fine," I replied curtly, crossing my arms over my chest.

He rolled his eyes at me. He was insufferable.

Whatever he was about to say was interrupted as Mom walked around to the front of the house, catching us closer than I would have liked. Her eyes rotated between Chase and me, completely misreading the situation. The mischievous delight in her irises had me on full alert. She was up to something.

"Mom, this is Lexi's cousin." I reluctantly introduced him.

"You live next door. That's wonderful." The sweetness in her voice made me want to gag.

"Chase Winters," he said, grinning. His face completely transformed. He looked almost … nice.

"It's nice to meet you, Chase. Would you like something to drink? It's unbelievably hot today." She gave me a wink.

I wanted to crawl into the nearest hole and die.

"Sure, that would be great," he agreed, much to my annoyance.

She gave him a pearly smile and then mouthed, *"Oh. My. God,"* at me as she turned toward the house.

I elbowed him in the chest the second she was safely inside. It was like ramming into an iron door.

"What was that for?" he asked, utterly unfazed.

"Please, I barely touched you, pansy. Suck it up." I wanted to rub my arm but didn't dare admit that it had hurt me. Not in front of him.

"I never said it hurt." His eyes latched onto mine. "You are something else, brat."

"I've been called worse."

"Oh, I bet you have. Stay away from my cousin. She doesn't need your drama."

I gasped. "*My* drama," I squeaked very unflatteringly.

Mom chose that moment to walk through the screen door with two glasses of lemonade. I bit my tongue from screaming out.

She handed us each a cool glass, eyeing the two of us with too much exuberance. It was starting to make me uncomfortable. Shifting on my feet, I cleared my throat.

Aiming a smile at Chase, she said, "You know, Chase, I would appreciate it if you could show Angel around before school starts. I want her to feel … comfortable here. Are you busy tomorrow?"

My eyes just about blew out of their sockets. Was she trying to set me up? On a date? With a practical stranger?

"*Mom*, really. He doesn't have to do that. I'm sure he has plans," I added between clenched teeth. My jaw was starting to throb.

She looked at him expectantly, her puppy brown eyes sucking him right in. *No. No. No,* I screamed inside my head, willing him to hear me.

He grinned wolfishly. "You're in luck. I have no plans at all and would *love* to show Angel around."

"Perfect," she cried gleefully.

This was turning into a horrible nightmare. No way would I survive a day in Chase's pigheaded presence.

The moment she retuned back to the house, I whirled on him, thinking we could reason. "Look, slick. You don't have to do this. I can make up an excuse for you."

He arched his brow. I wanted to rip that silver bar right off. "Now what kind of guy would I be if I backed out now?"

A decent one, a smart one, an alive one, because I swore I was going to kill him. "I don't expect you to show me around just because my mom asked." There was no misleading in my tone. I was pissed, and it was oozing from my pores.

Leaning casually against the tree, he angled his head. "Maybe I just want to keep an eye on you."

"Jerk." Talking to him was like hitting my head on a brick wall.

"That's no way to say thanks." He tsk-ed. "After all, I did mow your lawn."

My eyes brightened with anger. "You can shove your thanks where the sun don't shine. I didn't want or need your help."

His eyes got eerily serious. "Maybe that's your problem."

I was pretty sure *he* was my only problem at the moment.

"Guess I'll be seeing you at noon tomorrow, Angel Eyes."

I propped myself alongside the porch railing, watching the devil himself walk across the yard. He looked over his shoulder once at me.

With as much decorum as possible, I flipped him off.

His laugh echoed, carrying in the wind.

CHAPTER 5

My Saturday nights were no less lame than they were in Tucson. Sure, I had occasionally gone out with friends, but mostly I'd hibernated in my room and played CoD on my Xbox. I never did things normal girls my age did. They were all into their hair, nails, and clothes. I guess I was somewhat of a tomboy, though I didn't like putting a label on me. There wasn't anywhere that I really fit in; I was just me.

Sitting on my bed, I logged into my Live account, selecting a Call of Duty match and waiting for the game to load. There was another player in the match with the gamer tag B4DB0YSUX.

How relevant.

Chase popped into my head. He was the epitome of a "bad" boy. Dark. Sinful. Arrogant. An ass.

The match was in full swing by the time I chimed in. Before long, I was engrossed in the game, but Chase was never far from my thoughts, our looming, so-called date taunting me.

Biting my lip, I groaned as my player was taken down by a Scar-L assault rifle. With Chase lurking in my mind, I was distracted and way off point. He was driving me bonkers with distraction without even being in the same room.

There was a nice breeze blowing through my bedroom window. The sheer curtain was flying, casting odd shadows on the ceiling. I was so lost in the game and my hatred for bad boys, meaning Chase, that I nearly hit the ceiling when a howl rang out in the night.

I twisted my head toward the window. *It's just a dog*, I coaxed myself, burying myself deeper into the covers. We only had one neighboring house, and I was pretty sure the Winters did not have a dog. A few minutes later, it sounded again, only this time it was magnified by ten.

Sweet baby Jesus. There were werewolves running around in the woods behind my house. Nothing like being surrounded by wheat fields and towering trees to make a gal feel secure.

My interest in destroying the other team was gone, and it now laid on how I was going to sleep with whatever creepy animal was out there. Switching off my Xbox, I closed my eyes and clutched the pillow.

As the first streaks of morning light shone through my curtains, I groaned, instantly wanting to stay in bed all day. Half asleep, I still curled up in the same fetal position, listening to the sounds outside. An irritating bird sang repeatedly, leaves rustled in nearby tree branches, but other than that … silence. No howling.

Then the room filled with my drawn out moan when I remembered that today I had to spend the day with Chase.

Like the night before, his eyes chased my dreams—no pun intended. Now they were accompanied with the howling of … wild dogs? It did not make for the most restful sleep. After tossing and turning most of the night, I was sure my eyes were going to be puffy like marshmallows.

My stomach ached from nerves as I rubbed a gentle hand over it.

Maybe I could fake being sick. I mean, I already had a bellyache, and my tan was slowly fading. I could almost pass for pale. It might work.

But then Chase would know that I had chickened out.

I wouldn't give him the satisfaction. If I was stuck with him, then he was stuck with me. Throwing back the covers, I got out of bed and cleared the sleep crud from my eyes.

I hit the shower, letting the warmth from the spray soak into my body. Calgon, take me away. Before I turned to a raisin, I stepped out, wrapping myself in a towel, and headed for my room.

Riffling through my closet, I skimmed over my clothes, wishing I had something sexier. Normally, I wouldn't call myself sexy by any means, but there was a time in a girl's life when she needed to at least feel sexy once. This was my time. I wanted to make him suffer.

Sighing, I tossed aside another boring gamer shirt and thought about searching Mom's closet, only to quickly reject the idea. I didn't want Mom to think that I cared what Chase thought of me.

I picked out two very different tops. The black number was a one-shoulder top, and the other was a plunging halter that showed more of my girls than I was comfortable with. Did I want to show a little skin and leave something to the imagination, or did I want to go for full-out slut?

Ugh. I groaned. Why was I making this so difficult?

Fine. We'll just do this the simple way. I closed my eyes. "Eeny, meeny, miney, moe ..." I opened them.

Shit.

I hope Mom didn't mind a peep show. Wiggling into the ever so tight halter top, I then stepped into a pair of kickass jeans.

Examining myself in the full-length mirror, I checked out my ass. Hell, I looked pretty rockin' in these jeans. And I was shallow enough to admit to myself that I wanted him to check me out.

I wanted him to want me.

As an afterthought, I left my hair long and loose. Carefully, I applied a light coat of makeup, finishing the look with my favorite wild berry scented lip gloss and a mist of peachy body spray.

I looked damn good, and my confidence spiked.

Satisfied, I trotted downstairs. The aroma of freshly brewed coffee scented the air. It wasn't Starbucks, but I'd been coffee deprived for too long. At this point, it was better than sex. Or I assumed it was, as I was still part of the virgin club. Don't get me wrong, I was totally for doing the deed; I just hadn't found a guy worthy enough.

The fact that Chase's name echoed in my head just then irked me. No way was I allowing that jerk to put his hands on me, I thought, forgetting the fact that two minutes ago, I had fully admitted to myself that I wanted him to find me irresistible. My mind was warped.

Mom was already in the kitchen, coffee in hand. "Wow, you look fantastic." She said nothing about showing too much skin or the lack of appropriateness in my clothing choice. Nope. Not from my mom.

"Thanks," I muttered, still miffed about being maneuvered into a date with the d-bag of the century. I poured a cup of steamy coffee into my *Nazi Zombie* mug, adding cream and plenty of sugar.

Mom eyed me. "Are you having any coffee with that sugar?"

"Funny." I took a seat next to her, blowing on the steam rising from my cup.

She put down the book she was reading. "Honey, I know you are not exactly thrilled with me right now, but you are going to have fun today. It will be good for you to get out and see the town."

"What's there to see? It has only one stoplight," I moaned.

I realized then that she might be getting tired of the redneck remarks. "How can you complain? Have you seen that boy's butt?"

I dropped my head onto the countertop. "Mom, *please* don't check out anymore butts," I said, muffled against the granite.

"I'm not dead, Angel."

No, but I might wish I were after today.

She brushed a hand over my head. "Just try and have fun ... Okay?"

I lifted my head and looked into her concerned eyes. "Sure," I agreed for her sake. Who knew? Stranger things have happened—like my dad being behind bars. Who would have thought?

Precisely at noon on the dot, the doorbell rang.

Ugh, he would have to be punctual.

Scurrying to get to the door, I knocked over my cup of coffee. Thank goodness it was empty. Inhaling a deep breath, I opened the door, and my heart lurched to the bottom of my feet.

I thought that I looked good, but Chase outshined any guy I could

43

imagine, even Johnny Depp. He was like hotness incarnate. It was ridiculous how good-looking he was.

He stood in the doorway with his hands tucked into the front pocket of his jeans. Everything about him was fine.

Those unusual eyes looked me up from head to toe and back again. Whoa. From the look in his guarded eyes, I couldn't tell at all what he was feeling, and it racked my nerves. I was sure he could hear every single beat my heart pattered. And it pattered fast.

"Look, you don't have to do this," I said, stepping onto the porch and closing the door firmly behind me. "I'm sure Lexi wouldn't mind …" I offered, praying he would take the escape.

"She can't. She and Travis are gone with their dad. It's just me." He quickly shut down my only out.

"Oh, joy," I scoffed with an unwelcomed mixture of relief and anxiety.

We walked off the porch, and I got a good look at the car that was idling in my driveway. It was some flashy foreign sports car and stuck out like a sore thumb here—black, shiny, and new. I was expecting some kind of beat up truck. I should have known better.

"This is your car?" I asked, narrowing my eyes at him.

"Yep. Get in."

So much for southern hospitality, someone was awfully chipper today.

I sunk into the plush leather seat. "So where are we going?"

He drove the car with such effortlessness. We seemed to glide along the road. "It's a surprise. Just sit back and relax. We're in for a cruise."

Ha. Easier said than done. My stomach was fluttering, and I was getting light-headed. "We're not staying in town? 'Cause I thought that was the whole point."

His fingers tapped on the wheel in beat with the low music. "Have you seen our town? Trust me, you will get the whole five minute experience as we drive out."

That was the same thing I had tried to explain to Mom. The interior of his car smelled like him—pure wickedness. I closed my eyes for a moment and just inhaled the scent. Dark. Dangerous. Heaven. Everything that he was. I glanced over only to be swarmed by the intensity in his silver eyes. The sun seemed to reflect light off them like a prism.

Weird.

I tugged on my lip. "So how far is this *surprise?*"

"Not far. We're almost there. Did you enjoy your tour of Spring Valley?" He smiled disarmingly.

I had forgotten about the town and could barely remember my name. That smile distracted me in so many ways. "Um …" I mumbled.

He chuckled.

A half hour later we pulled up to Starved Rock State Park. I eyed the giant wooden sign as we passed through the gate. He parked the car and got out. Just as I was about to grab the handle of my door, it opened. There he was, waiting expectantly.

Literally two seconds had elapsed. "How did y— Never mind," I said, shaking my head.

This place was huge, nothing like anything in Arizona. There was so much green.

"You ready?" he asked, watching my awed reaction.

I angled my head at him, feeling uncertain. "Are you going to lead me out into the woods and then leave me stranded to fend for myself?"

He stroked his chin in consideration. "That has possibilities."

I gave him the stink-eye.

"Look, you seem to be under the impression that everything here is *country*, for lack of a better word. I wanted to show you that there is more to this area than meets the eye."

Did that just come out of the jerkwad's mouth? "Wow. Did you just have a moment of sincerity?" Sometimes I needed to learn to curb my tongue.

Of course, the ever so brief moment was ruined, and he was back to throwing up his badass shield. "I hope you can hike," he said taking off, leaving me to follow on his heels.

"I hope you can hike," I muttered, mimicking him to the back of his fine ass.

He stopped in his tracks and turned around. I bumped right into that wall of muscle. "Did you say something?" His brow arched.

I looked up, salivating. "What?" I dumbly asked, stunned by his body brushing up against mine. I swore his eyes were glowing. There were flecks of topaz that seemed to have come from nowhere.

"Stay close. I don't want you getting lost. Got it?" He reprimanded me like I was two.

I nodded, unable to speak. My body hadn't yet recovered from the proximity of his; otherwise that tone would have never flied.

We traveled deeper down the trails, heading off the beaten path. Carved rocks surrounded us on either side. Moss and plants grew in the crevices of these large sandstone rock formations. It was sort of magical.

In the distance, I could hear the rippling of moving water. Who would have thought such mystic beauty and artistic formations lived so close to all that flat land?

When he finally stopped walking, my legs rejoiced. Pride kept me from even hinting at being tired.

Taking a seat against a nearby tree trunk, I looked out. The exquisiteness of the rocks and the gushing water falling over them were out of this world. Everything was so alive and vibrant. If I were an artist, I would have been compelled to paint this place.

"Welcome to utopia, Angel Eyes." His voice was husky and seductive.

"It's lovely. I've never seen anything like it. Do you come here often?" I asked, staring up at his face. It was as captivating as this place.

"Every now and then. You should see it in December. It's like a winter wonderland."

"I would love to see that." I tried to imagine it, and I could almost see the frost-covered branches, the frozen ponds, and the huge icicles dripping from the rocks.

He tossed a pebble into the little lake. It skipped on the surface of the water at least twenty times, like a frog jumping on lily pads. I wasn't even going to attempt a try.

Sauntering like he owned the world, he sat next to me under the canopy of a tree. Our shoulders rubbed, and I angled my head, watching him. "Thank you for bringing me here."

He studied my face. "Don't thank me now. The day isn't over yet."

"Are you implying something?" I asked, my voice scrutinizing him.

"Maybe ... You're just different than I expected."

"How am I different?" I couldn't fathom how. It was becoming impossible to ignore the tingles I got from being so close to him.

His piercing eyes cast to the side. "I haven't figured it out yet," he replied, sounding puzzled as he twiddled with a blade of grass.

What I needed was space. Lying back on a cushion of lawn, I closed my eyes and wallowed in the sun. I missed its warmth. The sun here lacked the intensity of Tucson. "Well, please let me know when you do. Until then, I'll just be on standby."

"You have a sharp tongue," he informed me.

A shadow fell over me, and my pulse raced uncontrollably. Without even opening my eyes, I knew that Chase leaned over me. His scent was everywhere, teasing my skyrocketing emotions. If I opened my eyes, what would I see? Would they reflect what I was most certain shone in mine?

My heart couldn't take the rejection, but keeping my eyes sealed was one of the hardest things I'd ever done. Every nerve ending in my body was begging me to look at him. My head, on the other hand, thought that it was a bad idea.

I lost track of time. It could have been hours or seconds as I lay there with him hovering so near. When I finally realized that his shadow was gone, I slowly peeked out from under my lashes.

He was gone.

I should have been relieved. Then why was I filled with such disappointment?

Sitting up, I searched for him, my eyes scanning behind me. I turned, tiny prickles of unease starting to work their way up my spine. Getting to my feet, I walked off a little, looking in every direction. He was nowhere in sight.

Panic started to weasel its way into my chest. I had no car, no idea where I was, and only a cell phone with questionable service. There hadn't been a single person walking by the entire time we had been here.

And just like that, in a blink, I was feeling utterly alone.

"Chase," I called out over the washing waters. "Where did you go?" My shoes stepped on leaves, crunching them underfoot as I turned in circles. "Chase, this isn't funny." He wouldn't just leave me here, would he? I mean I know we joked about it, but really?

"I'm serious. Where are you?"

Still nothing. Not even a whisper of movement. My breath started to come in short pants with the real possibility of hyperventilating. I never had before, but there was a first for everything, like being abandoned in the woods by a selfish asshole. Thank you, mother, for suggesting such a life-altering experience. I was going to wring someone's neck when I got home. Mainly Chase's, the second I got my hands on him.

"Chase!" I screamed.

CHAPTER 6

My voice echoed, and my heart pounded triple time in my chest. "Chase!"

This cannot be happening. Stuff like this does not happen to me, nor would it if we had just stayed in town. Girls don't get left alone in the woods in the city. A gazillion thoughts flipped through my head.

Slasher movie quality. No way was I going to be strung up for some psychopath nut job just to eat my body parts later.

What if he had gotten to Chase first?

If some wacko had gotten the jump on Chase, I was in deep shit. I'd seen the arms on Chase, and he wasn't someone I would have taken lightly. There was a darkness that lurked in those unusual eyes.

Behind me a rustling sounded in the bushes. I bent down ninja style, arming myself with a fallen branch not much bigger than a ruler. Looking down at the wimpy weapon clutched in my hand, I rolled my eyes.

Worthless.

It wasn't much in the way of protection, but in a bind it would have to do.

"Chase," I called out hesitantly.

Zilch.

Sidestepping, I backed up, the branch in a death grip.

The bush shook again, its leaves dancing with movement. Raising the stick for an attack, I waited, poised ... and out raced a twitching squirrel. He took one look at me with his black beady eyes and ran back the other way.

Exhaling the breath I'd been holding, I turned around feeling like a dumbass. My scream rippled out into the air. Chase stood directly behind me, scaring the living shit out of me.

I punched him in the arm. Hard. "You ass. You scared me to death. Where the hell have you been? I thought you were mauled by a mountain lion or something." I hugged my throbbing fist to my chest.

"This is Illinois, not Arizona," he retorted, smirking.

I wanted to backhand that smirk. "You didn't answer the question."

He huffed. "You fell asleep, Angel. I didn't want to disturb you, and I had to make a call, but the service here sucks, so I went to find a clear signal. I was never far away." His eyes turned gentle. Maybe he could read the fear that had been in my expression. "I came as soon as I heard you."

It hadn't been soon enough. "I thought—"

"I know what you thought. I might be an ass, Angel, but I do have some standards. And leaving you stranded is not on the list."

Well, that was good to know.

My shoulders slumped in relief now that there wasn't anything ready to eat, slash, or dice me. Or worse.

He looked up at the sky. "We should get going."

I ran a slightly shaking hand through my dark hair. "I'm ready to blow this joint. It's giving me the willies." The night had already started to descend upon us.

He laughed. "Has anyone ever told you how impossible and heavy on the sarcastic side you are?"

"Sarcasm is just one of the many things I offer."

He lifted a brow at me. "I can only imagine what else you have to offer." He eyed me, over appreciating.

Promptly the blood rushed to my cheeks.

"Red suits you," he commented on the heightened color staining my face.

Ahhh. He made me want to hit him again. I tightened my fist and clamped my mouth shut.

Rushing us back through the woods, he pushed me faster than my bronze legs could keep up with. "Why are we running?" I was going to break something at this pace, probably my neck.

"It's getting late, and I need to get you home," he responded over his shoulder.

Looking to the treetops, I saw the sun was lowering, coloring the horizon in oranges and reds. He kept the grueling pace, and just like I had predicted, I tripped. My toe hit a fallen log, and I felt the ground slip out from under me. I gasped.

Before I fell flat on my rump, Chase was there. His arms secured around my waist, bringing our bodies together. My head swarmed with dizziness from the quick loss of gravity and our proximity. Holding me for a prolonged moment in his embrace, he slowly put me back on my feet, and every rational thought floated away.

I bit my lip as our hearts beat together in a heavy rhythm. I wanted to press my mouth on his mouth like I needed air to breathe. My tongue darted out, wetting my lips, and his eyes narrowed in on the movement. Held suspended by his gaze, I waited. Shimmering silver burned into my eyes and began to not only glow, but shift colors. Like a chameleon, the gray melted into amber.

I should have been freaked out, not intrigued.

But then he slammed his eyes shut, breaking the spell. His hands holding my waist let go of me, and I stumbled for entirely different reasons. My head was still spinning from all the heat infused by our bodies. It felt like an inferno burned between us.

A disciplined control hardened his features, and I took a step back, putting a hand over my chest. My stomach dropped in disappointment, which didn't make a lick of sense. I did not *want* Chase Winters to kiss me. I did not even *like* Chase Winters.

I love when I lied to myself.

After a deep gush of air, he opened his eyes. They were pure titanium again. No hint of dark yellow. I was getting kind of tired of this trick. Maybe I needed glasses. Maybe they were some new kind of contacts. Who knew?

"We need to go now," he growled.

Whatever had just happened between us was gone. I felt an icy barrier being thrown up, separating us, and the jerk was back.

My spine stiffened. "Fine. Don't get your boxers in a wad."

He gave me a look that screamed *don't mess with me.*

We walked a few minutes in silence while I let him stew in his own annoyance. The eye thing was gnawing at me. I just couldn't let it go. "What's wrong with your eyes?" I blurted out.

"What do you mean?" he asked, not stopping. At least he had slowed his pace. I was sure he'd done so for my benefit. He didn't even look like he was breaking a sweat.

"They change colors."

"That is the most absurd thing I've ever heard. Are you sure you didn't hit your head or something back there?"

I might have dropped it if it weren't for the tiniest hitch I heard in his voice. He knew exactly what I meant. "You caught me before I even touched the ground." Those words were a fresh reminder of being in his arms, and the thought made my cheeks instantaneously flush.

Blast it.

"You must have imagined it, or maybe it was a trick of the moon," he said, trying to brush it off as nothing.

"I know what I saw, Chase Winters," I replied, refusing to be discarded.

He looked a little astonished when I said his name, like he'd never heard it from my lips before. "We don't have time for this," he argued.

I wanted to stomp my feet like a two year old and refuse to go any farther until he told me what was going on. The only thing that stopped me was I could only imagine too well how he wouldn't have the slightest problem hauling me over his shoulder fireman style and carrying me kicking and screaming to the car.

We made it to his overpriced car in no time. I slumped into the leather seat, exhausted. Closing my eyes, I listened to the engine purr as we rolled along the road. Being in Chase's car was the closest thing to being engulfed in his arms. His scent was everywhere.

Teasing me.

When he pulled into his driveway, our street was as dead as ever. I couldn't have gotten out of the car fast enough.

Space. I needed loads of it from him before I did something incredibly foolish and stupid, like grab a handful of that dark hair and seal my lips to his.

I wasn't normally the aggressor. He did something to me that had me flying from one extreme to another. It was draining.

Just as I was about to grab the handle, something caught my eye and Chase's. He frowned. A man in his late forties stood directly in front of the bumper, headlights blaring in his eyes. He had short sandy hair, irritated hazel eyes, and a week's stubble growing on his face.

"Who is that?" I asked softly, trying not to freak out.

"That is a pissed off Devin—Lexi's dad. *Shit*," he muttered under his breath.

I stiffened at his distress.

Chase got out of the car, and I followed, feeling unsure I should be here. I kind of wanted to tuck my tail between my legs and scamper home. As we approached, neither Chase nor Devin spared me a glance.

Devin was good-looking for an old dude, with that distinguished Brad Pitt look going for him. There were traces of white in his hair and facial growth. "Where have you been?" He punctuated each word at Chase.

This was not the first impression I had imagined, but it was very clear that Devin was not happy with Chase. It wasn't late enough that I could imagine Chase breaking curfew, if he had one at all. Chase didn't seem like the kind of guy who adhered to curfews.

"Out," Chase responded, shoulders squared.

There seemed to be some kind of internal argument here and a bit of an authority complex. I hoped there wasn't going to be any bloodshed.

"*Jesus*, Chase. What were you thinking?" Devin indicated me with his fired up gaze.

"I wasn't," he admitted, not sounding at all sorry about it either.

"You know better, damn it. What if something happened? Did you happen to notice it's dark out?"

Uh, duh. It was night. What was up with these people? Were they some form of warped vampires? I mean, seriously, I didn't get it.

Chase never flinched. I couldn't say the same for me. "I lost track of time, but I rushed her home as soon as I realized my mistake. It's fine. Nothing happened. She's fine," Chase defended himself.

Well, not if you considered my mental state. I felt like we were being scolded, but I didn't have the foggiest clue what we had done that was that "wrong."

"That may be. But next time, you won't be so lucky. I've tried to warn you, both you and Lexi. Travis is the only one who seems to get it, but he had to learn the hard way."

Why did I get the sneaking suspicion that he was warning them about me? *I* seemed to be the common ground here. I kept my mouth tightly sealed, regardless of the fact that I had plenty to say. Lexi's dad terrified me. And I didn't agree with the way he treated his nephew.

"You need to be more careful. Especially now." Devin's pointed gaze looked right at me.

"I know. Devin, it won't happen again," Chase assured him.

"Damn right it won't."

Chase's jaw flexed. His eyes started to do that thing again that he claimed they didn't do. They flashed brightly in violence, lighting the darkness surrounding him like twin high beams on a car.

He stepped in front of me, putting himself between Devin and me. "You don't want to push me right now," he warned, his voice dropping low and dangerously. The air around us vibrated in tension, thick enough to cut with a knife.

Devin nodded his head in some kind of understanding that was lost on me. I hated being the last to know what was going on. This whole conversation was freaking me out to the max, and I'd already had more than enough of freaking out for one day.

"Just be careful, Chase." Devin looked at me one last time and shook his head in disgrace.

With long strides, he ate up the driveway. The moment the door swung shut behind Devin, I jumped down Chase's throat. Not with my tongue, either.

"What the flying *f* is going on?" I asked to the shadow of his back.

He had yet to turn around and face me. I watched his shoulders move in an even tempo with his breathing. Long. Deep. Breaths.

When he finally looked at me, I wished he hadn't. The menacing expression he wore was worse than being abandoned. The daggers aimed down at me made me shiver.

"If you know what's good for you, you'll stay away from us," he warned me.

"What makes you think *you* know what's good for me?" God, he knew how to flip my switch.

"If you value your life, you will."

"Are you threatening me?"

He shrugged. "Take it however you want."

"You're despicable. I never want to see you again." I stomped across the yard and slammed the door as hard as I could. Chase Winters could go to hell.

CHAPTER 7

The following days crawled by. There was less than a week before school started, and I was dreading it. Being the *new girl* sucked. At least at my old school, it was easy to get lost in the crowd. At Hall High, I would be an oddity. In the small school I pictured, everyone knew everyone; that's how it had been in town. Why would school be any different? Blending in wouldn't be an option.

At least I had Lexi.

Or did I?

Lexi called or texted me almost every day. She could tell something was amiss.

I felt bad for lying to her and making excuses. I just wasn't in the mood for company. The rain we'd gotten for two days hadn't helped. On the bright side, I got a lot of game time in, and that was worth its weight in gold.

Messing around on my Xbox, I'd gained two new gamer friends this week. The storm had knocked out our Internet access for the duration of the storm. So this was the first time I was able to connect back up. We'd become like old friends again, much to Mom's dismay.

It was sort of my crack to an addict.

I went ape shit without it.

Since the rain had ruined my plans of finishing the paint on my furniture, I decided to make it a top priority today. The sun was beaming through my window without a cloud in the sky. Plus, I was sick of digging through a suitcase trying to find my bras and socks.

Slipping on an old T-shirt and shorts, I skipped downstairs.

Mom was sleeping and would be up soon to get ready for her shift. Clucking my tongue, I tried to remember where I had stuffed the art supplies I'd used to prime earlier—no simple task in a house that was still unorganized. Rummaging in the miscellaneous boxes in the laundry room, I found the one marked *artsy fartsy*.

Yup, that would be it.

Classy.

Gathering my paints and brushes, I opened the garage door. A stream of light lit the black musty space. After dragging each piece from the garage—a workout for my arms—I began to apply the base coat.

Not even twenty minutes into my tedious project, a shadow fell over me, blocking my natural light. Looking up, I locked my gaze with a pair of eyes that could have been polished silver. There went my solitude.

And my mood.

"You haven't finished that yet?" Chase asked, angling that dark head of his at the nightstand I was just about finished with.

"I'm putting the last coat on, nosey. Don't you have someone else to bug?" I scooted the bucket I was sitting on, trying to allow for more light.

"Well, aren't you a ray of sunshine?" he said, examining my work.

"Should I be? I'm pretty sure that last time we talked, you told me to stay away from you. Voilà. Your wish is my command." I was feeling pretty snarky.

His brows drew together as he sized me up, probably wondering if it was my time of the month.

Guys were so hard to understand.

And guys like Chase were impossible to understand.

I shielded the sun from my eyes, watching him. He was so tall.

His lips lifted at the corners. "I said if you knew what was good for you. It's obvious you are one of the girls that don't listen to reason."

"Obviously," I dragged out. Then I did what any girl would do. I flicked my paintbrush at him, splattering his white T-shirt with silver metallic paint.

"You are definitely going to pay for that," he threatened me with a halfhearted attempt.

"It's no more than you deserve," I reasoned.

"Maybe," he agreed.

"Um, excusez-moi. Did you just admit that you might have been wrong?"

"Funny." He examined the damage, which wasn't as bad as it could have been. There was a tiny splat of paint marring his cheek.

I busted out laughing. It was just the most comical thing to see jerk-of-the-year with paint on his beautiful face.

"You think this is funny?" he asked.

I couldn't even respond. I was in such hysterics. It had been so long since I'd laughed with such zeal. Before Dad became a drunk. I clutched my stomach because it was starting to cramp.

He stood by and just watched me convulse with laughter. "Are you going insane?"

Taking in a gulp of air, I grinned widely. "Here, let me get it." I took my finger and wiped at the spot. It only made it worse, smearing it. A giggle slipped out.

"Is it gone?" His voice was soft.

I shook my head, my ponytail swinging with my movements. "Not quite." I licked the end of my finger and moved in closer. Then I pressed it against his cheek again, clearing the remaining paint.

"Did you just wipe your spit on me?" he asked, his gray irises twinkling and his breath heating my face.

Shit. Not *again*.

My toes curled. My stomach swirled. My hormones went into overdrive.

"It's good for the skin," I said.

He leaned back on the garage. "What have you been doing all week locked up in that house?"

"Xbox," I replied, returning to my chore.

"What do you play?"

"What *don't* I play is more the question." The brush moved in long easy strides under my hand. "I'm a total gamer," I admitted, unashamed at my geekdom.

He rolled his eyes. "God, you and Travis are made for each other. He monopolizes the TV downstairs all day with that damn war game."

"You mean Call of Duty?" I supplied.

"Whatever," he said, uninterested.

It made me grin. The awkwardness that I had been sure would be there the next time we saw each other was nowhere to be found.

Strange.

"I kind of pegged you for a smarty-pants, not a gamer," he commented. "Did you know that Native Americans named this place the Valley of the Spring? It is found at the only point where the high bluffs from Spring Creek are close together."

"What other kind of useless knowledge do you have stored up there in that hot head of yours?" I was enthralled by his voice.

He changed the subject. "Are you done with this?" he asked, his hand resting on the dresser.

"Yeah, it should be dry by now."

"Good." He lifted the dresser like it was a paperweight.

I tried desperately not to notice the muscles straining through his shirt or be impressed.

And I failed splendidly.

Standing in front of the door, he cleared his throat.

I jumped up, tearing my gaze from his chest, and grabbed the handle. "Thanks." I smiled sheepishly and felt confused.

One minute he was threatening me, the next he was sweet and helpful.

· · ·

THE SECOND CHASE WENT HOME, I felt achingly alone in this quiet house with all its creepy noises. What I needed was an activity. After being cooped up inside for most of the week, I decided to go explore the world. I had yet to leave my yard since we moved here. It was past time I learned my way around.

Changing into some old jeans and a pair of cozy tennis shoes, I headed out the back door. My legs were begging for some exercise. If I didn't use them for some strenuous activity, I wouldn't be able to sleep, again.

I refused to believe that Chase had anything to do with my restlessness.

The front of my house was bland with windblown wheat fields, but in the backyard, it was nothing but miles of woods. Some ten-year-old boy would have a heyday back here with all these towering trees. They were perfect for climbing and tree houses—large, thick branches, yet low enough for you to climb.

I wasn't feeling *that* adventurous today. My feet were staying on the ground.

The sun was still high and provided plenty of light. No need for a flashlight. I didn't plan on being gone that long, just a swift hike around the property and back again.

Maybe I should have left a breadcrumb trail.

Dried brown leaves crunched and twigs snapped as I entered into the forest. It was so serene, as if nothing had touched it. There was a reflective quality in walking alone with nature. With each step I took, a piece of the unease I was feeling slipped away. Being the new girl, feeling out of my element, the emotional loss of Dad.

Then there was Chase. It all fell back to him.

Shaking him from my head, I stopped and took in my surroundings, realizing I had daydreamed for most of the walk. Typical. My sense of direction was lost somewhere between a new school and my teetering emotions.

The woods took on a gloomy aura. Believe it or not, a mist swirled over the moss and the rocky ground. Talk about mystical. Pulling my cell phone out of my pocket, I checked the clock. Time had vanished—fast—which explained the fading darkness that snuck up on me.

Okay, not a big deal. I just needed to go back the way I'd come. Hastily.

Backtracking, I felt my confidence start to waver. Doubt slipped in. Maybe this wasn't the right way, but I wasn't about to give up. With each step I took, I became more certain that I was screwed.

And crazy lost.

No need to panic. Yet.

I had my cell phone. I would just call Lexi. Retrieving the phone again, I punched in her number.

Shit.

No service. Of course. There was never service in this godforsaken, stupid, country hellhole.

Okay, think, I scolded. I know that the sun rises in the east and sets in the west. My room had a clear view of the sunrise every morning, along with a fantastic view of Chase's bedroom.

Totally beside the point.

But it meant that the road in front of my house faced north. So if I kept the declining sun on my left, I should hit the road some time. Was walking alone in the woods safer than walking the street at night?

At this point, I didn't think it mattered.

Now that I had the sun in my sight, I started walking again. My feet ached, my head hurt, and I could feel the rise of tears burning the back of my throat. This day had gone down the crapper.

And then the nightmare began. The same howl from the other night rang out in the near distance behind me—somewhere in the forest with me.

Now it was time to panic.

I waited a beat before I took off at a dead run.

Every muscle in my body was tense with fear, making my movements clumsy. Sure, I wasn't the most graceful person, but add a good dose of terror, and I'm a klutz.

Leaves smacked my cheeks and arms, but I didn't notice. I was running on pure adrenaline. So it was no surprise when my feet tangled in some brush, sending me sprawling over the solid ground. My elbows skidded over rocks, wood slivers cutting into my flesh. I called out as the pain stung my eyes. Covered in dirt, leaves jumbled in my hair, I pushed myself to my feet. Blood trickled down one of my arms.

Ugh, that was going to leave a few nasty bruises and scrapes. How was I going to explain that to Mom?

The animal cried again, only closer this time. It wasn't even a normal howl and sounded more like a tortured soul.

Scrambling, I ignored the pain cutting through me and forced myself to keep running. The seconds turned to minutes as my pounding feet were accompanied by something much stealthier—its movements graceful compared to my clumsy loud-ass feet.

Turning my head around, I scanned behind me, looking for a wolf or some other kind of wild beast. Whatever it was, it was nipping at my heels, gaining ground fast.

The sun was all but gone. Nightfall submerged the forest, making it nearly impossible for me to see. I could hear the puffs and heavy breathing before it appeared in front of me. Skidding to a stop, I realized I was royally screwed.

Its red eyes pierced through the blackness as it stalked me on all fours, circling its prey. A sob escaped my trembling lips. This was like no dog I'd ever seen. Black as spades, his sheer size alone was ungodly. Disgusting foam dripped from its teeth down its matted and scarred muzzle. Maybe it was a scientific experiment gone wrong—a rabid dog.

Whatever *it* was, *it* wasn't friendly and only made my fear spike.

The thing's front paw stomped on the dirt floor.

Without warning, the creature lunged in the air and in perfect precision took me to the ground with it. Heavy paws pinned my chest, razor-sharp teeth bared, and it drooled something that smelled like sewage and probably burned like acid. I didn't want to find out.

The hideous thing growled low in its throat, eyes staring at my neck. If I didn't do something soon, it was going to gash into that exposed flesh, tearing into a vital vein.

I was going to die.

Mom's face flashed into my mind. She was going to be devastated. I was all that she had left, and I couldn't leave her alone. She needed me.

Its jaw snapped in my face, and there was no way I could stop the instinctual flinch. I thought for sure it was going to maul my face. Twisting my head to the side, I closed my eyes, and sharp pain radiated through my shoulder as the hound sunk its teeth into my flesh. I screamed from the intense throbbing, like poison blazing through my arm.

The bloodthirsty wolf-like creature was jostled from my bucking, easing some of its weight off my crushed chest. Just the small window of opportunity I needed. This probably was the worst plan in history, but it was the only one I had.

With the sting radiating down my arm, I opened my eyes and brought the heel of my foot up underneath it. I used all the strength I had left behind the kick I delivered to its chest and neck. Yelping, the mutt rolled off me before crashing into a nearby tree trunk. I didn't wait to see what happened next.

Bolting to my feet, I took off again. My lungs were heaving in loud pained sobs. Even over my own breathing, I could hear the racing thump of paws behind me. That thing had recovered far too quickly, and I didn't have a clue if there were any more of those *things* out there.

My body was starting to shriek at me when I stumbled. The shooting agony in my arm was blurring my vision and impairing my movements more. I knew it wasn't long before I would lose consciousness and tumble to my death. I'd never fainted, so of course this would be a hell of a time to start.

As I was just about to give up, every ounce of my energy depleted, a blur of movement shot out of nowhere—straight toward me.

No. Not again, I screamed inside my head. A warm hand snaked out from behind me, covering my mouth.

My eyes bulged.

"Shhh, don't scream," a voice whispered, tickling my ear with his breath. Even faced with the worse kind of horror, even faced with death, I knew that voice.

I slumped against his chest, giving him the bulk of my rundown and battered body.

Chase.

He turned me around to face him, a finger on his lips, signaling for me to keep quiet. I nodded in understanding. Feelings of safety, security, and protection rushed through me. His eyes were lit up like the moon against the black night. They ran over my dirt-smeared face. His mouth tightened, and the pulse at his neck throbbed.

Sadly, his inspection was cut short. Another round of ear-piercing screeches vibrated through the air in threatening frustration. I didn't think about what I did; this was not the time for shame or embarrassment. So, of course, I threw myself into his arms and whimpered. Pulling me to his chest, he shielded me against the harrowing sound. His scent wrapped around me.

"You're safe," he whispered close to my ear. "I promise. Nothing will harm you."

I snuggled against his secure embrace, doing everything I could to forget the throbbing bite on my shoulder.

"Can you walk?" he gently asked.

I gave a slight nod.

"The road is close. Come on, we need to get you to my car," he instructed me, taking charge.

The knowledge that his car was near gave me the push I needed. With his arms holding me up, he led us through the winding forest. Those things were still out there, hunting us. Every now and then, they would make a short bark. When we broke across the tree line, relief like nothing I'd ever experienced before poured over me.

"*Shit,*" he muttered.

CHAPTER 8

"Don't run," he muttered beside me.

Easier said than done. Every muscle, every fiber of my being was screaming for me to run. I shut my eyes as a sickening growl thundered in front of Chase's car. It was followed by a deep grumble from his chest. I could feel the vibrations under my fingers.

I risked a glance up at him. He looked downright ominous and dominant, like an alpha, keeping with the whole dog theme. His flaming eyes had flecks of topaz that grew, overpowering the silver. The rumbling was low in his chest, and the bands of his arms were bunched for an attack.

"Did you ... did you just growl at them?" I asked, my voice quivering.

"Angel. Get in the car now!"

That was totally a growl. "But you just said—" I countered.

"Are you really going to argue with me *right* now?" he shot back, pushing me toward the car.

He had a point. "What about—"

The haste in his voice caught my attention. "Run!" he thundered, right before the topaz took over completely, like fireballs, and the mad hound ambushed.

Finally, it sunk in, and I ran toward his car. Fumbling with the handle, my dirt-covered nails scratched against the chrome. Once I was in the car and the door was secure, I heard the crack of bones. Oh. My. God. Please don't let that be Chase with a snapped neck.

Sitting on the edge of the seat, I waited. One minute. Two minutes. Five minutes. With each passing minute, dread pitted in my belly, making me want to puke. The heat from my crazy rapid breathing began to fog the windows. Hastily, I brushed away the haze with my shaky hand.

At last, the driver door swung open, nearly giving me a heart attack.

He was alive. A wave of faintness struck me.

Trembling, my teeth chattered and the dizziness and queasiness increased. It felt like I had just gotten off the worst Tilt-A-Whirl ride of my life. I knew I only had seconds before I would hit the floor of his car, like a fallen tree.

Chase.

My last thought before I was consumed with blackness.

"ANGEL."

My name whispered in the back of my mind, floating through the fog. When I opened my eyes, I was gazing at soft lamplight and crickets chirped from the open window. The air had cooled considerably, and a breeze caressed my face, teasing the curtains. Sluggishly, the events started trickling through my memory as my cheek rubbed along something soft, like cotton. I was secured up against something warm and solid.

A heart beat under my ear, steady and strong. It took only a nanosecond for me to figure out it was Chase. His arm curved around me, resting comfortably on my hip. The thumb of his hand was tucked into the side of my tattered jeans, searing my flesh. Casually, he leaned against the back of my couch, my head on his shoulder, and my entire body supported by his.

I was afraid to move.

I was afraid to breathe.

Unfortunately, the torment of my injuries also returned painfully, along with the awareness of every blessed inch of his body. The tangled mess he was causing inside my gut was so foreign. I didn't know what I was feeling, or if what I was feeling was anything more than my overactive imagination. Nothing had prepared me for this kind of intensity.

The pad of his thumb moved, skirting the hem of my jeans, and I sucked in a gulp of air. I felt hot and feverish. Nibbling on my lip, I tried everything to not think of the hard body molded to me in so many intimate ways.

He stopped breathing.

Wincing, I lifted my head off his shoulder and looked up into his face. I swear I could lose myself in the pools of his silver eyes. They were crystalline metal now and clear of any alien glow or color muta-tion. Sometimes they reminded me of the end of a kaleidoscope.

Was it possible to have a dark knight in shining armor?

His eyes made my heart skip. There was so much going on inside them, and yet, I couldn't get a read on him. Shifting in his arms, I put some needed breathing room between us. He hissed.

I looked down at his arm, and there was a wrap soaked with blood. Concern instantly swept through me. "You're hurt."

"It's nothing."

"*That* does not look like nothing." The bandage was more red than white.

"Trust me, I'm fine. I heal fast anyway. It will be gone in no time." He said it like it was no big deal.

Yeah. Okay, Superman. Just like a guy to brush off his injuries.

Remembering that we were on the porch, I asked, "How did we get in my house?" I wrapped my arms around myself.

"I picked your lock," he stated.

"Oh."

"You know this isn't the big city. No one locks their doors."

"Some habits die hard." Did I also need to mention that it was illegal to break into someone's house and that I was just hunted down by some wild, freak of nature?

"How are you?" His fingers brushed over my chin, tilting my face upward as he examined my face thoroughly.

"I don't know," I answered honestly, casting my eyes downward. Rubbing a hand over my newly bandaged shoulder, it didn't look anywhere near as bad as his. I didn't want to be a wuss, but it hurt.

There hadn't been any time to process just what the heck had happened. Memories of how close I'd come to being mangled into some kind of crazy-ass animal's dinner branded my mind. But for the first time tonight, I felt safe, with Chase nonetheless. *Figures.*

"Do you remember what happened?" His dark voice was pleasant and sincere for once.

"Mostly. What was that thing?" I asked.

He leaned his head back, unfazed by the events of the evening. I couldn't say the same. "Probably a rabid dog."

That's what I had originally thought too, until I had stared into its red eyes. "I'm not sure. Its eyes … I saw evil in its eyes," I reluctantly admitted, afraid he would think I was nuts.

"I wouldn't doubt it," he mumbled.

My face scrunched in confusion.

"It was obviously sick and demented."

"Did—did you kill it?" I ran a hand through my ratted, leaf-strewn hair. Gawd, I must look atrocious.

He shrugged as if killing evil, dog-like creatures was an everyday occurrence. "If I hadn't, it would have tried to kill us."

I knew what he said was true. It had bloodlust on its brain, and there was no saving a creature like that. The humane thing to do was to put it down. "You snapped its neck, didn't you?" The crunching of bones echoed in my head.

"Do you *honestly* want to know the gory details?" he asked, frowning.

Point taken.

SAVING ANGEL

"There is one thing I can't piece together." I scowled.

He raised *that* one brow of his, smirking.

"How did you find me?" I whispered. The burning question lingered in the air.

Before he could answer, a bolt of lightning struck in the distance, lighting up the yard. Acting like a frightened ninny, I literally jumped into his lap. His arms caught me, steadying us at the same time and keeping us from falling off the couch.

He lowered his head, resting his forehead against mine. Now *I* stopped breathing. Why did he keep doing this to me? I didn't even *like* him.

Lie, my mind screamed.

Fine. He didn't like me.

There might be a storm blowing outside, but my focus was only on Chase and his startling eyes. His hands shifted around me, bringing me closer against him, all the while never breaking eye contact. The smirk he'd had earlier was gone, replaced with a scowl of his own. I trailed my hands from the front of his chest to up around his neck, making our position more comfortable, nothing between us but the thin annoying barrier of material.

Searching my face, he angled his head, bringing his lips closer to mine. Holy hell, he was going to kiss me. So caught up in my own heady feelings, I almost missed the eerie glow of his eyes a moment before he closed them. My mind told me to pull back. My body, however, had entirely different plans as it leaned in, waiting impatiently.

Chase was trouble with a capital T.

To kiss me. Or not to kiss me. It was as if he was plucking the petals of a flower, trying to decide.

I felt the moment his decision was made. His head fell back from me against the back of the couch—away from me.

"Angel?" Lexi's voice called out from somewhere near the entryway.

Suddenly, I found myself properly dumped on the porch in a suitable span. The jarring impact knocked the wind out of me, and it happened so fast. I hadn't even realized I'd been moving until my butt hit the floor—hard—and I landed with an *oomph*.

"Oh, Chase, I didn't see you," Lexi said sweetly.

What were they? Ninjas? Why was it I could never hear them until they had already scared the piss out of me?

"What are you guys doing?" she asked, grinning, implying that she had a good idea what we were doing.

My cheeks were painted crimson.

"Nothing for you to worry about," Chase replied, not altogether thrilled to see his cousin.

"Are you sure? Because from this view—" she was properly cut off.

"Don't go there, Lex," he said in a don't-question-me tone.

Wow, someone just went to douche mode in zero to sixty seconds.

A curious look passed over her expression.

Chase got to his feet and looked at me once before twisting toward Lexi. "You coming?" he growled lowly.

She shook her blonde bouncing hair. "Not yet."

"Lexi," he warned.

"I just need ten minutes. Is that too much to ask for?" Her voice was sugary and hopeful.

"You know it is." Gee. He was like sour patch kids. One minute he was sweet, the next he was sour.

"It's okay for you, but not the rest of us? Please. Chase, cut me some slack." She pouted, puffing out her glossy lips. "I just want to see how she is doing." Those turquoise eyes pleaded with him for some understanding, which was so over my head.

"I'm not leaving you with her." He stood, feet planted, arms crossed, and seriously unhappy.

She smiled at him. "Ah, *now* I understand."

She did? 'Cuz I sure as hell didn't.

"Rest assured, cousin, she's safe from me. I promise and cross my heart." She made an X over her chest.

That sounded ridiculous coming from Lexi's mouth. She couldn't hurt a fly, but I was sure that I didn't have the slightest idea what was *really* going on.

His eyes softened, like he found it difficult to deny her anything. I guess that might be the perk of being the only girl in a house over-filled with testosterone. A look passed between them, and his shoulders relaxed.

"Fine, but hurry," he conceded.

She gave him a winning smile, perfect pearly teeth and all.

I glowered at his back as he walked across the lawn.

"Did you guys—" Lexi sprung on me the second he was out of earshot.

I cut her off before that sentence went to an uncomfortable place. "No, nothing happened."

"Hmm," she murmured. "What *did* happen?"

I sighed at what a mess this day had turned into. "I got lost in the woods. He found me."

She looked at me expectantly. "Were you rolling in the dirt when he found you?"

Crap. I had totally forgotten about how shit-eous I looked. Running a hand over my head, a leaf fell from my hair. "Um, I sort of got attacked by a ... I don't know what it was. A mutated mutt."

A deep, thoughtful expression creased her brows. "Well, that explains his mood. How is the shoulder?" She was at my side in an instant.

I nodded. "Okay, thanks to Chase."

"He has his moments," she said, frowning at my injury.

Like the moment when he had almost *kissed* me? How was that for moments? "Far and few in-between," I mumbled.

A strand of lightning strung across the sky, shooting a ray of light into the room. As I looked at her, I noticed that her eyes were glowing like a cat's at night. Just like Chase's. They reflected off the lightning. Maybe I had overtaxed my ability to see things straight, or I could just chalk it up to the end of an extremely screwed up night.

"I came to ask if you want to go shopping for school supplies and stuff tomorrow," she invited me.

The "and stuff" made me groan. Lexi could shop until you drop, and the reminder that school started in a few days was like having ice water thrown on my face. "I guess we better. Ignoring it isn't going to make school start any later." I was a procrastinator in the finest.

"Great." She was the perkiest person on the earth at night. She seemed to come alive with vigor, whereas I just wanted to pass out. "You look really tired. I'll let you get some rest. See you tomorrow."

I glanced once at the window and then dragged my battered butt and pounding arm to bed.

CHAPTER 9

I popped a handful of purple and green Skittles into my mouth—my favorite candy on the planet, but only the purple, green, and occasionally red ones. The rest either got thrown away or given to Mom, who hated that I ate all the *good* ones.

This morning my arm was an annoying dull ache but nothing unmanageable. Self-diagnosed: I would live. Not poisonous after all, thank my scrawny butt.

Lexi arrived at my doorstep at an ungodly hour. Luckily, I liked ungodly hours. Mom ... not so much.

"Did I wake your mom?" she asked in a whisper, her eyes beaming.

"I doubt it. She sleeps like the dead. Are you ready?" I asked.

"Please, do you even need to ask? I'll drive." She squealed.

Lexi, of course, looked epic. Her car wasn't any less awesome. Apparently, her family had money.

"Nice car," I commented, a tad envious. How could I not be? She was drop-dead gorgeous, had fabulous clothes, and a kickass car. The only downside I could see with her life was she lived with Chase. Or maybe that was pure heaven.

"Thanks. How's the arm?" she asked, her brows drawn together.

I shrugged. "I think I'll live. How's Chase?" My voice fluctuated over his name.

"It was just a scratch; you can barely tell it's there," she reassured me. There was a strangeness to her voice, like she was uncomfortable talking about what had happened. She shifted in her seat, keeping her eyes on the road.

But I wasn't convinced. Was it just me, or had there in fact been a whole lot of oozing red stuff? It made me a little woozy just thinking about it. Blood and I were not good friends.

I wanted to press her for more details, but something in her expression told me I wouldn't get any more information from her.

There wasn't a whole lot I needed in the form of supplies, just the basics: pens, notebooks, paper, and pencils. Lexi, on the other hand, bought out the store with a little swipe of a gold card. She claimed she needed décor for her locker. I hadn't even known there was such a thing. You can decorate your locker?

It seemed like a waste of money—this coming from a girl who didn't have a lot.

She picked up magnetic picture frames, a cutesy dry erase board, locker wallpaper equipped with shag carpet, and a tiny blinged-out chandelier.

Holy cow. Seriously? Her locker was going to look better than my entire house. Even the supplies she purchased were puking pink, rhinestones, and glitter. She was worse than a bad drag queen.

I was starting to feel sort of drab and boring next to her. She didn't do it on purpose; it was just who she was, and regardless of her disregard for money, I couldn't help but like her. Her flaming ball of energy was such a refreshing change to be around. It could be because I spent so much of my time alone in that Frankenstein house. I swear, she was hopped up on Red Bull or something equally as energizing.

"I'm starved. Let's get something to eat," she suggested after we left like the tenth store.

Thank God, 'cuz I was dragging ass. Fuel and a place to plant my butt sounded like nirvana right now.

She took me to The Village Diner. The place was everything I thought about small-town diners—a hole-in-the-wall dive. It had the worn leather booths, a counter bar, a waitress named Sally, who snapped her gum, and everybody knew everybody.

But when we walked in, there was a uniform hush that overcame the room, accompanied by whispers and speculations. I hated to be the topic in a room.

"It might not look like much, but the food is amazing, and all the kids hang out here. You know, after football games, before dances, the usual," she informed me, completely ignorant of the crowd of eyes on us.

I was sure their choices were limited. Good thing I wasn't into team spirit. School functions were at the very bottom of my list of things to do on a Friday night.

"It's … quaint," I replied, trying to avoid the peering eyes. And it did have a cozy feel after everyone stopped staring at the new girl —namely me.

We took a booth in the corner with a window seat. Almost immediately after sitting down, two of the tables next to us got up and left. They took their bill and went to the register. Some still had half-eaten food on their plates, and now, it was just Lexi and me in our little corner.

A girl with short, cropped hair came up to greet us after what felt like too long. Didn't they have a quota on greeting the customer? She kept her head down, not making eye contact, and put plenty of space between herself and our table.

People here were strange.

We placed our drink orders with Jane, our not-so-friendly server, and then scanned the menu.

Swinging my legs under the booth, I asked, "So what do you recommend?" Everything looked good.

"Hm, I love their sandwiches. And their fries are ah-ma-zing."

"Sandwich it is."

"Are you nervous about the first day?" she asked over the top of her plastic menu.

I shrugged, biting on the end of my straw, more nervous than I thought. "I'd have to have elephant skin not to be."

She giggled. "Sorry, I was imagining you with gray, wrinkly, leathery skin. Not pretty."

I smiled in return.

"Don't worry. I'll be there, and so will Chase. I can introduce you to a few of our friends."

Slumping back in the booth, I thought about what kinds of friends Chase would have. Did I really want to meet them?

Jane came back to take our orders with the same rude behavior as before. They might have *good* food here, but the quality of the service sucked hardcore.

"What will it be?" Jane asked in a bored voice, sticking her pen in her mouth.

How about my foot up your ass?

"I'll have the roast beef, no cheese, and could you make sure to put my fries on a separate plate? I don't want them touching," I ordered in a bitchy tone. So what if they thought the new girl was a smartass. Let them have a taste of their own medicine.

Lexi snickered.

Jane just stared at me like I'd grown horns, no longer smacking her gum. She scribbled my order on a little notepad and waited for Lexi's.

"I'll have the turkey BLT with fries," Lexi informed her.

Not missing a beat or even lifting her head, Jane replied, annoyed, "We don't have the turkey BLT today."

After a minute when Lexi still hadn't said anything else, Jane finally looked up. I shifted uncomfortably in my seat, unsure where this was going.

Lexi leaned forward on her elbows, staring long and hard into Jane's huge eyes. In a voice steady with concentration, Lexi said, "I think you are mistaken. You *do* have the turkey BLT. It was on today's specials." Lexi never severed contact, and her eyes did that spooky color-changing thing.

Jane looked like she'd been zombiefied, and then just like that, she snapped out of it. "Oh, I'm sorry," she said sweetly and in a different tone than when she had greeted us. "Of course we do. How silly of me. I will put this order right in."

Lexi smiled brightly at her.

What the hell?

"What just happened?" I inquired of Lexi.

She turned her turquoise eyes at me all innocently. "What do you mean? I saw it on the specials when we walked in."

I didn't question that it was. It was more what had been up with the whole zombie dead-eyes. She'd had Jane in some kind of you're-under-my-spell trance. I would stake my sandwich on it and Lexi's.

"The whole eye thing you did. That was ... totally not normal."

She looked at me like I had just had a brain cramp and fallen off the deep end into some unknown abyss. "Are you sure you are feeling okay? School jitters?" she suggested.

I wasn't the one doing alien mojo with their eyes, I screamed in my head. Slouching against the seat, I realized I wasn't going to get any straight answers from her. Well, I would just figure it out on my own then. Somehow. I got the feeling that this was just the tip of the iceberg. There was a whole lot more under the surface.

Not to mention, this whole conversation was preposterous anyway. Luckily our food came in record time, a big improvement from when we were seated. I was sure I had Lexi and her super glare to thank.

"Angel, I'm sorry. I didn't mean to upset you," she apologized, noticing my silence while I stewed.

I didn't want to argue with her. "It's fine. You're probably right. I haven't been sleeping well, and I think I'm just being paranoid."

She looked at me, concerned, and I glanced around the room to avoid her gaze. Not a single person had been seated in any of the empty booths around us. Occasionally, the guy at the bar and his buddy would look over at us. It was like being in *The Twilight Zone*. I swear, I could hear the music haunting me in the background. Everyone wore the same kind of unsettling expression.

Fear.

Quickly, I averted my gaze back to Lexi, who didn't seem to be the least aware of anything abnormal. She eyed me expectantly, and the smells of bacon and beef hit me as I recalled that our food had been served.

Right, I needed to eat. "Do you come here often?" I asked, biting into pure bliss. This was good, homemade, but still not like Mom's.

"I told you it was the best," she said, nibbling on a fry. "But yeah, ever since Mom left, it's easier on my dad to eat out. He is not much of a cook. Sometimes Chase, Travis, or I will help out."

"I'm sorry, Lexi. I didn't mean to bring up something so hurtful."

She waved her pink manicured hand. "Don't even stress about it. It was a long time ago."

This was probably completely tacky of me, but I couldn't refrain from asking. "What happened to Chase's parents?" I knew it was invasive, but there was so much I didn't know about him.

That thought stopped me. Did I want to know more?

Her eyes deepened in sadness. "His dad ran out on him and his mom while she was pregnant. It was like, 'Thanks for the good time. Now I've got to run,' and run he did. Chase has never seen him, nor does he want to."

My heart sunk and sunk again. I could sort of relate to the whole Daddy is an SOB, but at least I had known mine before all the drama. Maybe it was better to have not known him at all. Then you don't know what you're missing.

She continued. "His mom died shortly after childbirth with complications. He never knew either of his parents and has lived with us his whole life."

"That is so sad." My voice thickened, and my eyes blurred. They filled with water, hurting for the little boy who had grown to have such a chip on his shoulder.

"I know he can be such a prick, but he hasn't had the easiest life, and he does have a good reason for it. He pushes people away on purpose, afraid to get close to anyone, except Travis and me. We're the closest thing he has to family. The only thing really."

Wow. That gave me a whole new perspective on Chase. He was definitely an asstard when he wanted to be, but I couldn't help my heart from softening toward him a little more. At this rate, he would keep chipping away the shield of anger I'd built up, reserved just for guys like him.

~

I WAS SITTING on the old window seat in my room in a pair of boxers, a tee, and polka dot knee-high socks. I looked like a mess, but I was comfortable. In my book, that overruled fashion any day.

The house was so quiet and dead you could hear a pin drop. Hugging my knees to my chest, I pulled up the blinds. A gazillion stars covered the night sky, bright and luminous. Not at all like Tucson. Sure they had stars, but *this* was cosmic.

What would it be like to be among all that spellbinding beauty?

No sooner had the thought crossed my mind when a prickling sensation spread over my skin, as if someone was watching me. Looking across the yard, my eyes locked on a pair of yellow specks. I blinked hard.

They were still there, and it wasn't dots, but a pair of eyes—a pair of eyes that belonged to Chase.

Goose bumps covered my arms, and my body was on full alert. I knew it was him. Not to mention, I was gawking at his bedroom window. Confession, I might have seen him pull off his shirt a time or two—accidentally of course. Chase might get under my skin, however I wasn't dead, and a little peek never hurt, right? I wasn't being overly stalker-ish.

Who was I kidding?

Transfixed, he looked at me. Slowly, my eyes began to adjust in the darkness, and I could just make out the poetic features of his face. None of it explained the creepy glowing of those topaz eyes.

I felt the challenge in his stare, daring me to look away, to see if he could scare me or warn me off. More than once he had implied that he wasn't *safe*, but all he had done was save me.

I couldn't look away, even if I wanted to. His eyes held me, frozen. My heart jackhammered in my chest, and my room clotted with

79

tension. His piercing gaze was doing something to me, like he was inside my head, coaxing me. It was a good thing we had a yard between us, because right now, I knew I would do something irrationally stupid.

Like kiss him, throw myself in his arms, and beg him to touch me. The possibilities of my stupidity were endless it seemed.

A gust of wind blew through the open window, brushing my burning skin. I swore to God I felt him stroke me with his eyes. Whatever was going on had just opened a whole new world of hotness.

Sweet Jesus.

How can something as simple as gazing be so mind-blowingly hot? My body felt like it had been hit by a lightning bolt. It was going to take a crane, a tow truck, or some kind of heavy machinery to move me from this spot.

What I needed was a cold shower.

Or Chase's blinds smacking closed with an unexpected blink that left me stunned. It was like a slap in the face, no down time from all that emotional high.

Whatever connection had been brewing between us was cut like a rope. I sat there stewing, turning all that heat into illogical rage. My heavy breathing fogged up the window again but with anger, and just when I was beginning to have some compassion for the jerk.

In a juvenile moment, I flipped off the darkened blinds and let out a string of F-bombs. It wasn't *him* I was pissed off with. I was mad at myself for letting him under my skin. For the way I responded to him, out of my control, like he was the last man on earth, and I was starving for him.

Pathetic.

Maybe *I* was paranoid, but something was odd about this town. I could sense it. The dogs from hell running loose, the bizarre behavior of people in town, the glow stick color of my neighbor's eyes, and not to mention how they moved like assassins.

I read somewhere that you're not really paranoid if something or someone is really out to get you. Right now, it felt like I was the main target in a horror novel.

Laughter flittered up to my window, interrupting my hissy fit. Casting my eyes downward, I saw Travis grinning up at me. It was obvious by the gleam in his eyes he had seen my little spectacle. I was just about to turn in and call it a night when his eyes trapped me. Utterly different than what had happened with Chase. There was no punch to the gut. I felt sadness—gut-wrenching sadness.

I don't know what happened next, and I couldn't explain it if I had to, but I found myself walking downstairs. Once outside, I padded in my fuzzy polka dot socks across the yard. It was the middle of the night, yet somehow, I felt compelled to traipse next door to where Travis stood on his porch. There was this murkiness clouding my mind, and I wasn't exactly sure what I was doing or why, but his eyes were lit up like the Empire freaking State Building.

"Angel," he murmured. "Such a pretty name." His voice had a weird quality to it—smooth and persuasive.

In the back of my mind, I wondered why everyone was so hung up on my name, when I should have been concerned that I was outside, in my PJs, exposing a whole lot of me to a guy I barely knew.

His hand brushed the hair out of my face gently. I tried to open my mouth, but my tongue felt heavy and nothing came out. Sadness was everywhere. We were swimming in it.

"You don't have a clue." He looked at me expectantly.

What was he talking about? It was hard for my brain to process what he was saying, as if he was talking underwater. Though, the longer I looked into his eyes, the more beads of fear were creeping up my spine.

"I can see why he is ... intoxicated with you. You're not afraid, like—"

Whatever he was going to say was cut short by Chase's sudden appearance. He came barreling through the front door, knocking into Travis. The two of them went steamrolling onto the grass, Chase coming up on top. Nailing Travis to the ground, he made a growling sound low in his throat.

The cobwebs cleared from my head, and I looked around sort of half dazed. There was an awareness of what had gone down, but at the same time, it was like a dream. As if I was watching from a distance. I felt like I had just been woken up while sleepwalking.

"YOU need to get yourself in control. Now!" Chase snarled at Travis.

Travis stared him down, looking anything but harmless. Right then, he looked like he could blast a hole through Chase's head with his eyes alone. Blowing out a rush of air, Travis finally relented. "I'm fine. Get off me." He pushed at Chase, getting to his feet, and then aimed a snarky glare at Chase before disappearing inside the house.

During the short exchange, I couldn't help but notice the golden glow in their eyes was no longer there. Shaken and confused, I leaned on the house for support. What was wrong with me?

Chase flashed in front of me. "Do you have a death wish little girl?" he roared lowly.

After everything that had happened today, I wasn't sure I could handle a tongue war with him. It was all too much. "No, I don't—"

"If you knew what was best for you, you would never step foot over here again. And I would advise you to keep your windows closed."

I gasped. His words cut through me and hurt way more than I cared to admit.

He stalked back into the house, leaving me conflicted and steaming furiously. My eyes stung with tears I refused to shed.

Why did I feel like I'd just had a brush with death?

CHAPTER 10

I was such a ball of nerves that I just might have blown chunks.

It did not help that it was absolutely pouring outside. What a way to start the day. Nothing like muddling around in a rainstorm to boost the confidence, and I could use all the confidence I could get. If possible, I would steal some from the egotistical Chase. He had more than enough to spare.

Downstairs, Mom was up and making breakfast—utterly unheard of. There was a plate with my favorite food and a glass of OJ waiting for me at the table. She drew a heart with Xs and Os on my napkin, a childhood tradition. It made me smile.

"I wanted to do something special for your first day. Things have been … hectic, and I just wanted you to know that I couldn't have done any of this without you," she said when she saw me. Her hair was a mess, and her eyes were droopy from lack of sleep.

"Mom, you didn't have to wake up just to make me breakfast. I love you, but you work too hard."

She waved her hand in the air. "So, do you think you will have any classes with dreamboat?"

Dreamboat? Who used words like that? "Hopefully not," I

mumbled, taking a forkful of stuffed French toast. Mmm, she was the best.

"Do the two of you not get along?" she asked, confused by how I wouldn't want such a perfect male specimen.

Like polar opposites. "It's complicated."

"Angel, baby, *you* make it complicated."

"I totally take offense to that."

She came to the table and kissed my forehead. "Have a good day at school."

I grumbled, shoving the food around on my plate.

Hall High was half the size of my old school. No shocker there. I didn't foresee any problems finding my way around. Now, if only I could stay clear of Chase. After the whole steamy, Titanic-worthy, window scene, I was kind of avoiding him.

Checking my class schedule, I went to find my locker, thinking about my shopping excursion with Lexi. Her locker was probably glittering like a disco ball or some kind of homing device. It made me smile in an otherwise belly-convulsing situation.

All eyes on the new girl please. I might as well have had a bulletin board on my back.

My homeroom class was a cinch to find. Sure, I got a few tentative glances and half smiles; mostly it was okay. I didn't feel as out of place as I'd built it up.

Making my way through the hallway to my second class, I heard my name. Lexi and a small group of my peers were standing around the lockers, Chase included. A part of me wanted to wave and keep on going, but I knew that wasn't what she expected, especially since she was gesturing to me excitedly.

Internally, I groaned. Captain asshole was the last person I'd wanted to run into.

"Hey, Lexi." I purposely ignored Chase.

"So, how was first period?" she asked. Her long blonde tresses framed softly around her face.

"I survived."

She grinned. "This is Hayden, Craig, and Sierra." She introduced the two boys beside her and the redheaded girl fused to Chase's side.

I had avoided him thus far, but it was impossible when I looked at Sierra. Her amber eyes were killing me with hate. I had no clue what I had done to this girl, but I guessed I'd just made my first enemy. The feeling was mutual as far as I was concerned. She even looked like a bitch.

Laying a hand on Chase's arm, she made it clear he was hers.

Red-hot jealously filled me. Ridiculous, since I despised Chase with every pore in my body.

He didn't acknowledge her hand. If anything, he looked indifferent. My eyes shifted to his, only to have him lift that annoying eyebrow.

"I should probably get to class," I mumbled uncomfortably, not wanting to stay another second in their presence.

"See you at lunch?" Lexi asked.

I nodded.

"Run along. You don't want to be late, miss Goody Two-shoes," Sierra spat.

My face bloomed red. I didn't know why I'd expected Chase to step in and say something, but he didn't. He just leaned back against the locker, watching me through those piercing silver eyes. This was going well. All I wanted to do was get the hell out of Dodge.

"Sierra," Lexi scolded, glowering. "Chase," she pleaded. No help from the douche. She turned and faced me. *I'm sorry,* she mouthed, her eyes brimming with an apology.

I hightailed it out of there before I did something to get myself expelled on the first day. Sierra wasn't someone I pictured Lexi being friends with.

By fifth period, I was back into the groove. No more run-ins with Chase. Thank God I had no classes with the ho-bag Sierra. My next class was chemistry. Ugh. I was not exactly looking forward to mixing liquids and, in my case, blowing shit up. Now give me an English paper to write, and I was all over that like white on rice. Science, however, made me lose brain cells.

Shuffling near the back of the class, I took an empty seat. I was early. There were only a few other people in the room and a stuffy looking professor with us.

A cheerleader-looking girl across from me caught my eye. "Hiya. I'm Brandy," she introduced herself. "You must be the new girl."

Would I ever lose the label?

I smiled friendly at her. "That's me. Angel."

"I know. Everyone knows your name."

Well, wasn't that comforting? It sounded like the theme song from *Cheers*. "Fabulous," I replied under my breath.

Another girl walked in, one I recognized from my homeroom. She took the desk beside Brandy. "I remember you. Creative writing, right? I'm Kailyn."

"Hi," I replied cheerfully. The two of them chatted and included me in the back-to-school gossip: Did you see what so-and-so did to their hair, or who broke up with whom over the summer, or who did who? It was nice to be treated normally, even if, honestly, I had not a clue who they were talking about.

Then the room suddenly erupted in silence. Looking to the front of the class, Chase swaggered sinfully through the door, looking dark and dangerously hot. Why couldn't he be grotesque?

Maybe he won't notice me, I thought, sinking lower in my seat. But then our eyes connected, and there was a zing that ignited the air.

Shit.

He flashed me a lopsided grin. Funny how this class just went from lame to crap on a stick. I pretended to doodle on the notepad I had out on the desk. *Please sit anywhere but by me.*

Brandy and Kailyn greedily lapped him up from head to toe. I couldn't help but notice their reactions.

Keeping my head down, I felt his body brush by mine as he settled in the seat beside me. Obviously he wanted to torture me. The room was on eggshells. I had been so caught up in avoiding him that I hadn't noticed at first. They treated him like something foreign, but appealing. I watched as the girls eyed him with yummy appreciation. He was the best kind of eye candy. Their goggling was accompanied by a reservation in their gazes, like they were afraid to look him in the eye.

I had the opposite problem: he was never close enough, or he was too damn close and making me want to cause him bodily harm.

The seat beside me creaked as Chase shifted his weight. I could feel his gaze drinking me in. "Angel," he called softly, causing more than one head to turn our way.

I ignored him, but nothing snuffed out the tingles that spread like wildfire inside me.

"Angel Eyes." He sneered like he was laughing at me.

I twisted my head only to find him disturbingly near, our mouths only a lip's length away. His intoxicating breath wafted through the air around me.

"Are you stalking me?" I asked.

"Don't flatter yourself," he snorted.

"Good, then let's get this straight. Stay out of my way," I hissed.

I knew we had drawn more attention than I'd ever planned. So much for skimming through senior year in the shadows. At the rate I was going, I would be all the buzz around campus.

"I like a challenge." He leaned back in his seat and crossed his arms, enjoying every second of this.

I rolled my eyes. "That wasn't a challenge, you pig; it was a threat."

His brow went up.

Chemistry couldn't end soon enough. I even silently prayed for a tornado, anything to get me the hell out of there. This was going to be the longest year of my life.

After school, I went straight to my locker to grab my homework assignments. Believe it or not, I actually had some on the first day of school. They didn't mess around here, apparently.

Shuffling the books around, a hand landed on the locker next to mine, banging the metal. I nearly jumped out of my skin as it hit with a crash, and I swore there must have been a dent from the impact. Glancing tentatively from under my lashes, I got an eyeful of red hair. This was going to be bad; I could feel it. Aggression rolled off her stance. Now that she saw that she had my attention, Sierra slammed me against the locker and got up in my face. Her amber eyes glowed wildly, sort of reminding me of Chase's or Travis' *that* night.

The *night* I was trying to forget, because it was just too freaking weird.

"I'm going to tell you only once. *Stay away from him. He's mine.*" Her voice had a skanky jeer to it.

"I'm sorry. I didn't realize he was on a leash." It was probably not in my best interest to provoke her, especially since she seemed bent on kicking my ass, but I couldn't help it. My tongue was flapping before I even thought about it.

"Keep your hands off him. I don't want him near you." She said it like I had an infectious disease and Chase was liable to catch it.

Why did she think I wanted my hands on him? What made me so different? Or did she give everyone such a warm welcome?

"Just so you know … I wouldn't let him touch me if he was the last dick on the planet." I wanted to rip the hair right from her ginger head, and I was pretty sure she wanted to obliterate me.

Just dandy.

I shoved at her. She stepped back, but didn't move as much as I'd hoped. What the hell? She must have been heavier than she looked.

"Good. I'm glad we got this straightened out before it became a problem. But I'm telling you, if it does … you'll regret it," she snapped, flicking her hair in my face.

Nothing like being threatened by an insanely jealous lunatic to kick-start the school year. I rested my head on the back of my locker as she sauntered away.

Lightning and thunder still splintered and lit the sky as I hurriedly weaved my way through the parking lot, trying to remember where I had parked. The curtain of raindrops that pelted the ground made it difficult to see two feet in front of me.

Just freaking great.

Now I looked and *felt* like a drowned cat. My eyeliner was running down my face, my clothes were plastered uncomfortably to my body, and these shoes were not made for tramping around in rainstorms, that was for sure. More than once I lost my footing.

Finally, I located my little car and rushed toward it. Probably not the best move on my part. My feet slid out from under me as I slipped on a patch of blacktop, hands waving wildly in the air. My momentum was going down, and it was palpable that I was going to crack my head on the ground. With nothing to use for balance, I started falling backwards, pulled down by the book bag slung over my uninjured shoulder.

At this point, what else could happen? I waited for the jarring impact that was going to hurt like a mofo. The wind picked up around me, and I braced myself, but the fall never carried through. A pair of strong arms caught me around the waist, pulling me securely against a firm chest. In almost an exact replica of the maneuver at Starved Rock, I knew whose arms I was in. Would it always be *him* that saved me?

My heart went pitter-patter in time with the rain. "Get your hands off me," I spat, unsuccessfully trying to jerk from his embrace. Wouldn't it just be grand if Sierra saw this?

"That's the thanks I get for saving you from having a sore ass or splitting your head open? Stop wiggling or you are going to fall again," he demanded, annoyed. His arms held me steady.

"Look, I have had enough shit from you and that redheaded slut. I just can't take anymore right now." Against my will, my eyes flooded with tears, and I relaxed in his arms—the fight gone from me.

He tilted my chin up until I was forced to look at him. His eyes brimmed with concern as my salty tears mixed with the fresh rainfall.

"Angel," he said softly like dark sin. His gentle fingers wiped away the tears on either side of my face. "Don't," he whispered.

Just like a guy to think I could control my tears. If I could, they wouldn't have fallen at all. I would have had the strength to walk away from him and the silver eyes that somehow were capable of looking into my very soul.

The gentleness of his hands and his voice pierced my heart as I shivered. "You're cold," he proclaimed, rubbing his hands up and down my soaked arms. That was not helping in the least, especially since I wasn't suffering from the cold; it was him. Being this close to him seemed to always make me feel *more*.

I didn't know what to say or do when he looked at me like that. Sniffing unflatteringly, I was too wet, too emotional, to care what I must look like. His hands cupped my cheek, and I swore he was going to kiss me. His eyes locked on mine, and I could see war waging behind them—should I or shouldn't I? A part of me wanted to lean in and take the decision out of his hands, but was this the best time to make such a bold move? When my emotions were crazy out of control and there were still tears in my eyes?

The pad of his thumb brushed over my bottom lip, and they parted on an involuntary gasp. The silver of his eyes blazed like the center of a fire, almost painfully, which in turn, caused my entire body to go up in flames. Steam could have sizzled from my skin as the rain poured on us. I bit my lip to keep from doing something stupid, like lick the finger that had traced my lips or take it into my mouth.

Why did he do this to me? *How* did he do this to me?

He bent down closer to me, and I held my breath, but he only rested his forehead on mine. It would take the slightest tip to press our lips together. I hated that he tempted me with something I so desperately wanted.

"I'll drive you home," he murmured. He smelled like heaven and hell all at once.

"My car's right here," I objected, a little dazed by him.

"You can't drive like this. I'll have Travis bring your car home." He grabbed my arm, probably afraid I would fall again, and he started leading me across the parking lot away from my Fusion.

I sighed. There was no arguing with him. I could hear it in his voice—he wasn't going to budge. Being trapped in close quarters with him while my emotions were on high alert, I'd be lucky if I didn't jump him on the way home. My body was still screaming at me to kiss him and protested when his arms released me.

"Fine," I agreed unpleasantly.

"What's with the redhead comment? You mean Sierra?" he asked when we were seated in his extravagant car. I was almost afraid to get his seats wet. He shook the water from his hair. Only he could look hotter dripping wet, while I, on the other hand, looked like a soggy muffin.

I nodded. "Look, I don't want to get between you and your *girl-friend*." I said that last word like it was hard to swallow, and the idea sickened my stomach. He and Sierra together made me want to vomit.

Steering the car with one hand, he rejected the idea. "She's not my girlfriend."

"Well, whatever *she* is, I don't want to be involved," I argued, folding my arms.

"She's nothing but a friend." He said it so matter-of-factly that I almost believed him—almost if I hadn't nearly gotten pummeled in the hallway earlier.

"It didn't look like nothing," I mumbled under my breath before I could stop myself.

"Are you jealous?" he asked, grinning at me.

"Please. As if." That grin put my guard back up.

He glided the car smoothly into the outgoing traffic. "It sounds like you're jealous."

"You are such an ass."

He arched his brow.

"I'm just calling it like I see it," I defended myself, leaning against the window. There wasn't enough space in this sleek car.

"What did she do?" His expression lost its luster and turned serious.

Sigh. I wanted to avoid this whole conversation and forget it ever happened. "It's nothing," I replied. "Nothing I can't handle."

He was unconvinced. "Angel, you better tell me. Either way, I will find out, from you or someone else." There was something in his eyes telling me it was true. I might not understand what was going on in this crazy little town, but I knew that Chase never lied.

"She just implied, very persuasively, that you two were an item. More specifically that you were hers," I begrudgingly admitted.

His brows burrowed together. "Did she hurt you?"

I looked at him, confused, wondering: How was it he knew that she had threatened to make mincemeat out of me? Or maybe she was prone to this kind of neurotic behavior. My silence was enough to convince him she had.

"I'm going to kill her," he growled.

Whoa. "Chase, really, it was nothing. She just didn't want me getting in the way."

"Bullshit, Angel, and you know it."

"Don't make things worse for me. Whatever half-wit idea you have in your head, just stop," I pleaded, sinking into the seat of his car.

"If she touched you—"

"She didn't, okay?" I was pretty sure telling him she had me shoved up against the lockers wasn't a smart idea. "We just exchanged words."

He glared at me like he didn't believe me, but let it go.

We pulled up to my driveway, and he twisted in his seat. "I texted Travis. He'll get your car here before your mom gets home from work."

"Thanks for the unnecessary ride."

He chuckled.

And it followed me all the way inside.

CHAPTER 11

"How was your first day?" Mom asked on the phone after I'd taken a long hot bath and soaked in bubbles.

The idea had been to calm my frazzled and fried emotions. I needed a good long crying jag—it had been a while. Giving into the frivolous need, I filled up the tub, lit a few of my favorite scented candles, turned on a sappy station on Pandora, and buried myself in the bubbles. With the mood set, I gave in and let myself heave those big sobbing tears.

Of course my eyes were puffy and red afterwards, but at least my emotional being was purged.

"Just peaches," I replied bitchily.

"That bad, huh?" she said, sounding sympathetic.

"The pits," I groaned. "It was like a page right out of a nightmarish horror script."

"Oh, honey, it will get better. It has to from here."

She had a point. The only place to go was up.

We hung up shortly after that, and I opened the fridge. My hand passed over a bottle of wine in the back. *I bet that would cure what ails me,* I thought for a moment. Then I remembered Dad. I would never be what he became. Alcohol was not going to solve my problems. Not today, and certainly not in my future.

THE FOLLOWING DAY AT SCHOOL, Lexi stopped me in the hall before homeroom. "Angel, wait," she called from behind me.

I paused, waiting for her to catch up. Her eyes were big pillows of anxiety. Plastering on a smile, I did not want her worrying about the little new girl.

"Chase told me what Sierra said to you." There was remorse in her voice. Those turquoise eyes were full with it. *If she only knew the half of it*, I thought to myself. "She is a complete bitch, and I'm ashamed most of the time that I know her."

The smile I'd been holding fell from my lips. What was the point of the charade? "Why do you? Know her, I mean?" I asked, unable to resist.

She cast her pretty eyes to the ground. "Our families are sort of associated. It's kind of expected for us to be friends, but I hate it." I could hear the torn conflict in her voice. "I—I hope we can still be friends?" she timidly asked.

"Lexi, of course we can still be friends. I'm not going to let Sierra the wench ruin that. She couldn't," I promised.

At lunch I sat with Brandy and Kailyn—the two girls I'd met in my chemistry class. I knew that I sort of hurt Lexi's feelings by not sitting with her, but I could not stand to be around that hellfire Sierra. The less contact we had, the better for me. I knew how conflicted Lexi felt, and I was hoping that maybe this would make it easier without impacting our friendship.

Both Brandy and Kailyn were on the cheerleading squad, and their boyfriends played football.

How cliché.

Brandy was petite with tight brown curls, while Kailyn was dark-haired and olive skinned. She looked exotic, and I was envious.

"How do you know Chase Winters?" Brandy asked, opening a

bottle of water. I looked at her salad and realized how she stayed so thin. She starved herself.

"He and Lexi are my neighbors. I met them when I moved in," I replied, taking a gooey bite of my pizza. Figure be damned.

"You are totally into him." Kailyn popped a pretzel in her mouth, her dark eyes glinting.

I bit the end of my straw, wondering how to answer that. *Was* I into Chase? I would have to be gay to not be into Chase, and even then, I would check him out. I didn't think it mattered what sex you were; Chase was just plain sexy.

"We have a sort of like-hate relationship. We like to hate each other." That about summed it up.

"That's not how it looked yesterday in chem," Kailyn commented with a grin.

Ugh. They would remember that. "It wasn't how it seemed. He does things just to get under my skin."

"I bet he would like to get under *more* than just your skin." Kailyn snickered.

"He doesn't scare you? Don't get me wrong, he *is* gorgeous with a capital G, but there is something about him that is frightening," Brandy proclaimed, forking a hunk of spring greens that looked like they came out of my backyard.

I thought about all the bizarre reactions from everyone in town whenever Lexi and I went out. They all seemed to be wary of her, never getting too close. "I'm not scared of him, no, but there are about a million times when I would like to chop his head off."

The two girls looked at me like I couldn't be serious and then burst out in giggles.

"He seems so dangerous," Kailyn replied, wide-eyed.

"They say his family is possessed," Brandy added in a hushed whisper.

I couldn't help it. I busted out laughing. "What? You're kidding, right?"

Kailyn glanced around. "Nope. Hayden, Sierra, and Craig too. Have you met them?"

Well, Sierra I could believe, but everyone else … people in this town had way too much time on their hands to make up such outlandish stories. Seriously, possessed?

"Yeah, unfortunately," I muttered.

Brandy scooted in, enclosing our little circle from eavesdropping ears. "So you know what we're talking about."

"Um. Not exactly," I confessed.

They stared at me, astonished.

"I can't believe you don't get freaked out by them. If I even get too close, I panic," Brandy said in shock. "Maybe you have some kind of immunity."

I almost spit out the swig of pop I'd just taken.

Kailyn's dark eyes sparkled. "People have claimed to see deranged dogs taken over by the devil himself. They run around at night. Their gruesome howling can be heard for miles."

I swallowed hard. *That* I could attest to.

"I shit you not," she continued, seeing the serious lines cross my forehead, "they say that there are demons walking the earth, looking for a vessel to take over."

I was officially starting to get sucked in. "And you guys believe this?"

Kailyn laughed. "Not a chance, but it makes for great campfire stories, which reminds me, you have to come to the opening football game."

I scrambled for some excuse. Football and I did not go hand-in-hand.

Brandy chimed in. "It is so much fun. Afterwards, we all go to the lookout for a bonfire. Say you'll come with us. I bet Chase will be there," she dangled as an incentive.

That settled it. I was definitely not going. "Does he often go?" I just had to ask.

Brandy shook her bouncing curls. "Nope, not really, but I swear it is a blast."

They both looked at me with pleading eyes, and I could feel myself caving. "Sure, why not?" I heard myself say. I was going to regret this.

The remainder of the day I was haunted with images of burning eyes, razor-sharp canines, and monstrous demons sucking the souls out of my friends. What kind of screwed up town did Mom stick us in? Or maybe it wasn't just this little Podunk town. Maybe it was everywhere.

What a frightening thought.

Heading upstairs to study in my room, I looked over at the unfinished novel on my nightstand. I sighed internally. What I really wanted to do was lose myself in that book, not my English assignment. Pulling my attention back to the textbook, I continued reading through the material. The setting sun was casting pretty rays of red and orange across my floor.

My eyes skimmed the next paragraph when I heard a voice peel out from the open window—a deep, enraged voice, clearly in a vicious mood. It was pretty obvious which house it was coming from. I hadn't seen Devin, Lexi's father, since the night we met, but I was almost positive it was his voice I'd heard. His booming outburst was followed by another in a deeper tone, more violent and darker.

Edging to the end of my bed, I listened to the ruckus next door, worrying about Lexi … and Chase. The voices had gotten quieter but not any less pissed off. Doors slammed, footsteps pounded up and down the stairs. Something big was going on next door.

I hadn't the foggiest clue how well Devin and Chase got along, but from the only encounter we'd had together, I sort of concluded that they were at odds about something.

I was brought out of my thoughts by the shattering of glass hitting the ground. Now I was almost afraid to look out my window with all the yelling and glass breaking. Completely freaked out and concerned, I thought maybe I should call the police.

Then I heard Chase's voice, except it was him, but it wasn't.

The conversation I'd had at lunch today came barreling back. Everyone thought my neighbors were possessed. Are they? I wondered …

Getting enough courage to peek out the window, I saw Chase slam the door shut and take off in the direction of the fields. Following him seemed like the dumbest thing I could've done—utterly reckless—but it was what I did.

Rushing down the stairs, I jumped the last four steps and bolted for the front door. I threw it open and just made out his form near the line of the fields. His stride was different, more aggressive about the way he swallowed up the ground. This wasn't like the forest, I reminded myself, no batshit-crazy dogs—I hoped.

Picking up speed, I entered the field right after him and made my way as quietly as possible behind him. You would not believe the amount of noise those wheat stalks actually make when you are poking around in them.

I was closing in on him, but something held me back. Watching him, I realized it was more than just his stance that was odd. His whole behavior was strange. He didn't seem to be going anywhere specifically, just blowing off steam. Wandering aimlessly. I thought about calling out his name, yet a part of me wanted to see if maybe, just maybe, Brandy and Kailyn were right. If there was one thing I was certain of, it was that Chase and his family were not like everyone else.

I needed answers.

Of course, I would have to step on a stalk and snap it. The sound vibrated through the impending nightfall, and Chase cocked his head in my direction just enough that I caught the glint of the blinding topaz in his eyes.

I'd had enough of the secrets, enough of the BS.

Making myself known, I stepped out. "Chase," I called tentatively. "Are you okay? I heard—"

He turned, and I gasped—loud. This wasn't Chase. Not the Chase that *I* knew. Sure, physically he looked the same, maybe stronger, I don't know. But his eyes blazed against the dark like nothing I'd seen before. He was poised to attack, muscles in his neck and arms coiled. I could hear the heavy and snarly breathing from where I stood.

And I swear to all that is holy, he looked possessed.

Holy shit.

Similar to what I'd seen in the mental dog that attacked me, I could see the pits of hell in Chase's eyes. The unearthly gold glow burned into my skull.

With a blink of an eye, this crazed Chase was in front of me, hovering over me. I'd felt fear before, but this was a whole new onset of distress. This Chase looked like he was going to deliver me to the front gates of hell and watch me burn alive.

I stepped back from him, panting hard. What were the chances of me getting out of this unscathed?

Not very good would have been my guess. Cautiously, I took another step in retreat.

He growled.

I guessed he didn't like that. Running out of options, I decided maybe it was time I got the heck out of there. Even as I moved to take off at a dead run, I knew that he would be faster. Isn't that how it is with the unknown, supernatural, or whatever *thing* he was? They always get inhuman powers. We never even stand a chance.

He leapt in the air like some drugged-out panther and landed on top of me, taking me to the ground. With an *oomph*, the air was knocked out of my lungs, and I struggled to breathe with his weight crushing me. We were so close I could count his heartbeats; they were completely irregular and faster than any human I knew.

He angled his head, watching me, so close I could feel his quick short breaths tickling my lashes. Suddenly, I could sense him inside my head like before with Travis, and my fear spiked a thousand times. *No. No. No.*

"Chase!" I screamed desperately, before he had me utterly at his whim.

He looked startled. Ever so slowly that creepy, abnormal yellow started to dissipate from his eyes, eventually leaving the pure, clear silver that I now loved. The Chase *I* knew was back. Releasing a gush of pent-up terror, I watched the clarity come back into him. It wasn't instantaneous but gradual, like he had to push back whatever had a hold of him—fight to be *him* again.

While he rubbed a hand over his face, I waited for the mist to clear. "Angel," he moaned softly.

My tongue was still stuck in my stomach, where it had dropped after being stamped to the ground, so I just nodded. "It's me," I croaked.

His hand moved to touch the side of my face. Instinctually, I jerked out of his reach.

I was scared out of my mind, and I wasn't certain what had possessed Chase, though I immediately regretted the action. His silver eyes filled with pain, almost as if he had expected the rejection.

The racing of his heart slowed to a more regular and human speed. His eyes darted over my face, piecing together what had just happened, and I wasn't sure I liked the scowl that darkened his expression. I had just escaped one brush with death, and I didn't want to face another. A variety of emotions passed over his features, mostly annoyance.

"Angel, damn it," he yelled.

Here it comes. It was almost a blessing. If he was yelling at me, then I was going to be all right.

"What the hell were you thinking?" he demanded between tightly gritted teeth.

"How is *this* my fault? I was concerned about you," I grumbled inaudibly.

"Did I not tell you to stay put? Did I not tell you that you were going to get yourself killed? I swear, Angel, I've never met anyone who was such a magnet for disaster."

I glared at him. He was crossing a fine line between me being happy to see him and me hating his guts, again.

Chase was on a rage roll. Lucky me. "You don't have the first clue what could have happened to you, what *should* have happened." He was making my head spin with all this mumbo jumbo.

I sat underneath him, watching his rant, and even in the midst of all this madness, butterflies danced in my belly at Chase's proximity. His eyes sharpened on mine, reading the sudden shift in my face. Hell, maybe he could hear the quickening of my pulse or worse … hear my thoughts.

Awareness seeped in the pools of his irises. My body apparently had the worst timing.

He sat up, leaning his elbows on his knees and his face in his hands. I pulled myself off the ground, sitting across from him, waiting. Watching me, he had a glint in his eyes. He couldn't figure me out, when in fact *I* should be the one trying to figure him out.

"You're not going to freak out, are you?" he asked, surprised. "And no running," he added as an afterthought.

I shook my head. I'd come out here for answers, and answers I was going to get. "What are you?" My voice quivered.

His eyes searched my face, probably trying to decide what he should or shouldn't tell me. Looking out in the distance, he heaved. "I'm a Divisa," he informed me.

Was that English? "A what?"

"In layman's terms, a half-demon."

CHAPTER 12

S hit.

I sucked in a breath. "Did you just say *demon?*"

"You heard me, Angel Eyes."

And suddenly it clicked. "That's why you say my name like that," I mumbled to myself.

"Like what?" he asked, eyes narrowing.

"Like it tastes like battery acid every time you say it."

He laughed. "It's true that at first I thought someone from heaven was playing nasty games with me, but mostly, I just like to get a rise out of you. It's so easy."

"Chase, this is serious," I scowled.

"You don't have to tell me. You're the one who is more worried about your name than the fact that I just told you that I am half-demon."

I rolled my eyes. "How is this even possible?"

A howl punctured the air behind us, and my trembling eyes sought his.

He shook his head. "Sometimes you are more trouble than you are worth." He got to his feet and brushed the wheat particles from his jeans, eyes zeroing in on something in the distance.

I looked at him expectantly. He wasn't going to leave me here. Was he? "Chase," I scolded.

He glimpsed back down at me. "We need to leave. You shouldn't be out here with me." And just like that, I was plucked off the ground and was sailing through the night. Stalks of wheat smacked against us, but never really hit me. He had his arms protectively around me with my face tucked against his chest, taking the brunt of the lashes.

I took one peek, only to get dizzy with the blurring of colors.

Literally nanoseconds later, he deposited me on the familiar cushions of my couch. I pushed the hair out of my face, glaring at him. He had plopped me down without much finesse, and I was pretty sure he'd done so on purpose.

Huffily, I snapped at him. "Will you tell me what the hell is going on?"

He smirked at me. "You are far more trouble then I need. I have my own crap to deal with." Coldness came into his eyes, and he started pacing in front of the couch.

The back and forth movement was driving me bonkers. I yanked on his arm, pulling him down next to me. "What do you mean you're a half-demon?"

He sighed, running a hand over his face. "Just that. I'm half demon and half human."

"How?" I wasn't yet buying into the whole *I'm part demon* thing, but I couldn't deny he was different.

He reclined back into the cushions, the couch shifting under his weight. "I don't even know where to start." He sighed. "My mom was seduced by a higher demon and impregnated. I'm the result of that hellish union. As are the other Divisa. There are very few females that survive the birthing."

I thought about his mom and what Lexi had told me about her dying in childbirth. Pieces were slowly starting to fit into the puzzle, but I wasn't sure I liked the picture I was seeing.

His tormented eyes held mine, searching for something. "It happens more than the hunters think."

J. L. WEIL

"Wait, what? There are hunters?" I asked, perplexed. He was throwing stuff at me, and I wasn't able to follow.

"There is a whole world of shit that you haven't got the first clue about, Angel. It's better if you don't. You shouldn't even know about me, and I will probably be in all kinds of crap if anyone finds out."

I scooted to the far end of the couch, tucking my knees under me. "I won't tell."

He held my gaze. Maybe judging my sincerity, I don't know. He let out a whoosh. "You probably wouldn't."

"So, does this mean that Lexi and Travis …" I let the question linger in the air.

He nodded. "Yeah, they are too. Except theirs is a rare case. The demon that came to earth was a female, and she sought a male—Devin. One day she came back and dropped an infant into his arms—Travis. I have no idea how many times she compelled Devin, but a year later he received another special delivery—Lexi. It was the last time he remembers ever seeing her."

Wow. Talk about some abandonment issues. "So Lexi and Travis have never met their mother?"

"No, and they are better off not ever seeing her," he replied harshly. "She would just as soon kill them than see them live."

I gasped.

"There is no love between a demon and their offspring. Actually, most of them try to correct the wrong if they ever find out." I knew he was trying to shock me.

It was working.

"Do you mean they kill them?" I asked bluntly, hardly believing what I was hearing.

He glanced at me, his silver eyes burning. "Don't look so shocked. This is hell we are talking about. Anyway, they usually send a lower-demon to do their dirty work or hellhounds."

Hellhounds.

"T-that dog? It was a hellhound, wasn't it?" I stammered at the dark memory.

"Yeah, it was, and you are damn lucky it didn't take your head off," he said coldly.

"Why is it *here?*"

He dropped his head in his hands. "I don't know, but if I had to guess, it was here for one of us. The hound could probably smell our scent on you and was hoping you would lead him to us."

I recalled him finding me in the woods. "I did. I led it straight to you."

"You didn't, Angel. I heard the howling and went out looking for it and found you instead. A good thing too, or it would have eaten you alive."

I gave him a snarky look, then recalled how lightning fast he had moved that night and many times since then, tonight included. "Does being half demon give you super powers?" I asked.

"I'm not a superhero, and you better remember that," he scolded.

"Fine, I get it. I was just curious about what you can do."

"We're faster, stronger, have heightened senses, and heal faster than normal, among other things."

"What other things?"

"You just don't quit, do you?"

I gave him a sarcastic smile.

He growled low in his throat. "Telekinesis, most can mind control, and see Death."

This was a crap load to process. I had a gazillion questions piling in my mind.

"Your eyes," I stated. "They change colors."

He smiled ruefully. "You just don't miss anything. Our eyes change the closer we get to giving ourselves over to the demon. Usually it is triggered by anger."

I got the feeling that anger wasn't the only trigger. Note to self: do not piss off Chase, or any Divisa for that matter.

Tonight it had been his demon I followed. *Way to go, Angel. Aren't you the smart one?*

"I'm not some lifesaver. I'm dark, dangerous, and evil," he warned in a deep voice.

Shifting on the couch, our legs brushed. "Are you trying to scare me?"

"Apparently, I have not been doing a very good job."

"You aren't evil," I argued.

"If you only knew how much," he muttered.

Half, I thought. And I wondered even about that half ...

"This isn't a game or a movie. This is my life. You are seriously going to get killed. That hellhound that was after you was a fly compared to a lower-demon. Do you get that? Your death wouldn't be painless or easy. You would beg ten times over before it would finally deal the deathblow, and that's only if you're lucky."

"I get it, okay. You don't have to be a jerk about it," I huffed, crossing my arms.

"You like that I'm a jerk," he sneered.

I rolled my eyes and hit him over the head with one of the pillows from the couch. He did not look pleased. I had to stifle a laugh. "Who else in this town is ... you know, like you?"

He tucked the pillow under his arm and leaned on it. "Only a few others," he said, not elaborating. I had to assume he was protecting them. Probably I should let him, but my tongue just couldn't hold back.

"Like Hayden and Craig?"

His eyes narrowed accusingly.

"Sierra?" I added her name to the list. That bitch had to be half-demon. There was just no other explanation for her heinous behavior.

"Are you sure you are not a hunter?" he asked, studying my face.

"Should I be offended by that remark?"

His shoulders slumped. "I just can't decide how much to tell you. But yes, they are all Divisa."

"I knew it," I mumbled under my breath.

He lifted his brow. "Don't underestimate them," he warned me. "Especially Sierra, she is nothing like Lexi."

"You don't have to tell me. Lexi actually has a heart."

He laughed. "I knew the moment I saw you that you were going to be trouble."

I shot him daggers.

Ha. He was the cause of all my troubles … well, most of them anyway.

His eyes sobered, and I knew his thoughts had turned in an ugly direction. "I just don't know if I can take the chance. There is so much at stake, and not just for me. I have Lexi and Travis to think about too."

I realized what he was contemplating, and I felt the blood drain from my face.

Compulsion.

He was going to use mind control to make me forget this ever happened, and I would go back to being blissfully ignorant. I didn't want that.

I'd be lying if I said that what Chase was didn't scare me, but I knew him, and I honestly believed he would never hurt me. Every bone in my body knew it. I just needed him to trust me. "Please, Chase, don't do this. I don't want to forget," I pleaded. Tears welled in my eyes. "I swear, you can trust me. I wouldn't do anything to expose you or Lexi." The appreciation I felt catapulted.

"Angel, don't you—" He was cut off as a tear rolled down my freckled cheek. "Shit," he uttered.

Cautiously he lifted a hand toward me, only to pull it away as if he was afraid to touch me. I wasn't scared of him but of losing what I was just beginning to understand. His eyes softened as he tried to figure out how to handle my fragile state. I doubted he had to deal with blubbering females often. If I hadn't been so upset, I would have found it comical.

"Please don't cry," he whispered.

I almost hadn't heard him as my chest heaved in a sob. He inched closer to me on the couch, his hand touching the small of my back. All the encouragement I needed. He was startled to find an armful of me soaking his shirt. Stunned, it took him a minute or two before he wrapped his arms around me, pulling me closer and encasing me in his exotic scent.

His patience was staggering considering. He didn't open his mouth to complain, didn't scold me on the uselessness of tears. Actually, he murmured in my ear, brushing his lips over my hair. When I finally got myself under control, every touch was like an electric shock wave to my system. He was driving me wild. My color came back in floods.

I risked a glance up. "Please *don't*, Chase. I don't want to forget."

He stared at me for a long time, the internal struggle clear behind his blustery eyes. I understood the responsibility he shouldered and the lives he protected, but I was only one girl. Surely letting me know couldn't possibly destroy everything.

"Angel, I—"

My bottom lip trembled, and I heard the regret in his voice.

"Okay, I won't. I promise, just don't …" At this point, I think he would have agreed to give me the moon if I asked. He just didn't want to see any more of my tears. His thumb brushed along my bottom lip, and they tingled from his touch. "I've never met anyone like you."

I couldn't decide if that was good or bad. My head was so absorbed with him that I couldn't think all that well at the moment. He was doing things to my body with those stormy eyes that no guy should be able to do.

Somehow during my crying jag, he had pulled me into his lap. Now I found myself in a compromising position, but I wasn't complaining. Biting my lip, I wondered if I should move. His hands spanned behind me, resting on places that I should be ashamed of, not turned on by, and his fingers scorched my skin even through my jeans.

It was suddenly extremely hot, and it got me thinking that the air-conditioning must be on the fritz. Silence spanned between us as the air crackled. Why him? How could he make me lose my head with just a look—a touch? He was probably used to girls losing their heads over him. I didn't want to be just another notch under his ho-belt.

If only my mind and body could communicate and come to a mutual understanding, instead of this yo-yoing hot and cold … and hot again.

Shifting, my knee accidentally rubbed up against him provocatively in an attempt to make our position less awkward.

Epic fail.

Oh. My. Gawd.

Did I just feel what I thought I felt?

My face flushed miserably. All I ended up doing was making the obvious known to both of us. My mortification could not be any grander.

His eyes flashed. I found myself underneath him on the length of the couch, and that part of him was evidently pressed up against me in the most intimate way. I shut my eyes.

"You want to play with fire? Watch out, Angel, or you'll get burned." His words rushed over my skin.

He is only doing this to teach you a lesson, a part of my brain insisted. I told it to shut the hell up. Right now, burning didn't sound so bad. Not if it involved him and what his lips could do to my skin. Tiny flames licked where his mouth skimmed along on my flesh. His lips nuzzled my neck not all that gently, and I swore a blinding light broke out behind my eyes. Those full, mouthwatering lips grazed the pulsing vein in my neck, nibbling a sensitive spot.

Everything inside me exploded like a nuclear bomb, and he hadn't even kissed me.

Yet.

I entangled our legs and ran my hands through his hair. He couldn't possibly be a part of hell, because this felt beyond heaven.

Did heaven vibrate?

Slowly the smokiness drifted, and I heard Chase let out a frustrated purr. Then I felt the vibration again against my leg.

His phone. Heaven hadn't called after all.

On the downside, the buzzing of his phone jerked us out of letting things go too far. Fast. I was surprised to find my clothes mostly intact and not already on the floor. Opening my eyes, a smoldering blend of shimmering silver and topaz bewitched me.

Not just anger, I thought.

He sat up, running a hand through his tousled hair before answering the call. My head lay on the couch, and I stayed as still as I could be.

"Lex," he answered. "I'm fine. Actually, I'm next door." He glanced over at me, snapping the phone shut. "She's coming over."

Her timing sucked. Royally sucked.

CHAPTER 13

He stood up, putting the phone back in his pocket.

"Are you leaving?" I asked, probably sounding clingy.

"Yeah, I have to get home and talk to Devin before he shits a brick. Lexi's already here."

Just then, she came through the front door like she was walking on glass, waiting for a nuclear explosion. Her eyes bounced from Chase to me. I fussed with my ratted hair and tugged on my shirt.

"What were you guys doing?" She was grinning.

"Nothing," Chase grounded out. "Look, Lex, she knows. Talk to her."

Her eyes got as big as a saucer. "She knows? What? Wait, how?"

"I don't have time for a rundown. Just stay with her. And no compulsion," he added.

I watched him stroll out the door with a weird, sad, and disappointed feeling I couldn't understand.

Lexi bounded into the room and sat down next to me like an energizer bunny. Was she always this excitable?

"Did you guys ..." she raised a perfectly arched brow.

"What? No. Definitely not," I said, outraged.

It didn't faze her. "Did you kiss him at least?" she asked, noticing my messy hair and disarrayed clothes.

I could still feel his lips on my neck.

"Lexi!" I exclaimed. "No, I didn't kiss him. We can hardly even stand each other."

She totally didn't buy that, and her glinting eyes laughed at my denial. "But you want to."

Ugh. This was highly embarrassing.

Her eyes turned serious. "You aren't freaking out," she commented like she had just realized it.

"Why would I freak out?" I asked, happy to be on a new topic.

"I did hear him, right? You know?" She warily took a seat beside me, tucking her feet under her.

I nodded. "Yeah. He told me about you being … Divisa." The word sounded foreign on my tongue.

"You aren't … scared of me," she asked under thick lashes, almost afraid of my answer.

"No, I don't think so. I just still can't believe my best friend is half-demon. It doesn't seem real."

"Oh, it's real. I'm so glad you know. It was so hard keeping it a secret from you," she said with über-glee.

I grinned at her. "Me too." Maybe some of her giddiness was rubbing off on me.

"I've never had a human friend before," she admitted.

Well, I'd never had a supernatural friend before. So it looked like we were both in for a few surprises. "Why?" I asked.

She shrugged, trying to act like it was no big deal, but I could tell that it hurt. "People are put off by us. They somehow feel the evil under the surface, and it keeps them from getting too close. It's a signal of caution—lonely for me, but protection for them. They just don't know it." She looked up at me, her turquoise eyes bright. "Except you. You don't shrink away or treat me any differently."

Odd. Why didn't I feel what everyone else did?

"That's not normal, is it?" I asked.

She shook her head. "I've only ever met one other person who didn't have that instinctual alarm and ..." her voice trailed off.

"And what?" I prompted, on edge. You can't leave a girl hangin' like that.

"Chase won't like it if I tell."

I rolled my eyes. "Screw Chase. He doesn't like anything."

She giggled. "You're right. Chase is a pain in the ass."

I couldn't agree more.

"She and Travis were very close. Of course that worried Chase." She sighed. "Emma was her name, Emma Deen. And she disappeared nine months ago."

"Like milk carton missing?"

"Yep. Travis went nuts—demon nuts. She was his girlfriend."

I tried to think what that would have looked like. Images came up of overturned furniture, walls with fist holes, complete chaos.

"Chase thinks she's dead," she said flatly.

Talk about a conversation downer. I leaned back against the sofa, slouching. Chase would be a Debbie Downer.

"What do you think?" I asked.

Her eyes looked lost. "I don't know, but she was the only person other than you that didn't treat us like outcasts."

"I'm sorry, Lexi. I'm glad that I don't feel what everyone else feels."

"Me too," she replied with a sad smile.

I couldn't imagine how lonely her life had been. It seemed so unfair.

"So Chase told me about the hellhound," she said, bringing up the nightmare I was still trying to forget.

"He seems to be constantly saving me," I admitted, not altogether happy about it.

She smiled. "Chase is more than capable of handling one hell-hound. That's like child's play for him."

That got me thinking. "How strong is he?" I asked with curiosity.

Her eyes lit up. "Chase is the strongest Divisa that I know of. From what little I understand, his father was some badass, powerful demon.

Like Chuck Norris of the underworld. But I think Chase is a little afraid to find out who his father is. Afraid of what he might have inherited. His strength comes with a price. He has serious anger issues."

No shit.

I was at the edge of the couch, hanging on her every word.

"He struggles with controlling his demon half the most, and because of that, he is the hardest on himself. Always pushing further then any human or half-human should."

"Is that why he didn't want us to be friends, because you might lose control?"

She nodded, sending her blonde ponytail swishing. "During the day it's fairly easy to control, even he does it without much effort. As the sun falls, the things that go bump in the night trickle out, and that connection we have with the underworld brims closer to the surface. It thins the line between human and demon."

Well, that explained a lot. "You are here with me now and seem fine."

She gave me a half smile. "It's not without effort, but I have the most control out of the three of us. Still doesn't stop Chase from being a bully. He is always sheltering us and is fiercely protective. I think because he is so much stronger, he thinks that he needs to take care of us. Even though I have way more control."

"Chase mentioned something about hunters?"

"You are the first person outside of us who Chase has ever opened up to." She sounded amazed. "The hunters, as we call them, are a group of people who have somehow found out that Divisa exist. It's almost impossible to hide ourselves from everyone, even as hard as we try. But I have to admit, with you, we could have tried a lot harder. I know a part of me wanted you to know so I wouldn't have to hide it anymore or lie. I can't say why on Chase's behalf, but he has been just as careless with you, regardless of all his threatening. The hunters have only one purpose. To kill us."

"Why would they want to kill you?" I got that they could be dangerous, but killing just seemed extreme.

"They believe that we're an abomination, a threat to the human race. In reality, they are right; we are."

I hated to hear her being so degrading. "I don't buy it. I have never seen any of you hurt anyone. How can you be a threat?"

She shrugged shoulders. "Not all Divisa are like us. Many never learn how to handle their demon. Or they were cast aside by family who didn't want them. Travis, Chase, and I got lucky."

"What about the other Divisa at school?" I asked, thinking about Sierra.

"Well, Hayden is cool. Sierra has issues, as you know."

Did I ever.

She continued. "And Craig's a loose cannon. Chase would not want you anywhere near him. He is constantly on Craig. I even watch myself around him."

"Thanks for the warning."

"Don't worry. Chase won't let anything happen to you," she assured me with the utmost confidence.

"Why do you say that?" He more or less despised me on most days.

"Just a hunch," she said, grinning secretly.

"What's their deal?" I asked, quickly changing the subject.

She pulled out her legs and sat Indian style, facing me. "Sierra lives with her parents. They are both Divisa. Her dad and mine kind of powwow together and find ways to keep us from being discovered. Without them, I'm not sure how we would survive."

I rested my head in my hand. "Does that happen often? Divisa marrying Divisa?"

Lexi grinned. "More and more. Hayden and Craig are like Chase, but they have it rough. Neither of them have parents. Whereas Chase has Devin and us, the two of them live with human relatives. It's extremely rare that more than one person in a family would have demon interaction. My dad and Chase's mom were brother and sister."

Okay, that was weird. It made me wonder if Devin and Chase butted heads because he was such a reminder of what Devin had lost —his sister. I wasn't claiming to be Dr. Phil, but maybe I was onto something.

"Hayden lives with his grandma, who is so old that she isn't in tune with the whole danger vibe. But Craig lives with his aunt, and from what I gather … she can't stand him. She collects her monthly check from the government and pretty much leaves Craig to raise himself."

Damn. The last thing I wanted was to feel sympathy for Craig.

I stifled a yawn. It was getting late, and I think my brain was fried.

She noticed my drooping eyes. "Do you want me to stay?" she asked.

"No, it's okay. I think I'll be all right. My mom should be home in a few hours anyway." I glimpsed at the clock on the DVR; it was after midnight. I was going to be a zombie for school on Monday.

THE FOLLOWING MORNING, Mom padded her way downstairs in her fuzzy slippers with bedhead and gave me a long hug. I needed it.

"I miss you, honey. It feels like forever since I've seen you. Has school gotten better?" she asked, concerned about how I was adjusting.

We sat curled on the couch, and I laid my head on her shoulder, trying everything in my power to not think about being sprawled underneath Chase on this very same couch just hours ago. I felt my cheeks flush a little.

"It's better, nothing like the first day. I met a few nice girls, and I already knew Chase and Lexi, so I think I'll survive the year."

"How are things going with Chase and Lexi?"

Somehow I thought this question had a double meaning. "Fine, I guess."

"Do you have any classes with them?"

"Actually, I have gym with Lexi and chemistry with Chase."

"Oh," she said.

"Oh, nothing," I barked.

"I didn't say anything." She grinned.

She didn't have to. It was written all over her face. I swear, sometimes she acted more like my sister than my mom.

CHAPTER 14

It was one of those lazy Sundays. Mom was at the station, and I was in my room catching up on some schoolwork when I heard the doorbell chime. I could only imagine who it was. It's not like we got a lot of solicitors in the middle of nowhere.

Rushing down the stairs, I caught a horrifying glance at myself. Why hadn't I showered today? Quickly tossing my hair in a ponytail, I opened the door, expecting to see Lexi.

But of course it was Chase.

I stared at him for a full minute and then slammed the door in his face.

Mature, I know.

Leaning my back against the door, I waited to hear his footsteps leaving the porch.

"Angel," he called through the door. "We need to talk. Alone," he stressed, in a voice that was now as familiar as my own.

And so grating.

My palms got sweaty. Talking. Fine, I could handle talking. It was the *alone* part that got me hot and bothered. I stayed silent, praying he would just go away.

"We have some unfinished business."

Did we ever. I couldn't keep the floating images of us sprawled on the couch out of my head.

"Don't make me break the door down," he threatened. Just like him to resort to destruction. "I can't imagine how you would explain that to your mom."

Righty-o.

He was such a jerk.

I opened the door. He was leaning against the frame with one hand, smirking at me. My hand twitched to hit him, pop him in his glorious mouth. He lifted the studded dark brow.

"Fine," I reluctantly agreed. "Do you want to come in?" I gestured dramatically with my hand.

"Nah. Let's walk," he suggested.

Okey-dokey.

"Is this the part where you take me out in the woods and take care of *the problem?*" I asked, wondering how smart this was when considering, just last night, he'd wanted to erase my memory.

He laughed. "How many crime games do you play? But no, Lex would never forgive me."

Right. And he wouldn't do anything to hurt her.

I shut the door behind me and walked in unison with him. His legs were so much longer than mine that I had to almost run to keep up. He was always in such a hurry.

"It's good that you are being cautious," he commented on the whole door-in-your-face thing. "You *should* be scared of us." His eyes lit with amusement.

"Wait, what did you say?" I asked, not entirely sure I understood him right.

He angled his head at me, reading my confusion.

"I told Lexi last night that I wasn't afraid of her," I said.

He shook his messy dark hair. "You might not think you should be scared of her, but you should definitely be afraid of me," he replied, like it was obvious.

"Um, I'm not really afraid of you either," I informed him, looking at him sideways. We'd just gotten to the edge of his property line.

He stopped walking and glared at me. "Don't take this lightly, Angel," he said, dropping his tone in warning.

I leaned against a nearby telephone pole and put my hands on my hips. "Look, I get that there is a part of you that is dangerous—"

"I could kill you. Do you get that?" he ground out, stepping forward aggressively.

Yeah, I understood loud and clear, but my impulse said he wouldn't hurt me. "I don't know that you would. You haven't yet. I just don't get—"

He cut me off. "You are stupid then."

That did it. My back stiffened. "You don't know anything about me," I said, poking him in the chest. He didn't budge.

"If you knew what was best, you would be afraid of me. Very afraid." There was a chill that settled in his tone.

I didn't like it. He might be a lot of things, but cold wasn't one of them. He was a hothead.

I recalled what Lexi had said about Chase being extremely strong. He made me feel safe, not afraid as he wanted. "I'm not though," I argued.

That seemed to piss him off even more. Before I had time to process the thought, he was in my face, flaming yellow eyes and all.

Crap.

"Are you scared now?" he growled lowly.

I gulped. "No," I squeaked, not backing down, but it was making my neck cramp.

"Liar. I can hear the quickening of your heart." He stepped closer, bringing us nose-to-nose. The heat from his body flirted with my skin. "Remember, I've got supersonic hearing."

I gave him a dirty look. Little did he know, most of my wildly thumping heart was because he was so darn close to me, not because I was afraid of him, though I probably should have been terrified.

A smart girl would have been.

"You are *trying* to frighten me, but you haven't hurt me," I pointed out. My back dug in to the wooden pole.

He roared in my face.

"All bark with no bite," I said, pissing on his flaming anger.

That did it. He hit the utility pole beside my head with his fist, and the pine cracked like a sonic boom. My eyes bulged from the earthquake movement. The pole literally rumbled under my back.

I looked at the fist-sized hole he left in the old weathered wood. It went clean through half of the pole. "Was that necessary?" I asked.

"If it gets my point across, then yes."

"The only thing ..." My voice trailed off as we both heard the creaking and crackling of splitting wood. I looked up.

Huge mistake.

The giant pole was teetering above us. I looked into Chase's eyes and saw my fears mirrored in his. This massive plank now plummeting toward us was something truly horrifying with its live wires flailing in the air. There wasn't time to run, to seek safety, or anything else for that matter.

There was only time to wait for the inevitable. I was going to either get crushed or electrocuted to death.

I kept my eyes latched on his, thinking he was going to be the last face I saw. His expression tightened, and he flexed his jaw.

"Get out!" his voice was a biting command. There was a hard line of concentration in his hellish gold eyes.

Looking above my head, the falling pole was suspended awkwardly in the air and held up by some unseen force. He had said he could move objects with his mind, I just hadn't believed him. It was much easier to deny what you can't see.

We both backed out from under the oddly levitating pole, and I prayed that my feet wouldn't get tangled. I couldn't imagine what someone might think if they happened to drive by. I was having trouble myself.

Once in the open, and a good distance away, he let his hold go, and the whole heavy thing plunged to the ground in an earsplitting crash. It vibrated the ground under our feet. Wires snapped and shards of wood sliced through the air.

I found myself sheathed in his arms.

Two seconds later, Travis came barreling outside, swinging the door wide open. "What the hell are you two doing?" he yelled, taking in the sight of the chaotic mess of rampaging wires and the enormous pole now blocking the road. "Dude, you just knocked out all the freaking power. Devin is going to have a shit-fit. I'm calling the electric company." He slammed the door shut behind him.

I gave Chase a piercing look. "The only thing hazardous to my life is your stupidity." As gracefully as possible for me, I turned my back and stomped off to my house. The sizzling and hissing sound of the downed wires followed me.

When I got inside, I realized I couldn't see a damn thing, and the house was spookier than ever. First thing, I needed a flashlight, candles, and a book.

"Damn," I muttered as my knee connected with the coffee table. At least I was in the right direction to the kitchen. Somewhere amongst the drawers full of junk was a flashlight. It took a few bumps and bruises before I finally had a working light.

Settling on the couch for a long-ass night, I surrounded myself with candles and dove into a book. I needed to keep my mind from thoughts of strangling Chase repeatedly.

I cursed him from here to hell.

CHAPTER 15

Believe it or not, I somehow made it through my second week of school without getting lost, falling on my face, or getting my ass kicked. Overall, I'd call that a smashing success.

The sun was beating in probably one of the last days of summer. Deciding to take full advantage of this glorious day, I slipped on a bikini, grabbed my iPod and the unfinished book, and went to lay out. I longed for the days in Tucson when my friends and I would go to the pool and soak up the sun all day. I missed splashing in the water, gossiping, the smells of tanning oil, and the sound of our laughter.

Popping in my earbuds, I selected a playlist and relaxed into the cushioned chaise. Before long, I was engrossed in my book with the sun warming my skin. It was therapeutic.

I must have dozed off.

A sharp beam of light glinted off my sunglasses, waking me. My eyes fluttered open, and Travis was sitting in the lawn chair next to me, staring. I have to say, seeing him more than freaked me out. How long had he been there, watching me?

I ripped out my earbuds, and my book tumbled to the grass. "Jesus, you scared me," I said a little breathily.

"Sorry," he replied, grinning. He didn't look all that sorry, actually.

The sun shone on his sandy hair, making him look more like an angel than part demon. It haloed around him, and the charming smile was easy on his lips. If it weren't for the eyes, I might have been convinced he was something from heaven not hell.

"I saw you out here, and I wanted to apologize for the whole mind control thing the other night. I noticed you at the window and ..."

Right. He saw me ogling Chase. I waved a dismissing hand in the air, trying to distract him from my pink-stained cheeks. "Don't worry about it. No harm done, right?"

He shook his head. "None at all."

I shifted, uneasy in the lounge chair, and lifted my sunglasses on top of my head. "So Chase told you that I know—"

"He did. My dad flipped a lid," he said, grinning before I could finish. "But it's cool. You really are different."

I recalled what Lexi had said about Travis and Emma—how she had been like me. "I guess," I admitted, pushing an escaped piece of hair behind my ear.

"I hope I didn't frighten you."

"Are you kidding? Have you met Chase?"

He laughed. "I guess you're right. He is way more intimidating than me."

You bet your ass. Not to mention, he had that whole dark, sinful thing going on, whereas Travis was just too lighthearted and carefree to be taken seriously as dangerous.

I grinned. Travis was so easy to get along with, like Lexi. I could see what Emma had seen in him. Why hadn't I met Travis first? Then maybe my heart would beat uncontrollably for him, instead of his foreboding cousin.

"You're just a nicer guy."

"You should meet my other half," he joked. "Lexi told me that Sierra has been giving you a hard time."

Lexi had a big mouth.

I shrugged. "She thinks I'm trying to move in on her territory," I admitted, screwing my nose.

He rolled his eyes. "She would. I don't think Chase will ever give her the time of day, and it pisses her off. You shouldn't take her lightly, but I'm sure Chase will set her straight."

Internally, I groaned. That was the last thing I wanted. It would just make it look like there was something *more* going on between us.

"I think that would just make things worse," I suggested.

"You might be right. I'll mention it to him." He really was a sweet guy.

"Travis."

I groaned. I would know that voice if I was dead and buried six feet underground.

Travis grinned mischievously. "Hm. Chase doesn't look happy. If you keep looking at me like that, he's going to think you like me better."

"I do like you better," I replied, unable to stop the smile.

His turquoise eyes sparkled. "You realize you are about to send me to a very early grave."

I doubted that. Chase stood looming over me, blocking out all my sunshine. *Figures.*

"Travis, Devin wants to see you." There was an edge to his tone.

"It was nice talking to you, Angel." Travis stood up and winked at me.

I swear Chase growled, which was followed by Travis' laugh.

I looked up at him. "Do you get along with anyone?"

He sat on the chaise where Travis had just been. "Not usually. What were you talking about?"

I smirked. "None of your business."

"Where you are concerned, I make it my business. Who knows what kind of trouble you'll bring?"

God, he knew how to get under my skin. "Hopefully the kind that knocks you off your pedestal."

"I have yet to find my match," he said cockily.

"Did you just come out here to annoy me? 'Cuz it's working."

"No, actually. Let's do something."

"Excuse me?" Did I hear him right?

He shrugged his muscular shoulders. "I'm bored."

"And why does that have anything to do with me? As you can see, I'm busy." I flopped my sunglasses back over my eyes, trying to sound indifferent.

His eyes traveled up the length of me, which did funny things to my belly.

Great. Now I felt completely naked and had to fight the urge to cover up. It was bad enough that I still had memories of those lips doing wicked things to my neck. They were etched into my brain.

"I think you have had enough sun," he stated bossily. "Let's go."

"Where?" I eyed him suspiciously. "And no surprises," I added.

He grinned wolfishly. "I know this great spot by the river. Boating, swimming, fishing ... you'll love it."

He had to be kidding. Did I look like the outdoorsy type of girl?

"You're already in your suit. What do you say, Angel?" His eyes did that thing again, making my pulse jump. When I didn't answer, he provoked me in the only way he knew would work. "You're not scared to be alone with me, are you?"

Reaching out, he held his hands for me to take. "Fine," I grumbled. "You'd better not make me regret this." I put both my hands in his. Literally.

He eased me effortlessly to my feet. "I'll drive," he said, grinning like a little boy.

In record time, I tossed a few things in a bag, and we were on our way, bumping along down the road. When he pulled over to the side of the road in the middle of nowhere and cut the engine, I figured he was screwing with me.

"You're joking, right?" I snarled, looking at him across the car.

Eyes sparkling, he replied, "Nope, we walk from here. Trust me, it's worth it."

I seriously doubted it. We trudged through a forest, which I wasn't very fond of. He must have picked up on my unease, because he never left my side.

"Lexi told me about Emma," I said, as we walked deeper into the woods.

"Lexi has a big mouth," he mumbled.

"Do you honestly think she is dead?"

"I think there is a better chance that she is dead than there is that she is alive," he stated honestly.

He was probably right.

"How do I know when I'm … safe with you?" I didn't know how else to phrase it.

"You are never safe with me, Angel Eyes."

I gave him a dry look. "Comforting."

He dazzled me with a smile, and I promptly tripped over my own feet.

His hands shot out to steady me. "Careful," he murmured in amusement. I shook him off.

And he laughed.

When we reached the clearing, the sounds of water lapped against the rocky shore. There was a wooden pier jutting out into the river. "Is this private property?" I asked, setting down my bag.

The scene was breathtaking and remote. Woods bordered either side of the water. There was a pearly white boat tied to the slip, bobbing up and down with the occasional waves. It was hard to believe that such beauty lived in the middle of the Spring Valley.

"It's my family's," he said over his shoulder as he walked on the dock.

The sky was cloudless, making the water seem bluer. "This is amazing," I said in awe.

He grinned at me dangerously. "I thought you might like it."

I shaded the sun from my eyes as I watched him walk to the edge of the pier. He tugged at the hem of his shirt, flashing me a quick smirk before pulling it over his head. Of course Chase shirtless was a far better sight than what Mother Nature offered.

My heart lurched.

The sun was still hot, and it baked my shimmering skin. Without hesitation, he plunged off the dock like an Olympian diver straight into the waiting water below.

"Show off," I called, laughing. Being here like this, without the bickering between us, was intoxicating. I felt drunk on Chase and high on summertime. God, that sounded like a country song.

I dangled my feet into the cool waters, waiting for him to resurface, and after a minute, I knew I was in trouble. I was sunk. In more ways than one.

His fingers snaked around my ankles, pulling me into the water before I could utter a protest. The scream died on my lips as I got a mouthful of cool water. It felt soothing against my warm skin.

I come to the surface sputtering and to the sound of Chase chuckling. Flipping my wet, tangled hair out of my face, I glared at him. "You are so going to regret that," I threatened with a smile. The white T-shirt I'd thrown over my bathing suit was plastered to my body.

"Angel Eyes, you look like a drowned rat."

Such a flatterer.

I splashed him with a wave of water, soaking him. He looked godly dripping wet. The water glistened off those sun-kissed abs. I turned, taking off in the opposite direction with my sights set on the shore. Two strokes later, I found myself plucked out of the water and in a pair of vise-grip arms. They enclosed around my stomach. My squeal echoed over the valley as my back connected with his solid chest.

"Where do you think you are going?" he whispered against my ear.

My stomach jumped and goose bumps covered my body. I swallowed thickly. His flattened hand on my belly moved lower, and my breath caught in my throat. Leaning heavily, I was pressed up on his chest and my limbs went to mush.

A few prolonged heartbeats later, I was soaring in the air, swallowed by depths of water. When I resurfaced, I was smiling from ear-to-ear.

Kicking to the edge, I sprawled out on my towel and let the sun dry my skin. He lay beside me on the pier, distracting my peace of mind. "Do you always live your life so dangerously?" I asked.

He tucked his arms under his head. "What have I got to lose? I might as well take life by the balls."

Nice analogy. My lips twitched into a smile. Hidden behind my sunglasses, I took full advantage of the cover. My eyes lapped up every glorious inch of his body, eventually landing on the black mark just above his shorts.

I studied the symbol. "What does your tattoo mean?" I had wondered about the black symbol since I'd first seen it.

"It's not a tattoo, but a birthmark. A mark of Divisa," he replied, turning his head toward me.

"So every Divisa has one?"

"Yeah, it's the mark of our impure blood, only being half-demon—divided," he informed me.

It sounded more like a curse. "Lexi told me about the hunters. Do you kill them?" I asked, wondering if my neighbor was a murderer, even though I thought it was mostly self-defense.

"The less you know, the better," he rebutted, dodging the question.

I stared at him, waiting, letting him know I wasn't dropping it so casually.

He sighed and looked up at the sky. "You have to understand. If I don't, Angel, then they will kill me or worse: kill Lexi. But the hunters, no, not if I don't have to. A huge part of me would love to. I usually compel them to forget."

"Do they come here often?"

He rolled over on his side, and I laid my head on my arm, mesmerized by those silver eyes. "It's sporadic. Sometimes years go by with nothing. Then we will get a hunter or two who got wind of someone spotting so-called demon activity. They'll come to investigate, and it doesn't take long for people to point fingers our way. With the right questions, they can weed us out. It's the special deliveries from hell that keep us on our toes."

"Is that why you live here, out in the country?"

"There is safety in numbers. We have sort of a pact with Hayden's, Craig's, and Sierra's families. It is easier to stay hidden in a rural area with a group. It is added protection from being wiped out by lower-demons. Not many Divisa can kill a demon alone."

"But you can," I interrupted, remembering Lexi mentioning that he was very powerful.

"Yeah. My abilities are unordinary. I don't really need the protection of a group, but I can't let anything happen to my cousins."

I unconsciously rubbed the tender muscles of my bitten shoulder. It had pretty much healed, but I was left with an unusual tiny scar. Occasionally, it tingled.

His eyes followed my movements. "Is your arm bothering you?"

I shrugged, not wanting to sound like a pussy. "Did your bite leave a scar as well?" I asked, remembering the sticky, bloody bandage.

He turned his head, looking at the sky and sighed. "It's not a scar, Angel. You've been marked."

"Marked?" I squeaked, afraid *marked* wasn't going to mean something pleasant.

He nodded, propping himself up on an elbow. "That bite from the hellhound put a homing signal on you. You've been put on hell's watch list. They think you can lead them to one of us."

Oh, hell no. I'd just been tagged by hell.

"It also bit you. Does that mean they can find you now?" I asked, instantly worried for them.

"No. Their venom doesn't work on us. Our demon blood and healing abilities make us immune," he said.

Of course. This was bad. Very bad.

I bolted up, looming over him. "And you are just now telling me this?" I shot back.

His pewter eyes flickered. "I didn't want to upset you," he argued, following my movements.

"You didn't want to upset me?" I echoed. "You don't think that I should know I am going to be hunted by ... by ... I don't know what?" I brushed a frustrated hand through my hair.

Those eyes flickered golden. "Nothing is going to hurt you," he snapped.

"I disagree. I have every right to know that I've suddenly become a priority on the underworld's hit list," I yelled. Would we ever be able to be in each other's presence and not argue?

"I didn't want to scare you." Some of his irritation dissipated.

Too late. I was way past scared. I trembled, thinking about my encounter with the hellhound.

He noticed. "We should get back. It's getting late."

Dusk had turned the trees gray and the water dark blue. I'd never been scared of the dark, but I was finding that with everything I'd recently learned, I was way more aware of things that lurked in the night.

He must have been in a hurry, 'cuz the next thing I knew, I was plucked off my feet and whizzed through the woods in some kind of vampire warp speed. When he set me back on the ground, I swayed.

Leaning on his car for support, I waited for the wave of dizziness to pass. "A little warning next time."

We didn't talk on the drive home. Stewing, I listened to the music as I rested my head against the seat, tired and relaxed for once in his presence. I caught his numerous looks angled my way, and it made my insides warm and fuzzy. I could smell the water, the sun, and his scent everywhere in the car. The gentle engine lulled me soothingly and traveled smoothly over the road.

The silence turned comforting between us—a feat that I never thought would happen with Chase and me. We always seemed to have too much emotional energy bouncing between us. It was incredible. I closed my eyes, on the edge of sleep.

So when I heard Chase drop the F-bomb, I was instantly on alert. Every muscle in my body tightened. My eyes flew open just in time to see a man in the middle of the road. He was dressed in a business suit and had large, black, soulless eyes. From the shock on Chase's face, he must have come out of nowhere. Chase clenched the wheel, and the vein in his neck pulsed. This was definitely not good.

CHAPTER 16

"Hold on," he said, his eyes a hard line of determination.

Everything happened in slow motion. Bracing myself, I heard the click of my seat belt and turned to Chase. He slammed the brakes, and the car began to spin wildly out of control. I knew immediately that his car was going to flip, tumble, and roll. At this speed, there was no way to prevent it from happening. Momentum just doesn't work that way.

My scream pealed over the screeching of tires, rubbing friction against metal. He ripped me from my seat, tucking me into his clutches. Wrapping his arms around me protectively, I was nestled against his chest. There was no time to second-guess what he was doing; I could only hang on.

The next thing I knew, we were sailing through the air, the wind dancing over my skin, and the sickening crunch of metal and glass rang throughout the night. We hit the ground with a jarring force, but his arms never let go of me, a testament to his brute strength. Rolling once, he made sure that he took the brunt of the fall as we slid to a stop. Debris scattered everywhere, raining with an explosive aftershock.

Too traumatized to move, I sat there listening to my shaky breathing. I heard Chase wince underneath me. His bands of steel still held me securely to him.

"Angel," he murmured in evident pain.

I lifted my stiff neck off his chest and looked down into his eyes. There were cuts all over his face and down his body. His clothes were tattered, torn, and smeared with black soot and blood—mostly his.

"Chase," I croaked. "Oh my God, you're hurt," I exclaimed in panic, touching a hand to his cheek.

His eyes closed in discomfort.

I rolled off him, numbly feeling only a few scratches and bruises— nothing like his. Looking across the street, I saw his car flipped on its top, smashed to the ground like a Swedish pancake. He had thrown us from the car before it had rolled.

Incredible. Stupid, but incredible.

He tried to sit up, and his arm gave out on him.

"Don't move," I ordered. "You might have broken something." I reached in my pocket to grab my phone. It was shattered to smithereens. "Shit," I muttered, throwing it to the ground.

"Angel," he called again. "I'm fine. I'll be fine. Are you okay?" He sounded battered.

In a daze, I nodded and watched as his eyes blazed like asteroids.

"Good, 'cuz I'm about to—"

He was cut off by a hideous, hissing behind us. I glanced over my shoulder. The man from the road glared our way with onyx eyes. Each step he thundered closer, his body jerked and flickered out of form. If I hadn't seen it with my own eyes, I wouldn't have believed it was possible.

Like some kind of robotic creature, its features shifted. The flesh color of its skin became a sickly gray. Its movements became more alien-like and less human with each step. I wouldn't have been surprised if it had started to grow horns and sprout wings.

Chase pushed me behind him as he crouched on his feet. I fell ungracefully on my butt and scrambled to back up. A low growl burned at the base of Chase's throat, and his eyes glowed like neon in the darkness. He was in full pissed-off, demon mode.

My mother was going to have a conniption fit when she saw me. I didn't know which to worry about more: demon-Chase or the thing that was advancing on us. Either way, as I saw it, I was chopped liver.

From what I could gather, that thing stalking us was a lower-demon. I tried not to make a single peep as I cowered on the ground. The creature gave Chase one long murderous hiss, flashing its razor teeth, dripping venom, and then it just disappeared like a bullet in the night.

Shit. That was one seriously scary beast.

"What the heck just happened?" I asked when I was able to find my voice.

Chase whipped around—those burning demon eyes zeroing in on me.

Uh-oh.

"Chase, it's me. Angel." I tried coaxing him and prayed that maybe the sound of my voice would snap him out of it. He looked ready for a fight, which made him a lot more frightening. The wounds on his face had stopped oozing before my eyes and were almost healed.

That was just plain freaky.

I scooted back on my hands, gravel digging into my already cut up palms. Those amber eyes never let me out of his sight. I was starting to become eerily familiar with this side of Chase. My back hit a tree, and I sunk against it. No place left to go, running was pointless.

I didn't see him move; he was just unexpectedly there, in front of me. My breath hitched. This close, I could feel the heat radiating off him. I kept waiting for him to make some kind of aggressive move. He just ... watched me.

Feeling bold and a little encouraged that I still had my head, I slowly sat up on my knees, bringing our faces level. His eyes never left mine. It was so surreal looking at him. Every gorgeous feature was Chase's, but he exuded power and danger. Mostly it was the eyes that changed him. Gone was the serious, arrogant, protective silver, replaced instead with something so much more haunting. I didn't know if I could ever get used to seeing him with the pure, radiant, yellow eyes.

Ever so cautiously, I lifted my hand. He didn't so much as blink as I edgily brought my hand up to the sharp planes of his cheek. Those citrine eyes darkened. I felt like I was on the brink of some great discovery. Tracing the outline of his jaw with my fingers, his fist clenched alongside him, but he never made a move to hurt me.

Maybe they weren't as bad as they thought. "Chase," I whispered.

With unnatural speed, his hand closed over my wrist. I jumped, thinking this was it. I had spoken to soon. When I peered up from under my lashes, his eyes were my favorite color again—silver.

I expelled a gush of air. "Chase."

He looked out across the road, inspecting the damage to his car. He didn't appear pleased.

"Damn it," he swore. "I really loved that car." He mourned a moment and then announced, "We need to leave."

"Where did he go?"

He shook his head. "I don't know. They don't usually retreat without a fight. He will be back; I guarantee it, but he will not be alone. You're not safe tonight."

I never felt safe anymore. "How are we getting home? My phone is trashed." I pouted, just a little.

"We're going to walk," he said matter-of-factly.

I closed my eyes and groaned. *More walking. Joy.*

After my second stumble down the road, Chase swept me up into his arms. My whole body ached in places I didn't think it could hurt.

"Put me down. I'm fine," I protested.

"Just shut up and close your eyes."

Crap. Here comes light speed.

It was like being rocketed into space. Kicking open the front door to his house, he only slowed when we were safely inside. A surprised Travis was spread out on the couch watching TV. He turned in our direction.

"Christ, Chase, what did you do to her?" Travis asked, outraged, sitting up.

Having the manners of a mule, Chase ignored his cousin and headed straight up the stairs. I gave Travis a sympathetic look.

He dumped me on Lexi's bed. "Here, I can't be around her," he said to Lexi and then walked right out the door.

Argh. How dare he? I couldn't believe I'd ever felt anything for this lout other than hatred.

I grabbed the first thing I could find and hurled it at the door. The little unicorn figure shattered to pieces on contact, littering the floor with its jagged chunks.

Lexi smirked beside me.

"Sorry," I muttered, ashamed at my outburst.

She eyed my ratted clothing and my dirt-covered arms and cheeks. "Please tell me you were mud wrestling and my cousin didn't go all commando on you," she said, plucking a dried leaf from my hair.

"Funny," I replied sarcastically, feeling moody.

She lifted a brow.

"Your cousin is such an ass." I sighed, lying down on her soft bed. It felt glamorous after the hellish night I'd just had. "We were sort of run off the road by a demon, which caused Chase to flip his car." That pretty much summed it up nicely.

She stared at me for a full minute. "Holy shit, you are not kidding." She climbed on the bed, occupying the space beside me.

"I wish," I muttered and closed my eyes. All too easily the events surged through my head. "He threw us from the car. Can you believe that?" I turned toward her.

She looked me up and down. "You look pretty good, considering."

"I think he saved my life ... again."

"I told you he has his moments," she said, beaming. "But he's mostly an ass," she agreed.

I cracked a grin. She'd hit it right on the nose.

"I've never had a sleepover before," she said gleefully.

Probably with good reason.

"Don't worry, you'll be fine. He wouldn't have brought you here if he thought otherwise," she said, trying to smooth over any anxiety I might have been feeling.

I called Mom and informed her that I was spending the night with

Lexi, and I would see her sometime tomorrow. She was ecstatic that I was making such good friends.

The joke was on her.

"So he jumped from the car?" Lexi asked next to me.

"He did," I assured her. "Lexi, when your other half takes over ..." I hesitated, unsure how to phrase the question. "Do you remember everything that happens?"

"It depends on the Divisa. For me, it's clearer. I'm always aware of what's happening and can even control the demon, mostly. For Chase it's like seeing through glass. Images are distorted and sounds are muffled. There are even some Divisa who blackout during a demon episode. They don't remember a thing. I think that would be the hardest—not knowing what you've done."

Wow. I had no idea the range of half-demons that were out there. None of them sounded the same.

"So, is it possible for Chase to recognize me?"

She looked at me funny. "It's not impossible, but it is unlikely. Why?"

I shrugged. "I could have sworn tonight he did," I said, staring at the ceiling. My hands fumbled with the covers.

"What made you think that?"

"After the demon ran, Chase was gone—yellow eyes and all."

"Wait, you saw Chase's demon?"

I nodded. "He just stared at me, and then ... he snapped out of it."

"That's *not* normal," she assured me, sounding serious.

Of course not. When was anything in my life lately normal?

"Do you guys have any dating restrictions?" The question came out of nowhere.

She tried to hide her smile. "No, it's just hard to find someone who understands all this and accepts us. It's almost impossible when they can hardly stand to be near you."

"I can see how that would be a problem. It's so sad," I murmured.

"You should probably get cleaned up. I bet you are exhausted. I'm beat just looking at you." She grinned, twisting her head toward me.

She was right.

I sighed, inhaling the hot steam, and let it wash away all the grime, caked blood, and overall dirtiness. Right then, I would have killed for a lavish bath bomb, infusing my skin with scented oils. It was an experience I could have gladly indulged in after a night like this. Lexi's French soaps were going to have to do.

Afterwards, I tiptoed back into her room and crawled under the covers. I was out like a light the moment my head hit the pillow.

THE FOLLOWING MORNING, Lexi and I walked down the stairs to a multitude of voices. Curious, I reached the bottom step, and my eyes immediately sought out Chase, who to my dismay had a very clingy Sierra suction cupped to his side. Slut. She was wearing some skanky outfit that showed off every inch of her fabulous body, looking more like a runway model than a teenager.

I hated her.

The flirty smile she aimed up at Chase turned downright sour when she got a glimpse of me.

Good.

CHAPTER 17

"**W**hat is *she* doing here," Sierra spat in disgust.

She was the last person I wanted to see, especially when I looked like complete shit. My arms and legs had a couple good-sized bruises that were a lovely shade of purple. At least Lexi had let me borrow some clean clothes, and a full night's sleep had made me feel almost human. Still beside Sierra, I stood out, but for all the wrong reasons.

The last thing I wanted was to battle against the she-devil herself.

"Cool it, Sierra," Chase warned coldly.

"Cool it? I want to know why this bit—"

"Finish that sentence, and I will throw you out of here on your ass," Chase threatened her.

"Just ignore her," Lexi said, looping an arm through mine.

She led me into the kitchen, while Sierra's glares burned holes in my back. She held her tongue, but I could tell she had a mouthful to say. The same question was in my head: What was she doing here? Had Chase invited her?

It kind of appeared that way.

She had removed herself from draping over Chase, but they were still huddled close, whispering. I wanted to gouge her eyes out and slice off her tongue. White flaming jealousy engulfed me.

"I can't believe Chase asked her here," Lexi said, sounding offended.

Travis came up beside me. "He didn't. She just showed up. You should have seen his murderous expression. I thought he was going to slam the door in her face."

It was a small relief knowing he hadn't invited her here. And it was just like Sierra to butt in where she wasn't wanted. She was probably here trying to protect her *property*.

I tried everything in my power to ignore them, but I sucked at subtlety.

"You look like you want to be rescued. It's painful to watch. Want to get out of here? Maybe get some breakfast?" Travis asked, flashing his lady-killer dimples my way.

"Are you asking me out?" I teased.

"Possibly," he replied, scratching the stubble on his chin. "Would you say yes?"

I looked over his shoulder at Chase and Sierra. He was acting like I wasn't even in the room, but every so often our eyes connected and teeny bolts of electricity shot through my system. "Hell yes," I decided.

I couldn't stand to be in the same room with Chase *and* Sierra another second. Travis and I stood up.

"Angel," Chase called as he noticed Travis and me walking out the door.

Feeling extremely put out, I stuck up three fingers and replied, "Read between the lines."

"Cute," he said, eyes flashing with anger. Sierra was watching Chase, who was glaring at me.

Travis laughed.

WE ENDED up at the same place Lexi had taken me: The Village Diner. There were limited choices in Spring Valley.

"Lexi took me here once," I commented as we grabbed a booth. She had decided not to come with us just in case Chase and Sierra needed a referee. Apparently she thought a fight would ensue after we left. I was glad I wouldn't be sticking around to see that.

"Good. Then you know how amazing the food is. Breakfast is my favorite," Travis commented.

I remembered what Lexi had said about them coming here a lot. "Does it bother you the way everyone treats you?" I asked, thinking about the alienating feeling I'd gotten the last time we were here.

He shrugged. "I think I'm just used to it. You have to remember that it has always been this way for us. I don't know anything different."

"It's so hard for me to believe still. Lexi doesn't have an ounce of ugly inside her." She was one of the sweetest people I'd ever met.

"Don't let that innocent face fool you. She can be ruthless when she wants to be."

"I guess I just haven't seen that side of her." I was still unconvinced that there was a part demon living in my best friend.

He took a sip of his orange juice. "Consider yourself lucky. You've noticed her bursting energy; imagine that inside a pissed-off demon. Not pretty."

I laughed.

He glanced wistfully out the window, and I wondered if he'd ever brought Emma here.

I lowered my voice. "Lexi told me about Emma. I'm sorry, Travis."

He fumbled with his fork. "She told me she'd mentioned her. I still can't believe she is gone."

"Did she know about your ..." My voice trailed off.

He nodded his blond head, gulping down a bite of blueberry pancakes. "Yeah, she knew. It was unavoidable, but she never cared what I was. She just wanted us to be together." I heard the incredulity in his tone.

"She sounds great. I would have liked to have met her."

"You would have loved her. The two of you would have gotten along so well. She was impossible not to like."

"Do you know what happened?" I asked, thinking about Chase

believing she was dead. I got the impression that Travis was holding onto the last thread of hope that Emma was still alive. There was an unmistakable glimmer of chance in his eyes—a part of him still clinging to hope.

"I repeat that day over and over in my head, and I still don't know what happened. I can't help but think if she hadn't ever met me, she would still be here."

"Travis, don't do that. Don't beat yourself up over what-ifs. It won't change anything and only hurts more."

"It's why Chase is so rough with you. He wanted to keep you at a distance. He figured Emma disappeared because of us, but I don't agree. There was something about that night that I just can't piece together. Regardless, Chase thought it was best if we never opened ourselves up again to outsiders. Until you." He gave me a half-hearted smile.

Of course I would be the one who made him break his sacred vow.

"What was she like?" I asked, because it seemed like he needed to talk.

He smiled softly, looking lost in memories. "She was a dancer, a fabulous dancer. Her family moved around a lot, something about her dad's job. We didn't talk a lot about her parents, but I could see how lonely she was. On her first day of school, she was so shy, and her dark green eyes just trying to soak it all in. She was tired of always being the new girl."

"I can relate to that," I mumbled.

"I bet you can. You and Emma would have had a lot in common. The strange part is, even my demon … recognized her." His eyes shifted a tad, revealing little bits of golden color.

"What do you mean?" He had me on the edge of the booth.

"When I lost *it* around her, I could feel *his* intrigue. For once, the demon and I were in perfect agreement. Nothing would harm Emma."

"And that's not normal?"

"Definitely not. The demon doesn't have feelings. It doesn't care about other people. I was confused and conflicted, afraid to trust. I didn't know what to think about it."

I thought about Chase and how he had stared at me. This must mean something; I just didn't know what.

"The worst part is," he continued, "I never even got to tell her how I feel." His aqua eyes pooled with pain and regret.

I laid my hand on his. "I bet she knew."

He looked at me from across the booth. "I hope so. We should do this again sometime. Maybe on a real date." He grinned at my stunned expression.

He was joking, right?

MONDAY MORNING WAS upon me in all its painful glory. My body was still stiff and sore. As expected, I had more than my fair share of bruises. They were doozies. Just what I needed. *The new girl looks like she got beat up.* With my luck, everyone would think it was Sierra who had delivered the ass whooping.

During gym, I regrettably found myself partnered with Hayden for tennis. I guess I should have been grateful it wasn't Craig.

Twirling my racket, I waited for him to serve. I wasn't athletic, so gym was by far one of my least favorite classes. Hayden, with his extra abilities, looked like he could go pro if he had a decent partner.

The ball whizzed past me before I had a chance to lift my racket. He grinned wolfishly at me from over the mesh net. Oh yeah, he was enjoying toying with the little human. Bending down, I picked up another tennis ball and tossed it in the air. It popped against my racket, buzzing straight into my side of the net.

Ugh. I suck at sports.

The supervision from our gym teacher was staggeringly awful. We mostly pretended a half-ass attempt at tennis. Most of the girls in my gym class were afraid to break a nail. *My* nails generally looked like crap thanks to my nervous habit of chewing them off.

Hayden served the ball short, hitting the net. I swore he did it on purpose. I trotted up the court to retrieve it. As I bent back up, I found myself face to face with him.

"So I heard you know our little secret," he said, his eyes carefully watching me.

My tongue got stuck to the roof of my mouth. He hadn't come right out and said, *Hey, I heard you know I'm half-demon.* It would have been simpler if he had. I wasn't taking any chances. No way was I putting Lexi in any kind of trouble.

He noticed my hesitation. "Look, it's cool with me. I'm just letting you know that Sierra and Craig aren't as easygoing as I am."

"I kind of already figured that out on my own." I bounced the tennis ball, only for him to swipe it out of the air before it hit the ground. I looked around nervously.

"Sierra has it in for you. She has some warped idea that her and Chase are destined." There was no malice or deceit. He just seemed to be giving me a heads up.

"She can have him for all I care, and she has made her claim very clear where he is concerned." The last thing I needed was him razzing me about Sierra.

"I doubt Chase feels the same."

"That's his problem, not mine. Thank God," I muttered.

"I bet it will be ... eventually." He smirked and tossed the ball in the air. "Just be careful. You already have a target on your back."

Great. Just what I needed ... another reason to look over my shoulder at every turn.

"What was *that* all about?" Lexi asked at the end of class. We were coming out of the locker room.

"Nothing. He was just giving me advice."

"Are you sure? Because it didn't look like nothing, and if Chase—"

"Chase," I ground out, "doesn't need to know. It was no big deal. He was just telling me what I already know: Sierra is crazy."

I left her staring after me and hurried to my next class.

CHAPTER 18

"You're coming on Friday, right?" Brandy asked.

Brandy, Kailyn, and I had just sat down for lunch, and I was already being steamrolled about the football game on Friday night. I could feel myself being caged into going.

Fresh start, I reminded myself.

Well, maybe in this *fresh start* I attended school functions, like football games, and actually enjoyed myself. Brandy and Kailyn claimed that it was a huge event for Spring Valley. Practically the whole town showed up.

Imagine that.

They were mostly excited for the bonfire afterwards. Couldn't say that I shared their enthusiasm, but maybe I should give it a whirl.

"Fine," I exclaimed. "I'll go." I expected some squeal of delight or display of excitement.

I got silence.

Their eyes locked above my head, and the chatter at my table died. The chair legs next to me scraped against the linoleum floor, and the seat filled with Chase's form.

I glared at him from the corner of my eye. Brandy and Kailyn looked like they wanted to bolt. It was still weird for me that people reacted that way.

"Did I hear you are going to the game on Friday?" Chase asked, smirking.

I leaned on my hand. "What does it matter to you?"

He shrugged. "It doesn't. I heard what happened in gym today." His silver eyes looked like glass.

I sunk in my seat. Nice Lexi. Throw me to the wolves.

"Maybe we should talk about this later," I said, clenching my jaw. My turkey sandwich became less appealing.

He leaned in close to me, and I heard the gasps from across the table. "Good, then I'll see you tonight, Angel Eyes." His voice had dropped deep and thick, and those full lips were kissable and close.

God, he smelled good. And why did he have to insinuate that we would be doing more than talking? I could feel the blood rise in my cheeks.

He winked. The silver bar in his brow glinted, and he sauntered off.

"That boy has buns of steel." Kailyn hummed, burning holes in the back pockets of Chase's jeans with her zealous stare.

The three of us watched him leave the cafeteria with our tongues hanging out. I might have sighed.

"You guys are totally hooking up," Kailyn purred. Her brown eyes were spilling with barely contained excitement.

Brandy leaned over the table. "I thought he was with the redhead," she said, looking confused.

"Sierra." I supplied the hoodrat's name. "No, they're not dating, but she would jump down his pants if given the slightest chance," I replied grumpily.

I needed to be more careful with my display of emotions, because if Kailyn could pick up on them, then surely everyone else would also.

"So you *are* hooking up," repeated Kailyn, milking every second of what she considered hot news.

I wanted to thump myself on the head. "No, we're just …" Hell, I didn't know what we were. "Friends."

"*Friends*, do not look at each other like that," Kailyn insisted.

"You totally want him," Brandy added, joining in on the fun.

I rolled my eyes. Well, duh. I'd have to be dumb to not want him.

Or just stupid and reckless.

I'd always thought I was a smart girl.

"I wish I had a guy who looked at me like that." Brandy sighed wistfully, pushing the fallen curls out of her eyes.

"Aren't you dating Tommy, the quarterback?" I asked all mushy and batted my eyes.

Kailyn giggled.

"He hardly notices me over his inflated ego," she responded, sounding put out and needy.

I could see that as being a problem. "Why not date a guy who appreciates you?" I said like it was as easy as shopping for candy, and this was coming from a girl who had never even had a boyfriend.

I was such a hypocrite.

"He's the quarterback," she replied, like it was a no-brainer.

I just stared at her. I didn't speak ditzy.

The rest of my day was pitiful. My heart beat erratically every time I thought about seeing Chase later.

He stressed me out.

When I pulled my Fusion into my driveway after school, lo and behold, there sat Chase on my front porch. I had no idea what he was driving now that his car was totaled. If I had to guess, I bet he had grabbed a ride with Lexi.

The sky was gray and kind of murky, casting dangerous-looking shadows over his face. It had been like that all day—the sun never breaking through the thick clouds.

"Aren't you going to invite me in?" He was leaning against the column as if he had all the time in the world. His jeans were frayed, and he'd probably paid a fortune for them instead of doing what I did. I was an expert at DIY.

"Do I need to extend an invitation, you know, like a vampire?" I asked over my shoulder, trying to steady my frantic heart.

"Funny. Would you prefer if I sucked on your neck?"

My cheeks turned the color of blood. The implication behind his words was an uncomfortably hot reminder of the last time I was alone with him in my house. "Is this going to take long?" I asked, trying to sound bored and failing miserably.

Opening the front door, he followed me inside. I ditched my bag at the entryway and headed for the family room.

"It all depends on you," he coaxed me, dropping his voice to a lethal low that hit me straight in the belly.

Totally not fair that he should have such a hold on me.

I cleared my throat to disguise the effect his words were causing on my insides. The couch sunk under his weight. "Let's make this quick."

He lifted that annoying brow.

Twiddling with my fingers nervously, I said, "So I'm assuming Lexi told you about Hayden."

What a narc.

"She was worried," he defended her, like always where Lexi was concerned. It was both endearing and nail biting.

"I'm listening," I replied, waiting for him to go on.

"I need to make sure that he isn't threatening our exposure."

"Him or me?"

He pointedly looked exasperated. "Not everyone is happy that you know, Angel. It's for your safety as well. We might have a truce, but that doesn't mean I trust them with my family's lives. I trust no one but myself where they are concerned."

His dedication was touching and hit a spot in my heart. "Are you immortal or something?" It sounded like a dumb question, but I had to ask.

"No, of course not. I'm just a lot harder to kill."

I thought about how swiftly his injuries had healed. "But you can be killed. That's good to know," I muttered.

He grinned. "You are not getting rid of me that easily."

I gave him a half-ass grin. "As if I could be that lucky."

"Angel, you have got to be the most unlucky person I have ever met. I swear a dark cloud of trouble follows you everywhere."

Only since I moved here, I added silently to myself.

He continued. "But to answer your question, we do live longer than the average human."

I found everything about him interesting. He was just so different from every guy I knew. Something about him appealed to me even above the urge to strangle him. "How much longer?" I tucked my legs underneath me.

"Are you always so inquisitive?" His voice dropped.

Warning, my mind cautioned me. Sexy voice.

That sinister tone was always trouble. Trouble of the good kind.

My heart pranced. "Always."

"Figures the little detective is a sponge for information."

I narrowed my eyes at him.

"It's something in the demon blood. We never get sick, we're extremely healthy, and our life expectancies are longer. It is not unheard of for a Divisa to live past a hundred. Some live two lifetimes."

"You're freaking shitting me."

He grinned. "Believe me, I wish I was. It's a curse. To be stuck with this burden for more than one lifetime."

I could see his point.

"Does your mom know what a dirty mouth you have?" he asked, smirking.

"Where do you think I got it?"

"I met your mom, remember? She couldn't have been sweeter." His eyes dropped the twinkle. "Lexi told me that your parents are divorced. Do you have plans to see your dad?" he asked, meeting my gaze.

I swallowed the large lump that formed in my throat and tried to push back the tears burning in my eyes.

His face softened. "Angel, I'm sorry. I didn't mean to upset you." I heard the anguish in his voice. It made it worse.

He brushed aside a tear streaking down my cheek. I realized then that they were rolling down my face. It had been so long since I'd cried for my dad. I didn't think it mattered anymore to me.

I couldn't have been more wrong.

He gathered me close, running a hand down my hair. "Tell me what I said."

I shook my head against his chest.

"I know. I'm the biggest ass on the planet," he added.

I let out a little laugh. True, but he had it all wrong. I pulled away from him, looking up into silver eyes brimming with distress. "Trust me, this time it's not you," I managed, wiping at the salty streaks. "My dad," I began and then took a breath. "God, this is embarrassing. I've never told anyone. No one. And I can't believe I want to tell *you* of all people."

"That should offend me, shouldn't it?"

I let out a nervous laugh. "Like I could ever offend you."

"True." He reclined back against the cushions, taking me with him. I laid my head on his shoulders. It was like a weight had been lifted off me. I needed to do this—get this off my chest so I could start to heal.

The steady beat of his heart was comforting. I placed my hand over it. "My dad was ... is an alcoholic. It started with just a drink after work or on the weekends. The pressure at his job was building, and it was too much he said. Then it quickly turned to six, to twelve, to him not being able to stand, to getting sick, passing out. My parents started fighting: scary fighting—furniture overturned, china broken."

"Did it ever get out of hand? Did he ever—" I felt the muscles in his arm flex.

I quickly shook my head. "No, never, but sometimes I thought he would. One night he didn't come home, which was becoming more frequent. He had stopped at one of his favorite bars, and after a full night of boozing, he got behind the wheel."

I inhaled a deep breath of his familiar scent. It filled me with security like I'd never felt before. "I don't even know how he was able to find his car, let alone start it. A family of four was traveling home from a vacation." My voice got heavy with emotion again. "He ... he swerved into their lane, hitting them head-on. None of them survived. None of them except my dad."

Why was it the drunk always lived?

Horseshit.

His hand stroked down my back, encouraging me to finish, comforting me.

"He was sentenced to six years at the Arizona Penitentiary. It doesn't seem long enough to me, and maybe this sounds coldhearted, but I am glad he's gone. He is not the dad I loved anymore."

"Sounds like you have some demons of your own, Angel Eyes. They are safe with me," he whispered against my hair.

Tilting my face up, I met his compassionate eyes, realizing I trusted him wholly. Fascinated, I watched as his stormy gray eyes intermingled with topaz. "Your eyes are doing that thing again," I informed him breathlessly.

His hands lingered at my waist, edging under my shirt. "I know. It means it's time for me to go," he said feebly. His voice was strained and sinful.

Tracing lazy circles at my hip, his fingers impishly played a dangerous game, causing arrows of heat to shoot through my body.

"And if I don't want you to go?" I proposed, shocked at my own forwardness.

His colored irises held mine for infinite minutes, keeping me suspended on some pivotal moment. He closed his eyes. "I would say that is just too bad." He leaned in, catching my breath, and kissed the tip of my nose.

I wasn't about to let him get off that easy. It was starting to royally piss me off. Constantly he was building me up to something, dangling it just out of my reach. I weaved my fingers into his silky dark hair, keeping his head a breath's length away. I heard his sharp intake of surprise.

Score one for Angel.

I didn't know when I'd suddenly grown such lady balls, but I was on my way to becoming a tramp.

Like I was in another body, I brushed my lips over his and uttered a helpless little sigh. I wanted his mouth more than I wanted oxygen. He made me feel everything I always longed to feel. Beautiful. Smart. Desirable.

That quick taste was like a fantasy. Wickedly delicious, leaving you aching for more.

He moved like lightning.

Before I could press my lips fully to his, he shot across the room. Without his body there to hold me up, I fell face down on the couch and not gracefully like a swan either. Blowing the hair out of my eyes, I looked across the room at him and sent him a murderous glare. His hand was braced against the wall, and his eyes were an unearthly gold. There was nothing he could say or do that would diffuse the anger now simmering in me. All the passion I had been feeling instantly turned to rage.

He bolted from the house like a blur of black.

I didn't think I'd ever be able to look at the couch again without thinking of Chase or having my cheeks flame pink.

CHAPTER 19

F riday night.

The crowd roared in the stands, stomping on the bleachers as the home team crossed the end zone for yet another glorious touchdown. Football here was like a royal event. All the stops were pulled out. There was a parade down Main Street with trucks piled with students, followed by the band. It was a real hoot. The town was decorated in school colors from banners to streamers to balloons.

Citizens of Spring Valley took football seriously.

I dragged Lexi with me since I promised Brandy and Kailyn I would come watch them cheer at their first game. She was a much better sport than I was, looking all cutesy in her school colors of red and black, ribbons tied in her bouncy blonde hair, and makeup to match. It was super freaky that our school mascot was a red devil.

What were the odds?

Lexi and I had quite a laugh over that.

There was a little bite in the breeze. The first sign of the approaching fall. I have to admit that I was a little nervous and excited for my first snowy winter. I'd never had a white Christmas.

Snuggling in my hoodie, I couldn't believe that I might possibly enjoy myself. I warmed my hands around a cup of hot cocoa and tried to look like I knew what was going on, cheering at the appropriate times.

The giant scoreboard blinked "Touchdown," and our cheerleaders broke out in a series of high kicks before chanting their victory cheer. I smiled at Brandy and Kailyn, feigning excitement as best as I could. This was so far off from playing video games.

"Hey, Lions, beware! The Devils have no fear, B-E-W-A-R-E. This will be, this will be, this will be the *Devils'* victory," shouted a bunch of overeager teenage girls in skirts that covered only half an ass cheek.

Brandy and Kailyn each did a perfect handspring and waved their red and black pompoms in the air. I might not be cheerleader material, but they really got the crowd in an uproar. The players huddled on the field, giving each other weird hand signs from the sidelines that ended in a unison clap. Very technical.

"You are enjoying yourself." Lexi grinned beside me, flashing her adorable dimples.

I smiled back. "Who would have thought?"

She giggled. Lexi was one of the girls that had a sexy giggle, not an annoying one like most.

"So does this mean you will be going to homecoming?" she asked sneakily.

Nice try. "Don't hold your breath."

"Come on. New dress. New shoes. What more could a girl ask for?" she tried to persuade me.

A date. And I definitely didn't have one of those.

During halftime, Lexi's little pink phone buzzed. I waved down at Brandy and Kailyn as they finished one of their stripper-pole-quality routines. Lord knows I would make the worst cheerleader. Overlooking that I was clumsy and uncoordinated, I just couldn't fake being that cheerful.

The panic in Lexi's voice caught my attention, and I started to listen in. Whatever had her upset, it didn't sound good. She snapped her phone shut and said hurriedly, "We have to go. Chase said there is a demon in the area. Close. He thinks he might be at the game."

Did that mean he was after Lexi?

My eyes automatically scanned the field like I knew what I was looking for.

Ha. As if I would be able to pick him out from the crowd of people. I could barely see the other side. One short interlude with a lower-demon and I instantly thought I was an expert.

Lexi grabbed her purse off the bleachers and started zigzagging her way down.

"Where's Chase?" I yelled over the horde. A wave of alarm for his safety rose up in me. It didn't matter that he was some big, bad, half-demon.

"He is on his way here. Sierra called him. He is going to lead him away from the game, hopefully," she informed me as we maneuvered between people.

We raced to the parking lot.

"I'll meet you at my house," she instructed as we split up to find our cars.

I nodded and started weaving in and out of the mass amount of cars until I came to my little white Fusion. Rummaging through my bag, my fingers slipped from nerves, and it tumbled to the ground.

"Hell," I muttered. Bending down, I retrieved the bag at the edge of a full-blown freak out.

My keys were missing, and I swore my heart fell out of my chest. I peered into the driver's side window. Sure enough, there sat my keys in the ignition.

Only me.

"Okay, calm down," I coaxed myself. There was no point in spazz-ing. I think my heart had stopped beating.

I'd just call Chase. He was on his way. Problem solved.

If I last that long, said that little voice in the back of my head.

I told that little voice to shove it.

Pulling out my phone, I dialed his number. It rang and rang and rang.

Voicemail.

I was going to kill him.

Trying to think rationally, I decided my best bet would be to head back into the crowd. I honestly didn't think *it* would openly attack with so many prying eyes nearby. Lexi was safely on her way home, and that was what mattered. I didn't give two flying pigs about Sierra, Hayden, or Craig. As far as I knew, the lower-demon was only interested in Divisa.

I hoped.

Turning around, I headed back in the direction I'd come. The parking lot of the school wasn't nearly as lit up as the football field, and it was deserted. My footsteps echoed in the spotty darkness, and my heartbeat roared in my ears.

A prickly sensation tickled my spine, and I looked over my shoulder, wanting to make sure I wasn't being followed. My human eyes saw nothing. Putting a hand to my chest, I picked up speed.

I swear I was being stalked.

Another minute and I would be surrounded by people. I could hear the crowd raving in the stands.

The creepy feeling came back tenfold. This time, I was certain something was following me. Rushing forward, I was relieved to see the field up ahead. I nearly broke out into a run.

Then the unmistakable sound of heavy footsteps clopped behind me. A chill skirted down the back of my neck, causing the tiny hairs to spike. All I could think was, *I'm not going to make it.*

Before my brain registered the thought, a scorching hand closed around my neck with brutal force, and razor sharp nails burrowed into my adrenaline-pulsing veins. My heart thundered against my ribs as his grip tightened. He held me in the air, feet dangling from the ground. The oxygen my lungs desperately needed was cut off as his inferno breath roasted my neck. A sickening scent of burning flesh twisted my stomach.

"Don't scream," he warned me. His voice growled in a foreboding command.

The next thing I knew, I was sailing through the air. I cried out as my body slammed into a nearby SUV. Metal crunched under the force of my hit, and I fell limply to the pavement. Teeny stars danced behind my eyes as I wavered toward darkness. At this point, I would have surely welcomed it.

Rolling onto my back, I greedily ate up the air and had barely enough time to fill my deprived lungs before he was on top of me again. Pinned under an unbelievably awful truck of weight, my chest felt like it was going to cave.

I stared into pools of sooty blackness, and little gasps wheezed in and out of my barely functioning lungs. What had been the face of a man swiftly turned into a gross depiction of nightmares as he shed his form. His ill, gray skin was tougher than leather, rotting shark-like teeth spewed vile venom, and he grew in size, hovering over me.

"Human, we meet again. Tell me, where are they?" he ground out, keeping my head locked in a death grasp. Finality resounded in his words. I wasn't getting out of this alive.

"I-I don't know," I croaked. My skin grated against rough gravel in blinding pain.

There was no question; apparently I had a death wish. I didn't even think about what I was doing. Looking into those soulless pits of black, I spat into his face.

He threw his head back, howling loudly and forcefully. The ground shook underneath him from the power.

Ah shit. I'd done it now. It was probably the worst time to remember what Chase had said about the lower-demons drawing out a human's death for pleasure.

"Stupid girl," he shrilled in a maddening voice. "I understand what the half-human sees in you." His ashen finger traced my face in a hard line. Turning my head, I jerked it away from his repulsive touch. It only made him tighten his grip, forcing tears into my eyes. "He will come for you. But that doesn't mean we can't have some fun while we wait."

"I wouldn't count on it," I choked out, my throat dry and burning.

He upturned his wicked mouth in a tormented grin. "You will fight until the end ... I look forward to it." Keeping his grasp on my head, he locked his onyx eyes on mine, making it impossible to look away. I could taste a bitter metallic flavor on my tongue—my own blood.

A sob escaped my lips as I felt the pressure of him inside me. I didn't know what he was doing, but I assumed it was very bad. Then he locked something onto my chest. I felt it attach and pull. The essence of my life was being torn from my body. I could feel the darkness weaving around my heart and taking pieces of me. My very life energy was being sucked away, flowing freely from me to him.

He laughed at the frozen shock in my eyes. Purely evil and without an ounce of remorse, those hollow eyes lit with pleasure and happiness, if that was at all possible.

My body grew weaker, and my eyes tired, while his seemed brighter and energetic.

Shit.

Hope seemed like a faraway island I would never reach. "Chase." His name was nothing but a whimper on my lips.

My ass had just been handed to me on a silver platter. This was it. The end.

I heard Chase before I saw him. Well, he was mostly a blur. Slamming into the lesser-demon above me with the force of an asteroid, his battle cry exploded as they tumbled to the blacktop. Fists battered against flesh and bone, over and over again. It was impossible to keep up with their movements. There was no telling who was thrashing who. He moved like Neo, from the Matrix, on steroids.

The instinct to survive had taken over. Forcing my legs to obey, I scrambled to sit up and pushed away from the fight. Propped against a nearby car, I leaned heavily on it for support. My legs were wobbling, and my whole body was shaking.

All I could think was: *he had come.* He found me. Chase was here, and I would be safe. My tense muscles relaxed as his rippled.

They rolled on the ground, delivering blows that would kill a normal human. I had to bite my lip hard to keep from shouting and distracting him.

"You think you can save her, half-breed?" the lesser-demon taunted.

"If I were you, I would quit while you can," Chase growled lowly.

His dark hair beaded with perspiration, whereas I broke out in a cold sweat from fear for him.

The demon licked his lips. "She's tasty," he said, laughing sickly.

Chase rammed him in the gut, taking them both to the hard pavement and cutting off his demented laugh. The grunts and moans were almost like something from one of my games, inhuman and wolfish.

Just as quickly, the demon got the upper hand, and my blood turned to ice. Chase groaned as he took an enormous hit to the face, and his head snapped to the side. I sucked in a sharp breath at the stomach-churning punch. Slowly he turned back, wiping the blood from his mouth. His eyes seared a radiating yellow. It was the first time I might have truly feared him.

"I think I'm done playing games," Chase hissed between clenched teeth.

He pulverized the demon into the ground, repetitively. Securing him with his weight and knees, Chase reached in his back pocket, eyes aglow, and pulled out a shining ruby dagger. Raising it over his head, he jammed it into the center of the demon's chest, uttering, "It's time to go home."

The being from hell howled and then promptly erupted into a million particles of raining ash. Breathing heavily, Chase dropped to the concrete, head hung in exhaustion. Blood oozed from the cuts on his face and arms, dried and smudged in spots. He looked more like a warrior than a half-demon.

My warrior.

Chase was a badass.

Closing my eyes, I heard my name in the faint distance.

"Angel ..."

A part of me recognized it was Chase, but with the immediate threat gone, I couldn't have opened them if I wanted to. My throat felt like it had been filed with sandpaper, my body like it had been hit with a battering ram, and my ribs felt shattered. Overall, I was a mess.

A gentle hand cupped my face. "Angel Eyes ... stay with me." His voice sounded muffled and far away. I knew that I was sinking fast.

Blackness consumed me.

CHAPTER 20

"**A**ngel," he called softly.

With a jolt I jumped, panic in my eyes. Disorientated, I didn't know exactly where I was. A bedroom was obvious. Staring up at the ceiling, I lifted a hand to my sore and swollen throat. I was going to be wearing turtlenecks for a while, or Mom was going to have a shit fit.

He sat on the other side of the bed, his shirt ripped, and his silver eyes loaded with concern.

This must be Chase's room.

I blinked a few times, trying to clear the dust from my fuzzy mind. How did I get here? Last I recalled, I was at the football game, in the parking lot.

Then the memories swamped me in a horrible, murky rush. The lower-demon, being bashed against the pavement, practically choking to death, and that *thing* doing something strange to me.

"Chase," I whispered. My voice was unrecognizable to my own ears. I tried to sit up, and my head rocked like a hurricane.

"Do you ever listen to anything I say?" he asked, sounding put out.

"Why would I start now?" I croaked.

"Do you remember what happened?"

I nodded, my head throbbing. "I think so. But I'm starting to wish I didn't."

"That can be arranged."

I gave him a snarky glare. "Don't. Even. Think about messing with my head."

"When Lexi called and said you weren't there ..." His words trailed off in agony.

"I'm okay. You got there in time," I reassured him.

"And if I hadn't? If I had been another minute, would you still be okay?"

Honestly, I didn't know, but he didn't need to hear that. "It doesn't matter. I hate what-ifs."

He pushed off the bed and went to his dresser. "How are you feeling?"

I put a hand to my head. "Like I just got choke slammed."

He snickered. "I'm pretty sure you did."

I laid my head back and closed my eyes for a moment. "Not funny. How long was I out?"

"At least an hour." I followed his voice, and my mouth watered. He had removed his nasty shirt and stood like a dark temptation in front of me. I almost sighed out loud when he covered his sun-dipped chest. "I was starting to wonder if you would regain consciousness tonight."

"I guess I should be glad I did, but I can't say the same for my body. God, it's painful."

Looking guilt-ridden, he walked to the nightstand. "Here, I got you some aspirin and water." He handed me a glass and two tiny white pills.

"Please tell me these are happy pills." I swallowed them with a gulp of water. It cooled my burning throat.

The corners of his lips turned up. "They will help; that's for sure." The mattress springs squeaked under his weight.

After a brief pause, I tilted my head toward him. "What did he do to me?" I asked, thinking about how I had felt him inside me.

His sigh was crowded with emotions as he clenched his hand. "He stole strands of your life. It gives him strength." His words were tight.

The strength part gave me concern. "Enough to kill you?"

"Enough to give me a fight," he replied with a cocky grin.

Did his ego ever not get in the way?

"They steal human life?" I asked, trying to understand the impossible world I found myself living in now.

"Yes," he confirmed, his eyes quickly turning serious. "The longer they hold you in their soulless gaze, the more it shaves off from the human's life. Sometimes ... they take it all until death," he said in doom.

Just freaking wonderful.

I swallowed hard. "Did he—"

His metallic eyes filled with anguish, meeting mine. "He didn't take much, not even a year of your life," he assured me.

"You killed him, didn't you? With that dagger." I remembered seeing him ram it into the demon's chest—like an avenging dark knight.

"Yeah, he is dead. I sent him back to the underworld," he said with finality.

There was an underworld. I was relieved, but it felt like I was living in one of my video games, like God of War. "This is crazy. The knife you had kills them?"

He pulled out a small dagger with a red hilt from a leather sheathe. What I didn't notice before was the engravings on the blade. "It's the easiest way to kill a lesser-demon, but not the only way." He twirled it once before putting it back on the nightstand.

Bits and pieces swirled back. "You said something before you ... um, struck him."

"Is there nothing you don't notice? The more I tell you, the more you get sucked into this nightmare. Don't you see that? It is a nightmare. You don't really want demons and hellhounds chasing you your whole life." He ran a frustrated hand through his black hair before sinking back against the headboard beside me. "The mark you are so curious about is a connection to the underworld. It not only brands me a half-breed but also links me to hell, which enables us to send the hellish beings back." There was a hardened desperation to his tone. A dire need to make me understand this wasn't a game.

"Am I really in danger?"

Some of the edge in his voice left. "Yes." He stared at the wall. "When he took your life energy, he also got your essence. It is like a signature for them, a way to track you."

"But he is dead now," I disputed.

"*He* is gone, yes, but the world is filled with demons. Hell has them positioned everywhere, always watching. Other demons will be able to see that you have been touched by one of their own. It will put a target on you."

Christ. I was a freaking walking demon life-support bank.

I gulped as difficult as it was. "For how long?"

He shrugged. "Honestly, I don't know. You probably shouldn't go home tonight," he suggested.

I couldn't agree more. "Probably not. One look at me, and Mom would call the SWAT team. I'll just leave her a message that I'm staying with Lexi tonight."

Chase stepped back into the room after a shower when I got off the phone. He tossed me a T-shirt. "I thought you might want to get out of those clothes."

I must look like a homeless person. "Thanks," I muttered and slowly walked to the bathroom. Every muscle screamed at me in protest.

Quickly, I changed, washed my face, and ran a brush I had in my purse through my knotted hair. Nerves fluttered in my belly. For the first time, I realized that I was about to spend the night with Chase. In Chase's bed.

Oh God. Inhale. Exhale.

The T-shirt he gave me came down to my knees, but that was all that stood between him and me. I'd never felt so exposed in my life, or so anxious. How was I going to sleep when my stomach was doing jumping jacks just at the thought of lying beside him?

Act cool. I mentally gave myself a pep talk before opening the door.

He was stretched out on his bed in nothing but lounging pants.

How I could feel anything after the night I'd had was beyond my comprehension. Where Chase was concerned, there was no reasoning. I stood in the doorway like an idiot, just trying to remember to breathe. His eyes zeroed in on me, taking in my bare appearance. I felt naked before him, and my cheeks blossomed pink.

With shaky legs, I forced one foot in front of the other until I reached the bed. I wondered briefly if Devin knew I was staying here. Mom would probably have given me a high five. She never reacted like a normal mom should.

Lying on my side, I faced him. My eyes were tired and droopy. "Will I ever *not* have to thank you for saving my life?" I felt like I had the weight of the world on my shoulders.

He grinned, looking dashingly dark and handsome with his hair still damp. His sinful smell followed from the bathroom, filling his room. "Doubt it." The teasing spark in his eyes faded. "Maybe the question is: Will I always be there to save you?"

His words shouldn't have sent a gazillion tingles through my system. They shouldn't have made me want to hope. That one word, *always*, filled me with a warmth I couldn't deny. What would *always* with Chase be like?

Bliss. And hell.

"You haven't missed yet," I reminded him softly.

"And the next time … if I do? I can't have your life on my conscious."

"You won't. You're like some Billy Badass Divisa," I said, stroking his already larger than life ego.

He smirked. "I'm not a superhero, Angel."

Pretty damn close as far as I was concerned. "Then what do you propose we do?"

"I just can't leave your side," he stated matter-of-factly.

I choked on his words. "Excuse me?"

"What choice do you have?" he asked, playing the devil's advocate.

Hardy-har.

"I don't want a shadow." Especially not one who drove me to

163

distraction and then turned around and drove me bonkers. My head was bound to explode.

"You want to live, don't you?" he asked.

I nodded my head in defeat. Duh. I wanted to live.

He lifted his brow mockingly.

Huffing, I guessed it was settled. Chase had suddenly become my personal demon bodyguard.

Oh, goodie gumdrops.

"Try to get some sleep," he advised, brushing the hair from my forehead. "Good night, Angel Eyes."

Right. Like that was possible.

I lay there listening to the evenness of his breathing, trying not to fidget. No way did I dare glance in his direction. With my luck, he wouldn't be sleeping. Forcing my eyes closed, I started counting sheep. It never worked, but hopefully my wrecked body would be too tired to care. I finally lost count somewhere after seventy-three.

WAKING UP, my legs felt heavy, and my body was humming. There was sunlight creeping through the thin curtains, casting a soft light into the room. Glancing down, I was able to figure out why every part of me was alive. I was entangled with Chase. His arm was draped over my hip, securing me against him. Where I was naked, he was clothed. Where he was naked, I was clothed.

It was distractingly sexy.

My hand laid on his bare chest, itching to touch him more. I listened to the steady beat of his heart and gave in to my bold impulses. With my breath held, I flexed my fingers, waiting.

I must be insane.

His heart still beat strong and stable. The same couldn't be said for mine. Feeling encouraged, I moved my hand a little lower. And a little lower. Until I was caught in the delicious feeling of his muscles under my fingertips. Our legs looked like pretzels, knotted together. Briefly, I wondered how we had even managed such a feat in our sleep.

I was lost.

Bravely, I traced my fingers lower, following the trail of dark curls edging out just at the waistband. Skimming between flesh and material, I paused, holding my breath.

The hiss I heard was unmistakable.

My heart skipped.

Peeking from under tentative lashes, I was bedazzled by a set of silver eyes. There was nothing more mortifying than being caught red-handed feeling someone up. His eyes burned a slow steady torch in places I didn't even know were possible.

My hand had a mind of its own, still on the move. Under my featherlike touch, his eyes darkened, and his skin jumped. There was no doubt … I was playing with fire. He had warned me before. Right now, I would risk being burned to death just to be kissed by him. This time, I didn't want any games or warnings.

Just him.

Slowly, he reached up and fisted a handful of my wild, tangled hair. This wasn't going to be sweet or innocent. It was past that point and had toppled straight into desperate need, madness, and recklessness.

"Angel" was all he said as he lowered his head. Just my name on those edible lips and my chest burst into a million shock waves.

His mouth covered mine, tumbling me into a surge of desire. I arched against him, offering, challenging. Greedily, I took his mouth with mine, reeling on the taste of both heaven and hell. He was an intoxicating mix of both.

Inevitable.

We both knew we would end up here eventually.

The blanket barely covering us was quickly tossed on the ground. Encircling my arms around his neck, I crushed my lips to his and threw caution to the wind. Who wouldn't when your body was singing like angels?

"You smell like peaches," he murmured over my tingling skin. "And taste like wild berries." His mouth moved everywhere, hitting pleasure points all over my neck, shoulder, jaw, throat, and back to my waiting mouth.

I couldn't have said anything if I had wanted to. I was convinced this was the best dream of my life.

Exciting.

Exotic.

Erotic.

God, yes. That about covered it.

I let out a little gasp of pleasure as he changed angles, deepening the kiss, our tongues dancing. His mouth was possessive, branding me with his scent, his taste, and my toes curled like in the movies.

Expertly his hand moved up my smooth leg, passing over my hip and into uncharted territories. My skin felt like satin under his fingers. I swayed. It seemed foolish, but he made me dizzy. Every touch and feeling was seared into my memory.

It was a good thing I was already lying down.

In the distance, there was an annoying buzzing that just wouldn't quit. It wasn't until Chase pulled reluctantly away that I realized it was his alarm. His topaz eyes stared down at my lips, swollen from his kisses. My shirt was bunched up, exposing my bare midriff, and his fists clenched against my sides.

Heavily my chest rose and fell as I tried to steady my racing heart. Clamping his eyes closed, I lay in a trance, wondering if being compelled felt like this.

When he opened his eyes again, I'd expected to see crystal clear gray, yet they were blistering gold instead, and my pulse skipped. He slammed his fist over the alarm clock, shattering it to bits. Someone hadn't been able to get under control.

A dark part of me was thrilled that he had been so consumed by what happened between us that he had been unable to control the demon inside him.

Twisted.

Without saying a word, he stalked from the room in long angry strides. The front door crashed shut, and I closed my eyes, smiling. I should have been pissed that he left without a word, but I wasn't.

CHAPTER 21

I sat on the couch with Travis, playing co-op MW3 on his Xbox Live.

"You totally kick ass for a girl," he said, flashing his dimples.

Lexi rolled her eyes as she filed her already perfectly manicured fingernails. I think they were on babysit-the-fragile-human duty while Chase did God knew what. He was so infuriating.

Why couldn't Travis be my shadow? At least he was pleasant and could survive a round of search and destroy, though he always had a trace of sadness underneath his free-spirited charm. It made me wonder if he missed Emma. He must have really cared for her. Lexi said he had gone berserk when she disappeared.

"Damn it," he swore. "Your kill-death ratio is better than mine, again."

"What can I say? You're a noob."

"I can't believe a girl finally moves in next door, and she has more in common with my brother," Lexi pouted.

She was bored out of her mind, and I was starting to feel guilty.

"I'm hungry," she announced, putting away her nail file. "You guys want something to eat?"

Travis and I both nodded in unison, eyes glued to the TV.

"Good. I'll do a food run," she offered.

"Why don't we just make something?" I suggested, thinking it would give her something to do.

Travis laughed his ass off, rolling on the couch, and Lexi looked offended. She sauntered out of the house, leaving Travis in his laughing fit.

"Oh my God, I haven't laughed that hard in forever," Travis said with the biggest grin I'd ever seen. It was the kind of grin ladies swoon over. I wasn't the swooning type.

"Um, glad I could be of service," I replied, still unsure why that had been so funny.

"I needed that," he stated, those adorable dimples winking.

I couldn't help but think all his laughter had perished when Emma went missing. "You still miss her," I commented, realizing this was probably none of my business.

His grin only fluctuated a tad. I gave him credit for the good face he put on. "Every day."

Those two words split my heart. "Did you help search for her?" The game was forgotten. I crossed my legs and waited for him to answer.

He shook his pretty boy head. "Not with the official investigation. Her parents wouldn't let me. They never approved of our relationship and forbid her from seeing me," he revealed. The hurt of their rejection was evident in his tone. "They didn't think I was good enough for their daughter. Her dad was military strict. We spent a large amount of our time devising ways to see each other. It was the only time I ever looked forward to going to school." There was a wistful quality to his voice.

"You haven't given up hope." I could hear it in his voice. He didn't believe, like Chase did, that she was dead.

"No. Never." The determination in his startling turquoise eyes was so astonishing that *I* even believed him.

I put my hand on his. "If you ever need any help, I'm here," I offered sincerely. He was a good guy and deserved more in his life than sadness, lost love, and isolation.

"Thanks." The corners of his mouth turned up. "I still don't get what the hell you see in Chase," he said devilishly.

I didn't know why I found that so funny, but I did. Of course, Chase chose that moment to walk in as I was laughing with my head on Travis' shoulder and with him grinning down at me.

"Speak of the devil," Travis said.

My laughter pealed into renewed hysterics all over again. I clutched my stomach in pain, and water stung my eyes. It took only one glance at Chase for my amusement to freeze. When he'd left this morning, I was sort of under the impression that he needed space to quiet his demon, but by the looks of it, it hadn't worked. His eyes shimmered gold.

Travis tugged on a loose strand of my hair, and I swore I heard Chase growl. Before I knew it, the two of them were on the family room floor, engaging in a wrestling match. The coffee table ended up upturned, and I lifted my feet off the floor just in the nick of time.

Boys.

I would never understand what the hell goes on in their pea-sized brains. Did they not do enough fighting against the hunters, the hell-hounds, and all the other scary shit that was out to kill them? They had to fight amongst themselves.

I'd never had any siblings, so this was a whole new ball game for me. *Do I just let them pulverize each other?*

Lexi came back with the food just in time to see Travis slammed up against the wall, knocking down a picture. She stood next to me. "Should I assume this is about you?" she asked. I think she enjoyed watching me squirm.

"Are you going to do something before they kill each other?" I was panicking.

"And break a nail? Hell no."

"You were supposed to keep her safe, not seduce her," Chase yelled, sucker punching Travis in the stomach.

Lexi lifted a brow.

Travis snickered—so not helping the situation. I swore they were enjoying themselves.

Who said anything about seducing anyway? I was done worrying about their foolishness.

Lexi handed me a slice of pizza. "Oh, I forgot to tell you. Did you hear that my dad asked your mom on a date?" she casually informed me in delight.

"What?" I screeched.

This day just kept getting better.

Food forgotten, I headed for the door.

"Angel!" Chase and Travis called in unison.

Funny how they noticed my departure but not when I had yelled at them to quit beating on the other.

"Kiss ass," I retorted and left. As I walked out, I heard Travis chuckle and Chase grumble.

"Mom!" I screamed, letting the door slam shut behind me.

She popped her head out of the kitchen, looking stunned by my abrupt arrival. "Angel, I'm right here. What's wrong, honey?" she asked, seeing the look of annoyance on my face.

"You're going on a date? With Devin!" I accused her like the idea made me sick, which it did.

She looked kind of stumped, not sure why this was a problem. Sometimes Mom could be so clueless. "Yes," she drew out. "Is there a no dating policy I'm unaware of? 'Cuz if so, you have broken that rule more than once yourself."

Ugh. Technically no. Dating was fine. I wanted her to date, just not Devin. And I wasn't dating Chase for goodness' sake. "No, dating is cool, but does it have to be our neighbor?" I whined.

She studied me with her motherly amber eyes. "Have you seen Devin? Or maybe you have been too enamored with his nephew."

I groaned. I did not want to talk about Devin's apparent hotness with my mother. "I am not dating Chase," I huffed, taking a seat on one of the bar stools.

She put her hands on her hips. "What are you calling it? Devin says you two spend a lot of time together." There was a secret smirk on her lips.

My eyes widened. Devin was a tattletale. "We're … friends.

Anyway, we were talking about you, not me," I reminded her. "I get that we live in the country and we want to fit in, but do we have to start dating within the same family? It's so Jerry Springer."

"Ha. So you are dating." Leave it up to Mom to completely miss the point.

I dropped my head to the counter. This was worthless. It was like talking to a brick wall. She brushed a gentle hand over my head. Did she want to hear that a few hours ago I was practically naked, getting hot and heavy between the sheets with Chase? That I nearly begged him to take me? And now she wanted to date his uncle.

Could my life get any more complicated?

"Did you hurt yourself?" Her eyes zeroed in at the slightly purplish marks on my neck.

Shit. Maybe I should have had Chase compel Mom.

All things considered, I had walked away from a life-threatening situation with only a few scrapes and bruises. It could have been a hundred times worse. At least I hadn't broken anything, though my ribs were pretty damn sore.

I brushed her hand aside. "It's nothing. I fell at the game yesterday. Oh, and to top it off, I locked my keys in the car." I was trying for a little distraction here.

"Hm," she replied, unsure if she believed my story. "I wondered where your car was."

"Do you think you could drop me off later to pick it up?" I asked, turning on the good daughter charm.

THE RETRIEVAL of the car was worse than I'd imagined. Every horrible detail came swarming back in vivid memories. I hadn't even realized that I had stopped walking and was just standing there ... staring.

"Angel," Mom called. "Everything okay?" she asked, a little confused by my behavior lately. First, I'd jumped down her throat for wanting to go on a date with Devin; then I'd spaced out in the parking lot. Next I'd be dying my hair green and piercing my nipples.

I was totally weirded out by being here. "Yeah, fine. Let's get out of here. I don't want to spend my Sunday in the school parking lot."

Rushing to my car, I sped out of the parking lot at Mach 10. I spent the rest of the day locked away in my room with my iPod and an unfinished history paper. Why did I need to learn history anyway when it was just going to repeat itself? My mind wasn't into the paper but was solely consumed with my crazy relationship with Chase.

We were like fire and ice. Hot as hell one minute and cold as ice the next.

CHAPTER 22

I wasn't sure how it happened, but somehow I got suckered into shopping with Lexi for homecoming. She needed a girl's opinion. Why she thought I qualified escaped me.

The dance was still a few weeks away, but Lexi just couldn't wait to get to the stores. She didn't want the crummy leftovers.

I had agreed to this shopping excursion under two conditions:

1. She stopped trying to set me up on a double date with Chase for homecoming.

2. She did not ask me again to reconsider going to homecoming. It was not going to happen.

Lexi finally conceded, but not graciously.

So here I was, with a hyped up Lexi, surrounded by expensive dresses. She was in pure heaven, and I was in shopping hell.

"Who are you going with again?" I asked, making a grotesque face at the lime green dress I stumbled upon. Who in their right mind would wear lime green to homecoming, except for Nicki Minaj?

"Hayden," she replied, shuffling through more silk, bows, ribbons, and lace then I'd ever seen. We were in some kind of bridal shop at the center of town.

"Are you guys dating?" A friend should know this kind of stuff.

"Not really. It's just easier for us to go together," she informed me, like it was no big deal.

I, on the other hand, thought it was a big deal, especially for a girl like Lexi. She was into all the high school traditions like dances, football games, and yearbooks. I thought that she should go with someone who would make the night special. Her admission got me thinking. "Do you guys only date other Divisa?" I whispered.

She pulled out a super short black dress that I was sure would look phenomenal on her. Her sea foam eyes met mine over the rack. "It's complicated. After Travis and Emma, we're all worried about us being with someone who doesn't know." She shrugged. "Chase and my dad think it would be in our best interest to stick together."

I wondered if that included me. "Is that what *you* want?" I asked, thinking how unfair her life was. Other people telling me what was best for me would just make me mad.

"It doesn't matter. We have already broken way too many rules with you. Everyone is on edge."

"I would never do anything to hurt you," I defended myself.

"I know, but Chase and my dad think we need to be extra cautious." She had an armful of sparkling dresses. "Here," she said, tossing a few at me. "Can you help me with these?"

Looking at the number of dresses we had between us, I internally groaned. We were going to be here for hours … days. "How many dresses do you plan on trying on?"

She grinned cunningly. "All of them."

I was following behind her to the dressing rooms and tripped over my feet at her words. "Tell me you are joking."

"At least humor me and try on a dress. Please," she pleaded, cutting off the swift rejection that I had on my lips. "I don't think I've ever seen you in a dress."

"With good reason," I muttered.

"It will be fun. I swear," she vowed.

Lexi and I had completely different ideas of *fun*. "Fine," I huffed. "Will it get us out of here faster?"

"Sure. You try on half. Then I can see what they look like." She gushed in Lexi fashion and grabbed my hand, pulling me like a crazy person through the store.

I was going to regret this.

Did I need to remind her that nothing I tried on would look half as good on me as it would on her? Closing myself behind the curtain, she tossed over a dress.

"Here, try this one on first."

"Whatever you say, *boss*," I muttered.

The first dress was midnight blue and elegantly simple. It was something that I might actually wear, if I had somewhere to go. The silky material felt like soft satin against my skin and very well might have been. I didn't know squat about pricey fabrics.

"You ready?" she asked from the other side of the partitioning wall.

I pushed the black curtain aside and stepped out. Lexi turned around and sucked in a breath when she saw me. She squealed in delight, making me cringe at her enthusiasm, which was drawing a lot of unwanted attention. "You look fabulous. Twirl," she demanded.

"Um, I'm not twirling."

I did however survey myself in a three-way mirror that highlighted every human flaw. I barely recognized the girl that stared back at me. Her eyes were wide and starlight blue. She looked taller, curvy, and she actually looked like she had boobs. It was amazing what the right dress could do.

Lexi stood behind me and lifted the hair off my neck. "See, I knew there was a bangin' body under those drab clothes you wear."

I should have been offended. She was lucky it was her. If it had been anyone else, I would have told them to go screw themselves.

"Chase would lose his shit if he saw you in this dress," she commented deviously.

"I don't see how, and do not get any ideas in that pretty head of yours."

Her smile only grew, those dimples looking dangerous. "So, have you guys …"

I narrowed my eyes. "Have we what?"

"I thought since you spent the night in his room that you guys totally did the deed."

Ugh. "Lexi," I hissed. "I can't believe we are talking about this. We didn't, okay?"

There was just no stopping her. "But you were thinking about it."

I smashed my face in an unflattering look.

"What? This *is* what friends talk about."

Annoyed, I angled my head. "Maybe, but not when it's her cousin," I countered.

"Hm." She pursed her lips, chewing on my words. Distracted, her jewel eyes looked me over again. "At least you would give Sierra a run for her money. She wouldn't stand a chance next to you."

Normally I didn't succumb to flattery, but any dig at Sierra brightened my day. We smiled at each other.

To my surprise, I ended up having more fun than I thought possible. Lexi was such a sunny contrast to my dark sarcasm. We made a great team—odd 'cuz she actually was part demon, and I was the good girl. Talk about role reversals.

After Lexi *finally* picked a dress with the wow factor, we strolled down the cobblestone path. Lexi's shopping bags were swinging merrily beside her. I glanced into one of the large shop windows. A group of little girls in leotards were doing some form of pirouettes. *Bare Feet Studios* was painted in bold, colorful letters on the glass. Ballet shoes hung from hooks in the storefront display.

Travis had said that Emma had been a dancer. I wondered if she'd ever come to this studio and looked out the same window I was looking in. Had Travis ever come to watch her dance?

Lexi noticed that I had stopped and was staring into the studio. She glanced in beside me.

A happy couple caught my eye, strolling toward the studio with a little strawberry blonde girl swinging between their arms. The little girl couldn't have been older than four and squealed in delight. Lexi stiffened at my side and watched the picture-perfect family walk into the studio.

"That was Emma's parents," she said softly. Her eyes shifted in the setting sunlight.

I looked at her, confused. How could that couple, who looked so content, be the parents of a girl who had only been missing for a year? It didn't seem possible.

"They don't seem … sad or affected at all." I didn't know what I'd expected, but that hadn't been it.

The petite woman, with hair like her little girl's, laughed at something her husband said. He lifted the girl easily into his arms and tickled her cheek with his nose. She giggled.

"I know. It's so weird. I remember the first time Travis saw them after they called off the search. He approached them, accusing them of giving up, not caring. Her father told him he couldn't possibly know what they were feeling and to stay away from his family. Travis got so angry I thought he was going to expose us to the whole town. It was after that when he lost it."

I wanted to walk right up to them and ask them how they could have so easily forgotten their daughter. Apparently they had another one to replace her. I could fully understand Travis' anger. There were plenty of colorful words on the tip of my tongue for Emma's parents. I'd never met Emma, but knowing Travis and what he felt for her made me wish I'd had the chance.

"Don't tell Travis," she pleaded, worried for him.

"I won't," I promised.

The ride home was somber. Lexi was the one to break the silence. "If anything happened to you …" Lexi started, her voice trailing off.

"Lexi, nothing is going to happen," I assured her, even though we both knew that wasn't exactly true.

"Angel, look at what has already happened. Look at what we have already exposed you to. It is probably only a matter of time." She slumped in the seat, her pretty mouth frowning.

"Don't say that. I'm not Emma."

"I know. It's just that this time it's not just Travis who will hurt. It's all of us." Her voice hitched on emotion.

My throat got thick with sentiment. I cared about them too. "How can anything happen to me when I have Chase looming over my every move?"

She smiled halfheartedly. "That's true. He is a badass."

I returned her grin.

She hugged me as we got out of the car. "Thanks, Angel. You are the best friend I've ever had."

Damn. Now she'd done it.

My eyes misted. "So are you, Lexi, even after you dragged me from store to store and made me try on a hundred itchy dresses."

She giggled even as she was sniffling.

Chase came out of the house as we were wiping our eyes. "Why are you crying?" His eyes clouded with concern, and his stance was ready for battle.

Lexi waved her hand. "It's nothing. Just girl stuff. See you tomorrow?" she said, grabbing her shopping bags.

I nodded.

Chase watched her walk inside. "I'll never understand the two of you. It was hard enough with just Lexi," he grumbled.

I tried to hide my grin. "So, did you need something?" I asked after it became clear he wasn't going anywhere.

"You want to watch a movie?"

Immediately I became suspicious. "Why?"

"I just thought we could hang out," he said, smirking. "You do like movies, don't you?"

Hang out? Was that even a good idea? Last time we were alone together, he was sucking my face. Extremely effectively, mind you.

What the hell. Why not?

"Of course I like movies." I just wasn't sure about him.

The house was dark and empty when we walked inside. Mom was at work, and I was secretly glad he had come over. This big old house still gave me the willies. We sat on opposite sides of the couch, almost as if we were afraid to touch or get too close. Who knew? Maybe we would end up attacking each other again. It seemed to be our style.

I popped in an action film. The last thing I wanted to watch was a sappy love story with Chase. Give me guns, explosions, and high-speed car pursuits. No awkwardness there.

Then why did it feel like there was a ghost sitting between us? I had to break the eerie silence or I was going to go nuts.

"We saw Emma's parents in town today," I blurted out.

His eyes roamed from the TV to me as my words sunk in, surprise shrouding them.

"Lexi doesn't want me to say anything to Travis," I quickly added.

"She wouldn't want to drudge up any old feelings Travis has just started to get over. And I agree." He rubbed his hands over his face.

"They were so ... happy," I noted, my tone laced with disapproval. "They didn't even seem like a chunk of their life was missing—their daughter."

"I saw them once, a month after she was gone. It took everything I had in me to control my anger. They were having a picnic in the park without a care in the world, while my cousin was at home suffering. Every. Single. Day. I decided then that they didn't deserve Emma. Not the way Travis did. He loved and adored her. Risked everything for her. His guilt ate at him for months after she was gone, and he is only a fraction of the guy he used to be. I don't know if he will ever be the same."

There was an underlying bitterness in his words. It made me curious. What was under the surface that had him upset? "He hasn't let go," I said.

"I know," he admitted, looking through me, lost in his own thoughts.

I fell asleep some time during the movie. My body was still worn from Friday night. It ached in places where a body shouldn't ache. When I woke up to darkness, a fuzzy TV screen, and a stiff neck, Chase was gone.

CHAPTER 23

My life sort of resumed as normal. I wasn't attacked by anything evil trying to steal my life. Sierra continued to give me hateful glares. Chase and I kept a safe distance between us. And Mom went on her date with Devin.

Okay, that part wasn't normal in my book. But she did have a good time, and it was nice to see a smile on her face. I think they even made plans for a second date. Before you know it, we were going to be planning a wedding.

God, I hoped not.

Brandy and Kailyn wanted to know what had happened to me after the game. I never showed up to the bonfire. I sucked ass at lying, so I tried to give them as much of the truth as possible. I got hurt at the game. Totally true. And then I had locked my keys in the car, so I had called Chase to come pick me up.

That perked their little gossiping ears up. I was positive by the end of the day everyone in school was going to think we were dating. Surely that was going to please Sierra. I expected a *pleasant* visit from her sometime after school. She was such a bitch prima donna.

Oh grand, something to look forward to.

I'd heard all about how someone had snuck booze into the bonfire.

Brody, a football jerk, got so wasted he'd ended up puking all over some poor girl. They both declared it had been a blast. I was almost sad I'd missed it.

Not really.

The halls were decked out in banners, streamers, and balloons of red and black. Our team mascot was plastered everywhere.

Earlier that morning, the nominees for homecoming court were announced. Brandy's name had been called along with puking Brody. Maybe she should ditch Tommy and go out with Brody. How cute would that be? Brandy and Brody. Wasn't that just the sweetest?

During chemistry, things got a little dicey.

Brody, the I-can't-hold-my-liquor football player, walked into the class. He smiled when he saw me. "Hey, Angel."

"Hey," I replied, returning the smile. He took the seat next to me, and I was finding it hard to keep a straight face.

"I didn't see you at the bonfire," he said, playing with the eraser on his pencil.

"Um, yeah, I wasn't able to make it. But I heard you guys had a great time." I fiddled with the spiral on my notebook, wondering where this was going. It wasn't like Brody and I were friends. Sure, we had said hi in the hall or lunchroom, but this was our first real conversation.

"That's too bad. I was hoping to see you." He looked me in the eye with those soft brown eyes.

He was? "You were?" I echoed my thoughts.

He scooted closer to me over his desk. "Yeah, I was hoping to get a chance to talk to you."

Before or after he was slamming the bottle? "About what?" I asked.

Someone walked into the classroom. I didn't have to look up to know it was Chase. He had a domineering presence wherever he went. Plus, Brody suddenly frowned and looked nervous as heck.

I looked up, meeting his intuitive silver gaze. He lifted that darn pierced brow, and I gave him a warning glare. "Brody," he greeted as he passed us by, taking the seat behind me.

Brody's eyes shifted nervously to Chase, and he cleared his throat. "Hey, Chase."

Chase and Brody were probably the same height, but Brody was broader. Still, Chase oozed badass, not to mention his supernatural strength.

"You were saying," I prompted him, bringing Brody's attention back to me. Trying as hard as I could to completely forget that Chase was there, I focused on Brody's harmless brown eyes.

"Um," he replied, losing some of his nerve. "I was wondering if you had a date for homecoming."

I blinked. *Crap.*

I heard Chase edge closer. This was going to spell disaster.

As luck would have it, Mr. Edgington started his lecture at that moment. And there was Brody waiting expectantly.

"After class," I mouthed, taking out my notes.

He nodded.

Now I had forty minutes to figure out how to let him down easy. How hard could that be? I couldn't believe this was even happening to me. Why Brody? Why now?

Shortly after class started, Chase flicked a strand of my hair and moved close behind me. I could feel the warmth of his breath on the back of my neck. Angling my head toward him, our lips were just inches away. This was the closest we'd been since *that* night, and I was beginning to see stars. How could he do this to me? In a room full of people?

"Smooth move, Angel Eyes."

I couldn't help myself. Inhaling his sinful scent, I finally admitted to myself that it was his darkness that attracted me to him. It was also his arrogance I hated. "You are the last person on this earth I want to impress."

He didn't believe me. I didn't believe me. "Are you sure about that?" he taunted.

Grrr. I wanted to slap that smirk right off his face. My fingers twitched on the top of my desk.

"Let's be honest. You don't want to go with him," Chase purred.

Turning around in my seat, I flipped my hair in his face. He chuckled. Brody looked at the two of us, jumping to all kinds of conclusions. I gave him a slight, reassuring smile, not wanting to hurt his feelings.

After the bell sounded, Brody caught me in the hall. He placed a light hand on my arm.

"Sorry," I said about making him wait all class for an answer. That was pretty shitty of me. A part of me almost said yes, just to spite Chase. But truthfully, I didn't want to go with anyone. "Look, about homecoming—"

"No, it's okay. I get it. You are going with Winters." And then not even waiting for me to protest, he took off in a hurry down the hall.

My mouth just hung open.

Chase's shadow was at my back, laughing over my shoulder.

"You." I turned, poking an accusing finger in his chest.

He held up both hands, grinning guiltily. "I didn't do anything. I swear."

My teeth were gritted. "I am *not* going anywhere with you."

He placed a hand on the lockers behind us. His voice got low as he boxed me in. "Good, then it saves me from disappointing you."

I slumped against the lockers and watched him saunter to his next class. "Prick," I yelled down the hall after him.

Everyone turned over his or her shoulders, staring at me. I clenched my fists in an attempt to restrain myself from stomping after him. His dark laughter bounced off the hallway walls.

By lunchtime, my temper had cooled slightly, though I was still convinced that Chase was the devil. When I got in the lunch line, Kailyn and Brandy immediately jumped all over me.

Small town schools sucked.

"Why didn't you tell us?" they said in harmony. It was frightening.

Grabbing a tray, I started down the line. "Tell you what?" I asked, half distracted by the food.

"That you are going to homecoming with Chase," Brandy said at the same time that Kailyn said, "That Brody asked you to homecoming."

These two were going to give me a migraine at this rate. The lunch lady piled a helping of lasagna on my plate. I almost dropped the tray. "What!" I shrilled, twisting around. "I'm *not* going to homecoming. With *anybody*," I emphasized, moving down to the end of the line.

"That is not what we heard from Sophie, who heard it from Amanda in your chemistry class," Kailyn informed me.

I gave the cashier my card to pay for the lunch while trying to process their information train. It was worse than playing telephone.

While they paid for their food, I set my tray down at our usual table. Lexi spotted me and waved animatedly a few tables over. I smiled shyly at her. I popped the top on my drink. Brandy's and Kailyn's plates clattered as they hurriedly took their seats.

"Why aren't you going with Chase?" Brandy asked across from me.

I twirled a forkful of noodles, mulling over how to answer that. "Because we can't stand each other."

"No way am I buying that," Kailyn disagreed wholeheartedly with a grin.

Neither of them seemed interested in their food. "Why is that so hard to believe?" She wasn't making any sense to me.

"You haven't got a clue, do you?" Brandy asked, biting on her straw.

I was starting to get offended and annoyed with this topic.

She indicated the corner off to my right side. "You don't see what I see every day at lunch. He is always watching you."

My fork paused in midair, never making it to my mouth. "Chase?"

Brandy rolled her eyes. "No shit, Einstein. See for yourself."

At first, I noticed Lexi talking excitedly to a bored-looking Hayden. He looked like he wanted to be anywhere but there. Poor Hayden. The corners of my mouth twitched. Then I shifted my glance and latched onto a pair of velvety silver eyes. *Chase.* My heart exploded, bursting in my chest and dropping to the floor. The noise and chatter of the lunchroom disappeared as time ceased. It was only him and me—eyes glued to each other, unable to look away. There was always something so wickedly hot in those color-changing eyes.

I couldn't think. I couldn't breathe. And I sure as hell hadn't expected to see him staring right at me. It was like some outside force was pulling us together. There was this uncontrollable urge to go to him.

Moments later, he lifted that glinting studded brow in my direction before turning to listen to something Craig had been saying to him. A gush of air rushed from my lungs, and I noticed Sierra was giving me the evil eye. Turning, I focused back on my friends.

"That was steamy. The two of you just about set the cafeteria on fire," Kailyn said dreamily.

Rolling my eyes, I tried to cool my flaring cheeks. I took a long swig of my drink, which did nothing to extinguish the flames burning through me.

"Did you see Sierra? I think she wants to slice off your head," Brandy added.

Kailyn sighed. "So again, I ask you why you are not jumping all over the extremely sexy Chase. He might scare the bejeebers out of me, but I'll be the first to admit he is by far the hottest guy at school. And he is crushing on you ... hard."

"Chase staring at me from across the cafeteria hardly qualifies as him liking me. He is probably scheming ways to make my life a living hell."

Kailyn picked at the lettuce of her salad. "I also heard you guys practically made out in chemistry."

I gagged on my soda, spraying the contents over my uneaten lasagna. "What? You have got to be joking."

She shook her head. "Amanda said your lips were like this." She indicated just how close by pinching her fingers.

"They have probably already been a whole lot closer." Brandy giggled.

I officially despised school and all its rumors. Well, in this case, they weren't entirely rumors. How did things get so out of my control? "Whatever, we can barely stand each other."

"If you say so, but I still think you guys should go to homecoming together," Kailyn said with a sly grin.

"No. Thanks. I don't think homecoming would survive with us in the same room together."

"You guys are sort of … explosive," Brandy commented, grinning.

"Funny," I replied sarcastically.

My appetite was shot. I half expected to be assaulted by Sierra in the parking lot after school today, which was why I ran from my last class to my car in record time. Forget my homework assignments. I just wanted to get home in one piece for once.

CHAPTER 24

The rumble of a bike outside my house broke my concentration. A crisp fall breeze blew through the open window, bringing in scents of an Illinois autumn. It was an entirely different experience, one I found I actually enjoyed. The burning leaves from a nearby farm, sharp pine from the woods behind the house, a cinnamon candle in my room, and the dampness of morning dew. That was my favorite: to look out my window in the morning and see the glistening drops of water on bold green blades.

I had to admit that the colors of fall were breathtaking. I'd never seen such vibrant oranges, reds, and yellows. It looked like an artist had painted all the trees and fallen leaves. If I was into photography, I would be taking the most amazing pictures.

And now there was the roaring of a motor interrupting my Call of Duty campaign. I hit pause on the game and ran down the stairs to check out the commotion. Throwing open the front door, I looked down my driveway.

Who else would be making such a racket other than Chase? There he sat on a powerful-looking motorcycle, grinning wickedly at me. His dark hair was windblown and sexy. He looked like a little boy on Christmas morning, and it was impossible to not return that infectious smile. Brandy and Kailyn were right. He was by far the hottest guy I'd ever laid eyes on.

And he knew it, which sort of added to his bad boy charm.

Leaving the door wide open, I walked down the path to where he stood beside the bike, a helmet dangling from his hand.

"New wheels?" I asked, hardly believing that Devin had let him get a motorcycle. Chase did not have the best luck with cars, so why not get him something with no protection at all? At this rate, he was going to kill himself sooner than later. At least he would look good doing it. I couldn't help but give him a once over. My eyes had a mind of their own.

"Hop on," he yelled over the idling motor.

"And why would I go anywhere with you? The last time we were in a vehicle together, you flipped it."

"You barely had a scratch." He grinned deviously. "But damn. I loved that car," he added as an afterthought.

True, he had saved me from getting seriously hurt. What the hell? I really wanted to go for a ride. Briefly, I wondered what my mom would say. She would probably ask for a spin around the block. "Fine. Let me run in and grab a hoodie." There was a chill in the air. Goose bumps had already spread over my arms.

"Here, take mine." And just like that, he pulled off the one he had been wearing. His T-shirt rode up a little, revealing tan abs and dark curls. My mouth watered. He held it out for me to take, and I tried not to drool.

"Thanks," I managed to mutter. My tongue was still stuck in the back of my throat where it had dropped moments ago.

Sliding on the oversized hoodie, I was engulfed by his lingering warmth and the heady scent that was uniquely his. It was erotic, wild, and dangerous. Taking a deep breath, I let the smell of him infuse my senses, making me a little light-headed.

His deep voice broke the embarrassing spell. The last thing I needed was to be caught sniffing his clothes. "Put this on. I wouldn't want that pretty head of yours splattered all over the blacktop." He handed me a helmet, eyes twinkling, and jumped on the bike.

Well, that was a comforting image. Straddling the bike behind him, I glided my arms slowly around his waist. The muscles on his stomach jumped at my touch.

He angled his head toward me. "Hold on, Angel Eyes," he warned right before he had the bike in motion. With a twist of his wrist, the bike revved, and we were flying down the road.

Instinctually, I plastered my body against his back, tightening my grip on his waist and locking my hands together. For the first part of the ride, I buried my face in his neck, getting adjusted to the speed. It wasn't long before I got a little braver, though I was still reluctant to lift my head. Having my face pressed against his back was just too nice to not enjoy as long as possible.

Smiling into the wind blowing against my cheeks, I laughed. The thrill of the ride, my arms pressed securely around Chase, and the wide-open roads, I'd never felt freer. Beautiful landscapes rolled by us in a blur, blending the colors into a waterfall.

As I clung to him, the bike hugged a curve effortlessly. Freshly plowed fields spread out as far as the eye could see. There was something so simple and basic about being in the country with a gorgeous boy. Never in a million years did I ever see myself here on the back of a speeding motorcycle, fastened to a guy so out of my league. I might have dreaded this move with every fiber of my being, but I'd never been happier.

Even when I wanted to strangle Chase.

He drove the bike like he was born to ride. When we arrived safely home, I was flushed and elated and absolutely energized. I felt the first inklings of being a reckless teenager, living on the edge of life—something my responsible self was unfamiliar with.

Grabbing ahold of my hand, his touch caused tiny tingles up my arm. "Come on," he said, laughing. He led us to our backyard, which was bordered by towering oak and maple trees.

I didn't have the first clue what he had up his sleeve, but as long as it didn't involve me going into the woods, I was game. He handed me a rake and leaned on the other one.

Angling my head, I asked, "And what do you expect me to do with this?" I found it hard to believe that he wanted me to do yard work now.

"Rake, Angel. I bet you never jumped in a pile of leaves in Arizona."

He had me there. "Do I get hot cocoa afterwards?"

"Deal." He smirked.

Side by side, we stretched our rakes, uprooting globs of fallen debris. Before long, we had a stack of colorful leaves as high as my waist.

"Jump," he said impishly.

His gunmetal eyes twinkled with a hint of topaz, and my blood heated with excitement. "You first," I countered.

Of course I never saw him coming. Before I knew it, I was swept off my feet and swishing through a pile of crunchy, dried leaves. Chase's laughter pealed out as he landed in a heap next to me, dusting up a layer of leaves in my face. I grabbed a fistful in my hands and smashed a stack of my own into his face, prepared to scramble out of his reach.

There was never a chance of escape. His hand clutched my ankle, pulling me into his lap. Twisting and turning, I fought playfully out of his grasp but failed. Effortlessly, he had me pressed under him and my back to the ground. Somewhere in the back of my mind I knew this was going to end here, with us wound together.

The blood in my veins rushed with excitement and anticipation. I knew by the look in his eyes that he was going to kiss me, and I would be helpless to do anything but respond with equal need. The intensity in his shifting eyes caught my breath.

He brushed the leaf-strewn hair from my face, his fingers lingering on my cheeks. Slowly his hand glided over my shoulders and down my arms, leaving behind heady shivers. He hovered above me with a wolfish grin and pinned my arms above my head. Our chests rose and fell in rhythm, panting from exertion. Eyes locked, I was seduced. Ever so leisurely, those full lips inched closer and closer to my eagerly waiting mouth, until they were pressed against mine.

Sweet Jesus.

His lips were tender, sweet, and irresistible. So different from the heated desperation I had gotten used to. It rocked through my system as I savored each prolonged sensation. His mouth slanted across mine, his tongue teasing in a game of tag. Deeply. Delicious. Intoxicating.

Who would have thought that the dark, arrogant, infuriating Chase had a soft side?

His free hand was sliding under his hoodie and up my shirt, flirting with my bare flesh. It was overwhelming. My gasp was lost in his mouth. There was an amazing tension building and building inside of me as I kissed him back wholeheartedly, holding nothing back.

Oh, God. What was he doing to me?

My hands were secured over my head, and I surrendered to his control, something I never thought I would want or like. And the way my heart was melting, I wasn't sure I should ever again. It was too dangerous.

But now … now I would take full advantage of it and enjoy every second. Or I would have …

A loud whistle rang out, followed by Travis' carefree laugh. We quickly broke away, collapsing on a crunchy bed of leaves. They were everywhere: in my hair, up my shirt, in my shoes, and everywhere in between. We must have looked a sight. I tugged Chase's hoodie down, covering my belly.

"I am going to murder him," Chase growled threateningly.

For the love of everything holy.

If Travis knew what was good for him, he would have gone back inside. Instead, his shadowy form materialized above us, smirking. "That was quite a show. I don't know about you two, but I definitely need a cold shower—"

The last word yelped through the air as he went tumbling to the ground, thanks to Chase kicking his feet out from under him. I covered my hands over my mouth to stifle the giggle that was bubbling at the surface and failed miserably.

Their bodies flashed in and out of my view, my human eyes unable to keep up with their lightning movements. In some bizarre way, I was getting used to their rowdiness, however more intense it was than normal. I just sat back, hoping I wasn't going to get trampled, and waited for them to finish one-upping each other.

I'd seen Chase fight before, and it was evident that he was holding back. Travis didn't have his speed or strength.

When Lexi came sauntering out, her hands on her hips, she didn't even bat an eye. "Why are these two idiots rolling around in this muck? And what happened to you?" she asked, eyeing me suspiciously.

Travis beat me to it. "I caught the two of them making out in the leaves." He was somehow able to rush the words out before Chase had him in a headlock.

Lexi pursed her lips, trying to hide a grin. "Well … all I have to say is … it's about damn time."

My mouth fell open. "Lexi!" I yelled.

"What? I was getting tired of being in the cross fire of all that sexual tension. It was suffocating."

Groaning, I just lay back down. She joined me on my bed of leaves, gazing up through the darkly outlined tree. Her dainty fingers clasped mine. I couldn't stay mad at her if I wanted to. She just made it so difficult.

"I'm happy. So happy actually." I could hear it in her gleeful voice. Grinning from ear to ear, she looked at me. "You have no idea how much you have changed all of our lives. For the first time in a long time, there is laughter again. Listen."

And I did. There were crickets chirping in the woods, a breeze rustled the leaves, and Chase and Travis behind us were chuckling between grunts, loving the horseplay, which wasn't normal. They took roughhousing to a whole new level. My chest filled with affection and warmth.

Home. This was my home now.

We smiled at each other, her bright turquoise eyes and my dark twilight ones shining in a great bond of friendship.

Just as we were having a girl moment, the guys had to go and ruin it. Piles and piles of oak and maple leaves just appeared, raining down upon us. They fell in our mouths, in our hair, and in our eyes. Damn demon levitation. Lexi beside me was shrieking, and I was laughing my ass off. You didn't want to mess with that girl's nails or hair, but I had to say, it was the funniest thing ever to see Miss Perfect riled. Chase and Travis were in for some hard core payback.

Bitch style.

CHAPTER 25

"Lexi. Your hair looks outstanding. Stop messing with it," I scolded.

She sat in front of her vanity, fussing with her hair for like the thousandth time. It was homecoming night, and I was suckered into helping Lexi get ready. Who knew why, since she knew way more about fashion than I did. I think she just wanted moral support from a friend. She was still pouting about the fact that I refused to go to homecoming. I think she thought I had been holding out for her cousin to ask me.

They weren't speaking.

She couldn't understand us. One moment he had his tongue down my throat, and the next we were at each other's throats. I think she was just about ready to give up on us.

It was better that way. No disappointment. And Lexi's heart was just too big for her to not get caught in the fireworks.

Her hair was piled on top of her head with blonde curls cascading over her bare shoulders and neck. Sprinkles of sparkles were dusted in the silky strands. The strapless dress she stepped into was the same color of her turquoise eyes. Those eyes were emphasized with smoky shadow, thick lines of eyeliner, and forever long dark eyelashes. She looked like she had just stepped out of a fantasy book. Everything about her was more angel than demon.

"So, what do you think?" she asked, turning in circles.

"Wow, Lexi. You look fantastic."

"You think?" She turned back to the full-length mirror and tucked in a strand of loose hair.

"Don't touch anything. You just need one last thing." I pulled her necklace from the box and secured it around her porcelain neck. "There."

Her reflection grinned at me in the mirror. "Thanks, Angel. I really wish you were coming with me. It just won't be the same without you."

"You are going to have such a fabulous time that you won't even have time to miss me," I assured her.

Her painted lips turned down slightly. "What are you going to do tonight?"

I shrugged. "Nothing really. Maybe hang out with Travis and play Xbox."

"Angel, really? My brother? It is our last homecoming, and you want to hang out with my brother? If we hurry, I know that I have something you can wear. You can come with Hayden and me. It will be so much fun, I swear—"

"Lexi. Lexi!" I yelled, cutting off her bubbling rant before it got completely out of my control. "I appreciate you wanting me there, but I just don't have the heart to go. I'm sorry."

"I know," she conceded.

The doorbell rang, saving me from having to endure any more of Lexi's pouty pleadings. As we walked down the stairs, we heard Chase and Travis razzing Hayden on his tie. Silence erupted as we entered the room. All eyes were on Lexi, as they should have been, except Chase's. I met his gaze, and my heart pattered.

Tearing my eyes from his, I focused back on Lexi.

Hayden stood in front of her, grinning like a kid caught in the cookie jar. "You look amazing," he complimented her, taking her hand.

They were just so cute together, even if it was BS that they were sort of pushed to be.

"Thanks," she replied from cloud nine. You could see the magic shining in her eyes and her dimples winking on her cheeks. I hoped tonight was perfect for her; she deserved it.

Travis swung an arm over Hayden's shoulders. "Do we need to have the *talk*? This is my sister, and I expect a 'hands off' policy."

"Travis!" Lexi yelled, outraged. "If I recall your homecoming, I walked in on you with your tongue down—"

Travis quickly cut her off. "Lex, I swear. I don't even want you to think in that direction." He cringed at the idea.

"What? It's okay for you, but not me?" she asked sweetly.

"Yes!" Chase and Travis chorused.

She folded her arms over her chest. "Hayden, let's go before they go mental over the room I got us for the night."

Hayden's eyes widened. Chase's narrowed. Travis' darkened a deadly sea green haloed in gold. And I smirked.

That was my girl.

"Angel … I still don't know how you can rather spend your night with these baboons than with me." She turned on her heels. "They're your problem now."

Hayden sheepishly closed the door behind him, totally unsure what in Hades had just happened.

Oookay, I didn't see that coming. Poor Hayden.

I plopped down on the couch next to a stunned and riled Travis. "Can you believe her?" he asked.

Yeah, I could. They could be so overbearing at times.

He looked ready to beat on something. "She was joking about the room, right?"

God I hoped so. For Hayden's sake.

And mine.

I watched Travis clench and unclench his fist as he was fighting with his control. Chase sauntered over, taking a seat between us, and I knew it was deliberate. He was putting himself in direct line of Travis in case things went sour.

"She was joking," Chase assured him. "You okay?"

Travis ran a hand through his blond hair, messing it up, and looked over at us. His expression noticed Chase's protective stance. It didn't go unnoticed by any of us. "Yeah." And he looked it. "Angel, some team death match?" he asked me with clear eyes.

Now he was talking.

"I didn't think you were ever going to ask." I grabbed a controller off the console and waited for him to start up the match.

"You two are pathetic," Chase huffed, irritated. "It's Saturday night, *homecoming* for God's sake, and the two of you are going to play Xbox all night."

"You got a better idea?" Travis asked.

His eyes looked at me, and my cheeks flushed as I could all too easily read his thoughts.

Travis chuckled beside me. "Would you prefer if I left you two alone?"

"No!" we both yelled hastily. It only made Travis laugh harder.

"Just start the game," I grumbled.

"Whatever," Chase snapped. "I'll leave you two to wallow in your utter lameness." He got off the couch like a spoiled two year old and went upstairs.

"He can be such a diva," Travis commented when he was out of earshot.

I reclined into the couch, feeling a little sad that he was leaving, which I wasn't about to admit. It was just the last few days I thought that we had gotten past all the crap and maybe even liked each other a little.

Okay a lot. He had just recently played tongue tag with me.

Travis and I started playing a round of MW3, but my heart just wasn't in the game. My mind kept wandering upstairs, wondering what he was doing. Was he in his room, lying on the bed we spent *that* night in? I briefly shut my eyes, and in the process, my player got his head blown off.

I didn't know what was wrong with me. He invaded more and more of my thoughts.

Travis noticed my lack of interest. "So I know you are probably sick of the question, but how come you didn't go to homecoming?" There was no ridicule in his tone, just curiosity.

I tried to keep my concentration on the game and answer his question. "Um. Dances really aren't my thing. I'm pretty sure I was born with two left feet."

"I'm totally going to step out of line, but does it have anything to do with Chase?"

No longer in the game, I set the remote aside. "No matter who asks, my answer is always going to be no. Did you go to homecoming?"

His eyes twinkled. "I took Emma to the winter formal, and I wouldn't have traded it for anything in the world."

I wondered if Emma had known how lucky she had been. "That's because you are one in a million. I don't think there is any girl that could say no to you."

"Even you?" he asked teasingly, those charming dimples on either side of his cheeks.

It should have been illegal to have a house full of drop-dead gorgeous teenagers. I nodded my head. "Even me. But I warn you, I would be the worst date ever."

"Somehow I find that hard to believe. Chase seems to constantly find reasons to see you," he said, grinning slyly.

"I think all that blond hair is going to your head."

He laughed, and it was nice to hear the lightness in it and in his eyes.

Maybe an hour later, I felt Chase's gaze on the back of my neck. Little hairs spiked, and my spine tingled. Glancing over my shoulder, he leaned against the banister looking dark, moody, and lethal.

I swallowed the large lump that formed in my throat.

"What are you still doing here?" he asked rudely. It caught me off guard.

"Chase," Travis hissed. "Don't be a dick."

I slammed down my controller. "What is your problem?" I said, raising my voice.

"Every time I turn, you are right there," he shouted, making little sense to me. It didn't matter. If he wanted a fight, I was going to give him a fight.

"If you want me to leave, fine!" I screamed, getting to my feet. "You don't have to be a bastard about it."

"I don't just want you to leave. I don't need or want you in my life. I didn't ask for this. For you," he yelled.

Travis sucked in a sharp breath.

I felt like I had just been kicked in the chest. His cruel words punctured a gap in my lung, and I couldn't breathe. Swaying unsteadily on my feet, Travis put a stable hand on my arm. Black dots swirled in my eyes and then quickly turned to a red haze. My eyes must have given away the pain that radiated within. Chase took a step toward me.

"Don't!" I threatened, stopping him. "You think I wanted this." I threw my hands in the air. "You think I want to turn every corner worrying if there is a demon waiting to torture me or kill me? Do you honestly think that I wanted this? I don't want anything to hurt Lexi." *Or you*, I added silently.

"I warned you," he cautioned lowly.

"You warned but hardly took your own advice," I threw in his face.

The vein in his neck ticked wildly, and I knew his blood pressure had skyrocketed. I was playing with fire and probably tempting fate. "You are nothing but trouble," he spat.

Travis was caught in the middle of our gunfire, looking bewildered. He put his hand on Chase's chest, though we all knew he wouldn't be able to stop Chase. "Will the two of you cut the lover spat crap?" he hollered above the blood roaring in my ears. He turned to Chase. "What crawled up your ass?"

"We aren't lovers. We aren't anything," Chase said, his face like stone.

It was like having a knife shoved in my back. Shock and unbelievable pain splashed across my face. I never thought we were dating, but I at least thought he was my friend. How wrong could I have been?

"I hate you, Chase Winters. Don't. Ever. Come near me again." My voice hitched at the end, full of emotions I couldn't control.

Travis' eyes burned. "What the hell is your problem, man?" And he shoved Chase up against the wall. Plaster cracked under the impact. Chase's eyes closed, and he didn't fight back.

I had to get out of there. Now.

Tears streamed down my cheeks in a flood of pent up hurt and anger. I was a hot mess. Running, I was out the front door, and I didn't stop, not even when I heard them both shout my name. Not until I was safely locked behind my front door. I hated that I'd let *him* see me cry.

Slamming my bedroom door behind me, I tossed myself on the bed and buried my face into the pillow, soaking it with tears. My shoulders heaved from the gut-wrenching sobs. I was blubbering on like an idiot over an asshole like Chase. He didn't deserve my tears, my compassion, my friendship, or my bleeding heart.

I was so pissed off at myself. My heart felt shattered like broken glass. More than ever, I wanted to be a million miles from here. I wanted to be anywhere but here.

There might have been a knock on my front door, but I ignored it. I was ignoring the world. As far as I was concerned, they could all piss off.

Rubbing my salt-streaked cheeks, I decided enough was enough. I refused to waste another ounce of thought or feeling on Chase Winters. He could roast in the fiery pits of hell for all I cared. If I could, I would send him there myself. Hand his daddy his head on a freaking platter.

After I had cried myself senseless, all that raw emotion turned to blistering anger. I hated him with as much passion as I had when he'd kissed me. Beating the pillow with my fist, I took out all my aggression on the down feathers.

I couldn't believe that I had let such a spawn from hell touch me. Never again, I vowed. I didn't want to even be within five feet of him. That was unrealistic, but in the heat of the moment, it sounded fabulous. Well, I'd just delete his number.

Grabbing my phone, I was startled when it started to ring. I glanced down at the screen. It was Brandy. The display of her name pulled me out of my mental hissy fit.

Weird.

She was supposed to be at homecoming with Tommy. My heart dropped. All I could think was that something had happened to Lexi. Whatever it was, I hoped it wasn't as bad as my imagination. Right then, it was pretty ugly.

I quickly fumbled with the answer button. "Hello."

CHAPTER 26

Her hysterical voice sent me into high alert. Something was wrong.

Very wrong.

She was rambling like a sloppy drunk, and I couldn't make out a single word. Apparently I wasn't the only one having a shit-tastic night.

Sitting up, I tried to calm her down. "Brandy, slow down. What's wrong?" I asked as gently as I could.

"Tommy," she sobbed.

Okay, very helpful, but at least Lexi wasn't in trouble.

I exhaled. "Did Tommy and you get into a fight?" It seemed like the most logical explanation. At this rate, it was going to be worse than pulling teeth trying to get information from her.

She broke out crying again.

I'd just take that as a yes then.

Pushing tangled strands of hair from my face, I sat on the edge of my bed.

"He. Broke. Up with me," she managed to get out between her crying jag. She made it sound like it was unfathomable.

"Are you okay?"

She sniffled into the phone. "I don't think so. Can you come get me?"

I pinched the bridge of my nose. There was the beginning of a headache working its way into the front of my skull, and I just didn't have any energy. But how could I say no?

"Of course. I'll be right there," I agreed. "Where are you?"

I heard her sniffle into the phone like she was rubbing the snot from her nose.

Lovely.

"I'm at school," she said, weeping. "By the football bleachers."

"Okay, I'm on my way."

Searching my bedroom floor, I pulled on a hoodie. The second it was on, I noticed my mistake. It was the one Chase had let me borrow. I had yet to return it. The dull ache started to spread through my chest again. His sinful scent was like a disease, eating through my organs. I clenched the hem, preparing to rip it off.

"Hurry," Brandy's shaking voice rang through the other end of the phone.

Screw it.

"Five minutes," I said and disconnected.

Running down the stairs two at a time, I scooped my keys off the counter and got in my little Fusion. The engine jumped to life. Shifting into gear, I pointed the car in the direction of Hall High. The road was deserted, as usual, and lit only by the shining moon and a tiny bit of starlight. Even then it was dark.

Eerily dark.

I tried not to think about the gloominess and focused on getting to Brandy.

Man. She was going to owe me huge for this. Like colossal.

When I pulled into the school parking lot, I could hear the music blaring from the gym. The school had been decorated in a gaudy amount of red and black. Stepping out of the car, I was glad for the warmth of the hoodie, even if it was douchebag's. I made a mental note to burn it when I got back.

There was a brisk evening breeze tinted with the smells of

perfume, musk, and country air. Fall was definitely in full swing. My footsteps on the gravel blacktop echoed in the night as I was swiftly assaulted with horrible memories.

How could I have forgotten?

It had only been a few weeks since I was in this exact parking lot with a demon hell-bent on sucking the life from me. I shivered.

Immediately I wished I had thought of calling Travis to come with me.

Too late now.

Suck it up, I told myself.

Every tiny sound made me jump. Picking up my pace, I hightailed it to the side of the school. The grass was damp from the evening fog, and my sneakers squeaked under the green blades. I gripped onto the ends of Chase's hoodie as I rounded the corner to the football field. At least the lights were on. They blazed on me like a spotlight.

"Brandy," I whispered, walking around the bleachers. Where the hell was she? I walked onto the football field, scanning for her outline. "Brandy!" I called louder. This was ridiculous. I pulled my phone out of my back pocket with the intent of calling her.

"Angel," I heard my name from behind me.

Snapping around, I squinted. She stepped out of the dark shadows into my view. Relief swarmed through me.

Finally.

I walked toward her. "I was just about to call you," I said as I got closer. It was then that I noticed her eyes. They were glassy, and she looked right through me. "Brandy, are you okay?" I asked hesitantly and stopped in my tracks.

She didn't answer me, but the voice that did made my blood freeze.

"Good job, Brandy. Such an excellent performance." He stepped out into the open.

My stance faltered as my knees almost gave out. There was something about lesser-demons; they all had the same human look, like the secret service but way scarier. He took off his sunglasses, throwing them on the ground. Looking into Brandy's eyes with his black pits, he said, "Go back to the party before your boyfriend notices you're missing."

And like a robot, she trotted across the field back to the school without as much as a glance in my direction. Technically, I understood that she was under his mind control, but I was kind of pissed she'd left me alone.

Shit.

I needed to think of something. Fast.

It didn't help that my brain had shut off. Close to an all-out panic, my fingers dug onto my phone in a death grip of fear.

My phone.

As inconspicuously as possible, I hit the speed dial that I prayed was programmed for Chase. And to think I had almost erased his number from my phone today.

"Well, now that we are alone ..." Agent Creep-o said, walking toward me. His voice was raspy, immensely spine-chilling.

I backed up, thinking I needed as much distance between us as possible. My quaking fingers fumbled for the dial button. I couldn't have been clumsier in my movements.

My surprise guest had other plans. I blinked, and he was in my face, intense heat rolling off him in waves of anger. The demon cocked his head. "You're not at all what I expected," he said, staring.

"So I've been told," I moaned.

He leered. "I'm going to enjoy this."

At least one of us was, because I was sure I wasn't.

My finger trembled, and I finally hit the button a second before it tumbled from my hand. Clutching my hoodie, he lifted me off my feet, leveling our gazes.

Whimpering, I met him eye to eye. "What? Do you plan on killing me here, in the middle of the school football field?" I asked loudly, praying that Chase had picked up.

"Angel," a muffled voice broke the evening silence.

I shut my eyes at the sound of his voice.

The demon's soulless eyes flicked down to the phone embedded in the grass. "Don't worry, I'll take *good* care of her," he cackled before bringing his foot down on the phone, smashing it to smithereens.

That was my second phone in a month. My mom was going to think I ate the things.

I closed my eyes, my death imminent.

His finger trailed down my cheek, drawing blood. "That wasn't very smart, but I heard you were spunky."

He wanted spunk, then how could I disappoint?

Twisting my head out of his painful grasp, I looked him in the eyes. Sometimes I wished I thought about shit before I acted on it. It was something I should probably work on.

Later.

With as much power as I could muster, I cracked my hand against his cheek, a perfect execution of a bitch slap. It was just enough for him to drop me to the ground, and I didn't waste a second of the precious time I was given.

Scrambling to my feet, I took off at a dead run, even though I knew it was pointless. The instinct to run was instilled into every beat of my heart. His angry growl behind me rumbled the ground under my feet. Stumbling, I felt his hands encircle my neck, pulling me against his iron chest.

I screamed out.

He had slipped from his human form, and I looked down at the ashen arms bounding me. "You didn't think you'd escape me, did you?"

Of course not, asshole, but a girl could try.

He squeezed, closing off my air supply, making it harder and harder to breathe. I gasped for air, and he eased off, letting the sweet taste of oxygen fill my lungs again. I inhaled ravenously.

A sickening wolf howled in the woods that bordered the school property line, and my heart beat in triple time. There were more of them. Dread hit the pit of my belly.

"Sounds like the party started without the guest of honor," he hissed, and then we were moving through the woods at stomach-churning speeds. He was just as fast as Chase, except nowhere near as graceful.

Branches and leaves lashed against my exposed skin, stinging like a bullwhip. Biting my lip to keep from crying, I pierced the skin, tasting metallic blood. He stopped swiftly in the center of a clearing and threw me on the ground. There was a horrendous whack as my body hit the hard surface, jarring my brain from my head and scraping every inch of my body.

I lay there dumbfounded, losing any sense of reality.

"Now we wait for your friends," he said, leering above me.

Lifting my head, I scanned the edges of the circle. Beady eyes of scorching red lined the perimeter with gnarling teeth barred in menace.

Hellhounds—a whole pack of them by the looks of it.

There were also two other lower-demons completely shelled of their human skin. Their large black eyes looked at me with tortured hunger. The sight turned my stomach into knots, and I thought there was a good chance I was going to puke.

Oh, God. What have I done?

They were going to use me as bait. And I just might have led my friends to a death trap.

"Sier, Oriax, meet our little spitfire. Don't take your eyes off this one; she's likely to gouge them out." He laughed at his own pathetic joke. It sounded demented and evil.

Sier and Oriax looked like they wanted to suck me dry. I wasn't sure they were the best keepers.

"Vassago, prince," one of the shadowy subordinates called. His onyx eyes looked at him with loathing. "We need strength," he said, licking his black lizard lips.

"She is not your vessel," he hissed. "Just make sure she does not escape. And prepare yourselves; our guests are almost here."

Pushing myself into a sitting position, I hugged my knees, shaking. Vassago hovered over me, looking ginormous. There was a shuffling in the trees right before I saw two pairs of twin golden eyes.

Casually, they stepped into the clearing. I was overjoyed with relief and panic. These demons had used me to get to them, and I didn't want them putting themselves in danger. There were just too many of the bad guys.

Lexi.

Her eyes burned like a cat's. She wasn't the fragile, prissy, and prim Lexi. She looked like a killer in a prom dress. Even I was scared of her, never having seen this side of her before.

Hayden was next to her. Together they stood, eyes shining bright.

"We came to play," she said, her voice toxic.

Vassago snarled beside me, while the hellhounds behind us howled. I'd never seen Lexi and Hayden fight before, but I was pretty sure we were in deep shit. How could the two of them take three lower-demons and a pack of hellhounds?

"Then come meet your death, *half-breeds*," Vassago invited, his dark voice wrapping around me.

"Lexi, no!" I screamed. "It's a trap—" Vassago kicked me in the gut, cutting off my words and cracking a few ribs in the process. The revolting crunch fractured above my whimper. I curled in a ball, clenching my stomach.

Everything turned into blinding chaos. Rolling on the ground in searing pain, I forced my eyes opened. Even as tears stung them, I searched for my friends. If I could just see that they were okay …

Lexi kicked ass.

The hellhounds were on her, coming from all angles. She grabbed one by the ratted muzzle, snapping its neck, then spun around unsheathing a blade, and rammed it into another's chest. Their death whines were almost instantaneous she moved so quickly.

Hayden was at my side, putting his arms under me. "Let's get you out of here before Chase cuts my head off."

I winced. "Lexi," I protested.

"She's fine and better at this than me. She trains with Chase." He said it like that explained everything. And maybe it did. Chase was pretty damn badass.

A demon popped into my view. "Behind you," I yelled.

Hayden didn't have enough time, and the lower-demon sent him sprawling through the air. The demon took full advantage of my precarious position. Pinning me to the ground, he immediately held me in his gaze, locked onto my beating heart, and started sucking the life right out of me. It was like having my innards ripped out by his bare hands.

"Sier, I told you she wasn't a feeding source," Vassago growled, tearing Sier off me and shoving him away.

As I lay there staring up at the stars, my chest felt like it was going to cave in. A tingling skirted down my neck.

He was here.

His war cry thundered over the grunts and groans of battle.

Chase.

CHAPTER 27

Travis was right beside him. Together they looked like an avenging angel and a dark warrior. Chase's eyes flickered to mine right before he jumped in, immediately dispensing of a hellhound without so much as lifting a hand. He moved with purpose, making his way to the center where I lay on the ground. I tried to move, only to have my body fail me.

Dispelling everything in their path like Tasmanian devils, Travis and Chase stood frowning in the center of the clearing, their glowing eyes piercing Vassago.

"So you're Alastair's bastard," Vassago leered, unaffected by the fighting around him.

Chase's golden eyes flamed. The mention of the father he never knew was a sneaky tactic. But other than an arch of his brow, Chase didn't flinch.

"Let's see if you are half the demon he is," Vassago taunted, his two minions jeering at his back. "Oh," he bent down putting his slimy hand on my neck. "You better hurry. Her pulse wavers," he said, right before slicing a crucial cut on my neck. "That should help."

Chase's bellow of anger drowned out anything else Vassago might have said as he went into turbo speed. Sier and Oriax stepped in, engaging Chase and Travis before either of them could get close. Bum-rushing the demons, who were so much bigger in height and girth, the impact thundered over the clearing.

I cringed.

Blood gurgled in my throat, and it slipped out the side of my mouth. I started to lose sight of Chase as I found it harder and harder to keep my eyes open.

The grass was damp, cold, and colored with my blood. I felt like I was freezing to death, my body racked with the shakes. While Chase and Travis were busy with Tweedledee and Tweedledum, Vassago decided I was no longer of use.

"Angel!" Lexi cried, zipping toward me.

Just my name was enough to distract Chase. Glancing at me cost him. Oriax had him to the ground with plummeting fists of iron. I heard the slaps of bone on flesh.

Oh, God, I thought. This was it.

I didn't even see it happen. Suddenly Chase was covered in Oriax's ashes. Black soot was smeared on his fierce face, and he was breathing heavily.

I looked up in relief. The moon was full—a definite bad omen—but Chase was still alive.

Yet it wasn't over. Vassago's hollow eyes captured mine. How could I have forgotten that he was dominating me? I thought about Mom. She was going to be beside herself with grief, and I couldn't help but think about her alone. As he latched onto my life essence, I blocked out all the terrible hurt and thought of my mom's face.

Somewhere in the back of my mind, I knew I was on the brink of death. With each breath, I knew it could be my last. Stillness came over me, easing the ache of all my pains and the end of my life. Everything moved in slow motion.

Just as I inhaled my final bit of air, Chase was overshadowing Vassago. Lifting the sparkling ruby dagger over his head, he ran it through the center of his chest, and Vassago erupted on a defeated roar into millions of immortal ashes. Chase dropped where he was to his knees. Lexi was screaming my name hysterically, her tears falling on my cheek as she pulled me into her arms. She looked like the Lexi I knew, her eyes a sobering turquoise.

Travis was beside her in a flash. "Angel, talk to me," Travis begged. "Say something," he demanded.

But it was too late.

"Don't … don't close your eyes," he yelled.

Lexi was sobbing painfully.

There just wasn't any fight left in me. I slipped into darkness with the sound of Chase's anguished cry following me, begging me not to die. His beautiful, arrogant face etched into my memories as they moved through my head like a motion film. Every single moment we'd spent together.

Then there was nothing.

No feeling.

No pain.

No Chase.

There was, however, a sense of weightlessness. I couldn't feel my body anymore, but there was a light airy tickle. It was refreshing, uplifting, and angelic. Surely this must be the path to heaven. All I needed to do was wait on my angel.

A swoosh of air passed over my shapeless form. Then I heard the faint mourning and denials of my friends. How could that be? Their sorrowing cries stabbed into my dead heart.

When I opened my eyes, I underwent the most astronomical out-of-body experience. I was literally floating above my own body with an extremely freakish shadowy figure next to me, cloaked in black tattered robes. Inside the hood, he was faceless, except for his white incandescent eyes.

I blinked again just to make sure.

This was definitely not from heaven. Apparently my nightmare wasn't over.

Tearing my gaze from the dementor-like figure, I looked down … at myself?

Holy shit-balls.

Lexi was crouched beside me with her hand clasped in mine.

There was a free-flowing amount of tears streaming down her beautiful face. Travis pulled her into his arms, and Chase stared down at me. He pushed the plastered hair from my face, mumbling my name repetitively. "Angel, I'm so sorry. I'm so sorry," he murmured against my already blue lips.

Blood trickled from my nose. My eyes were open and empty, and I lay in an awkward position. It was evident that I had broken something. My skin was sickly pale without any life in it. I'd never seen a dead body before, let alone my own. It was beyond messed up. It was just plain wrong.

Lifting his wet silver eyes to the sky, I thought he was going to see me, but it wasn't me he could see. I had forgotten. Divisa could see Death.

His eyes widened and were overcast with disbelief. "No," he whispered in agony. "No!" This time it was more forceful.

Travis and Lexi looked up. Neither of them took the sight well. Lexi shook her head, crying harder, and Travis buried her head in his chest, clinging to his sister. Her sobs jolted me to the core. I hated seeing them upset over me. I hated that I had put that overwhelming sadness in their eyes.

"You can't take her," Chase argued. Only he could think of arguing with Death. Some things never change.

The liquid black shadow hovered over me, and his voice was dark, raspy, and haunting. "It's out of your hands, half-breed. She has been tainted by the underworld. Hell is the only place for her."

Hell. Did he just say I was going to hell? I was starting to panic all over again. No way could I go to hell. I tried to scream Chase's name, but nothing came out.

"That can't be," Chase argued.

My thoughts exactly. I was no saint, but *hell*? He had to do something. Chase wouldn't let him take me to hell … He just wouldn't. My rationalization was astonishing.

"She has been touched by the underworld," the reaper insisted forcefully. I didn't think he was in a bargaining mood. You don't barter with Death.

"No!" Chase screamed. The terror in his voice was unmistakable. "No. That can't be. She is good—pure."

Images played through my mind—the lower-demons stealing my life force more than once, the hellhound hunt in the woods, being bit. I'd had more brushes with death and hell than any human should.

I knew it.

Chase knew it.

Death knew it.

"Not anymore," replied Death.

"Bullshit!" Chase bellowed. "It's because of me."

"Blame won't change her fate."

"There has to be something you can do. You're Death," he said, unable to accept the inevitable. I wasn't exactly gung-ho about going to hell either.

The reaper seemed to grow tired of this conversation. "Her outcome has already been decided. What will prolonging it do?"

"So there *is* something. You must help her. Please," he begged. "Please, I'll do anything. Just save her."

"Half-breed, what you ask will not only affect her; it will affect you as well. Her life won't be any easier on earth." He reached his cloaked hand toward where I floated beside him.

"Just save her," Chase whispered in sorrow. It broke my heart to hear him so dejected. "I'll do anything," he promised.

The reaper eyed him thoughtfully as he weighed my fate in his hands. "So let it be done, but you've been warned, Chase Winters. She is your responsibility now. Your lives have been intertwined, and the mark I give her is yours."

What?

Um, Mr. Death, I didn't quite get all that. Could you please explain it in terms I understand?

But it was already done, and it wasn't like he could hear me.

Without any kind of warning, that wonderful feeling of nothingness vanished. I was hurled back into the living, back into my battered body. On a gasp, I breathed my first breath of air again. It washed down my lungs and started my still heart. Blood flowed through my veins, turning from cold to warm, and tiny prickles came with it.

My dark blue eyes weren't lifeless anymore as they looked into Chase's shimmering silver ones. I could see the whoosh of breath he'd been holding. The tension and agony left his body.

"Chase, what have you done?" Travis asked.

Just as fast as my heart beat again, so did the flare of pain. I thrashed on the ground, my eyes stinging with tears. I cried out as my hip burned like it was on fire. I curled into a little ball, and the smell of searing flesh permeated the night's air. My hand gripped Lexi's, and her tears turned to concentration.

"Oh my God, Chase. You bargained for her life," she said, understanding lighting her eyes.

I didn't think either of them had been paying much attention to Chase while he was wheeling and dealing with Death. They had been too clouded with their grief.

"What's wrong? Why is she in pain?" Travis demanded, unsettled.

"Chase!" Lexi cried.

He rocked back off his knees, putting his head in hands. "She is being marked," he told them.

They both snapped their heads up. "Marked?" Travis repeated.

He just nodded, looking utterly defeated and tired.

"Are you nuts? Do you know what you have done?" Travis said between gritted teeth.

"What would you have me do? Let her die?" he yelled back.

"And you think this is a better option for her?" Travis shot back.

"Hell came for her. Do you hear me? *Hell*. I wasn't going to let Death take her there."

Travis' turquoise eyes searched his cousin's. Whatever he saw there made him nod in understanding.

"I couldn't," Chase murmured, quietly dejected.

Ever so slowly, the pain receded, degree by slow degree. Lexi, the compassionate friend that she was, never left my side. I was eternally grateful. I didn't know how to explain the pain. It was worse than dying, and that had to mean something. There was nothing I could compare it to.

When I was finally able to speak, I lay on my back with Chase leaning over me. "What did you just do?" I croaked.

"Don't ask," Travis muttered.

I glanced from Travis to Lexi. Her eyes were brimming with fresh tears. "Don't you *ever* die on me again," she said, her voice clouded.

"I can't make any promises," I said, my lips upturning at the corners. "Is someone going to tell me what just happened?"

"Later," Chase said, grinning foolishly. "I need to get you home."

Home. The word had never sounded so sweet. Spring Valley was my home.

CHAPTER 28

I t killed me to not be able to play Xbox. As it so happens, being brought back from the dead does not instantly heal all wounds.

What utter crap. Who makes these rules?

After everything that had happened though, I sustained only minimal injury. Death seemed to have repaired most of my body's damage. The cracked ribs were just sore, and the cuts on my face and neck were invisible. It was the mark on my hip that gave me the most problems. Occasionally it flamed, like it needed to remind me it was there.

Lexi was on the chaise lounge examining her nails. "My manicure is shot," she complained, pouting.

Everyone ignored her. Travis nudged me with his knee. "How are you feeling?"

The question of the hour … or every hour it seemed. They were all so worried about how I was doing. I couldn't really blame them. None of us had any experience with what had gone down. I kind of got the feeling like they were waiting for something gargantuan to happen.

Truly, I wasn't sure how I felt. There was definitely something different about me, but I was too much of a wimp to try and figure it out. Being blissfully ignorant sounded pretty darn good at this point. Look where being a nosey neighbor had gotten me.

I didn't want to sound like a whiny bitch. Don't get me wrong, I was glad to be alive, yet sometimes I couldn't help but wonder if we had defied the laws of nature too much and my being here was wrong.

I shrugged. "Better than I would have thought," I admitted.

He leaned his elbow on the back of the couch. "This is just too crazy to even think about."

"You have no idea," I muttered.

His expression fell flat, losing the glisten in his eyes. "I do understand why he did it though. If I was given the chance to save Emma, I wouldn't have even hesitated—not for a second."

A part of me felt guilty that I had lived. Travis lost the love of his life, and I … well, Chase and I did not share that same kind of all-consuming love. What we had was more like combustible lust.

Casting my eyes down, I fumbled with the fabric on the couch. "I'm eternally grateful that he saved me. More than I could ever say, but our relationship is complicated. It isn't a fraction of what you and Emma had. He doesn't care about me like that." Risking a glance up, I found Travis' eyes sparkling.

"I wouldn't be so sure about that," he said, his lips curling secretly.

Lexi couldn't wait to give her chatty two cents. "You wouldn't know love if it hit you smack in the middle of the forehead. You are so oblivious. There are at least a dozen guys at school who check out your ass every day and you couldn't be the wiser."

"You. Are. Nuts." I emphasized each word for dramatic effect. She didn't have a clue what she was talking about.

She rolled her eyes. "Just saying, I don't think you give yourself enough credit."

Maybe not, but when I was up against girls like her and Sierra, I didn't stand a chance.

Chase came into the room and flashed a disarming smile my way. He'd been doing that a lot lately, and it was making my head spin. I didn't know what kind of game he had going, but I wasn't going to play.

He sauntered like he had all the time in the world. The whole room was bursting with his presence. I, on the other hand, was filled with a calm relief, and it wasn't the first time I'd felt that way when he was near. He still made my heart go bonkers, but it quieted the jumping anxiety I was hit with when we were apart. I figured it was the aftershock from the ordeal I'd just gone through. There probably wasn't anybody who wouldn't feel some apprehension after being a demon's toy.

"Let me see it," he demanded in a voice that made my stomach drop.

I gave him the stink eye. He only grinned, loving each uncomfortable moment.

Crossing his arms over his chest, he added, "We can do this the hard way or the easy way. It's up to you."

Huffing, I stood up, meeting him toe to toe, and whipped up my shirt. The smile on his face only grew at my exaggerated actions.

His fingers skimmed the tops of my jeans, flirting over the still slightly red skin around the black mark. My belly jumped on contact, and I glared at him with challenging eyes, daring him to be a smartass.

"It looks like you have a little bit of demon in you, Angel Eyes," he just said, holding my gaze. His hand lingered on the mirror image to the one he had on his hip. I couldn't figure out if he was talking about the symbol or my attitude. Probably both.

He seemed to be always finding little ways to touch me. It was disconcerting to say the least.

I studied the intricate design with its tribal swirls as his fingers traced the lines. Swallowing hard, I fought the wave of hormones swimming to the surface. If I didn't stop him now, I was going to do something outrageous and embarrass myself. "I'm fine," I assured him, swiping at his hand and tugging my shirt down.

Chase and I had matching tattoos. Wasn't that just too cute for words?

It made me gag.

Slouching back down into the couch cushions, I scowled when he sat on the other side of me. I felt like I was smooshed in a demon sandwich. Chase on one side and Travis on the other.

Chase casually put his arm behind me and was twiddling with strands of my hair. There he went touching me again. It was like he couldn't be near me and not touch me somehow. The fact that I liked it way too much was reason enough to put an end to it.

I knocked his hand away. "Stop it."

This only made him smirk. "You know that only makes me want to do it more."

My eyes narrowed. "Find a way to control yourself."

"I'm finding it harder and harder to do just that."

Travis snickered beside me, and I elbowed him in the gut. "Try harder," I advised.

His laugh was dark and sexy. I wanted to not be affected by it. I really did. This tie we knew nothing about made me question everything I was feeling. I didn't know what was real and what was a byproduct of our being linked.

How had my life derailed so drastically? My future was looking sort of bleak. Chase had explained what he could about what had happened, but even he wasn't sure of all that it entailed. The best he could tell me was that our lives were intertwined in a way that kept me alive, but at the same time, put me in constant danger.

The best thing for me would be to stay as far away as possible from Chase. But I couldn't. I now bore the mark of a Divisa, except I wasn't half-demon. Though I wasn't even sure I was human anymore either.

What do you call someone who has died, only to come back from the dead with the mark of a half-demon on their hip?

I'll tell you: screwed.

In my book, that would make me a vampire or a zombie, but I wasn't one of those either. I didn't have any special powers. I didn't have any crazy speed. As far as I could tell, I was just me: Angel Morgan, a girl living next to a family of half-demons.

Yes, I had died. Yes, I had come back from the dead, and in that transition, I was tied to Chase and his demon for … well, eternity.

Lucky me.

SAVING ANGEL

Because of the pact he'd made with Death, I was now *marked* with Chase's *family crest* so to speak. So I got all the hellish pleasantries of being hunted. Every dark, nasty, and scary thing from the underworld would be looking for me. That included the human hunters.

I was not sure the bargain he'd made was worth saving my life. Who knew what was out there, ready to suck me dry again or put a bullet through my chest. I never did ask how the hunters killed a Divisa. I guess now I'd have plenty of time to find out.

So yeah, the best thing for the old Angel would have been to stay as far away as possible. That was all hindsight and didn't do me a flying monkey's ass of good.

The new Angel?

Well, what choice did she have but to stay as close to Chase as possible?

Being bonded to Chase Winters was going to suck. And probably be more drama than I bargained for. Everything else in my life was just groovy.

My body was still healing, and I was easily drained. "I should probably get home," I said, getting to my feet.

Chase stood with me, walking me next door. He leaned in the doorway, filling it with his presence. I'd had my quota of Chase Winters for one day and all his little touches. A part of me wanted distance and another part of me was pleading for him to stay. He must have sensed my inner turmoil.

"You can run, Angel, but I'll always find you," he said, smirking.

My humor vanished. "Bite me." We were really going to have to get a handle on this whole bond thing.

"Gladly," he returned, arching his pierced brow.

How I'd ever thought that was endearing escaped me. Smiling sweetly, I gave him the only hand gesture a jackass like him could understand. "Kiss ass." Then I slammed the front door in his face, smothering his sinful laugh.

Ready for the next part of Chase & Angel's story?

Grab your next Chase fix in *HUNTING ANGEL* the second book in the Divisa Series!

HERE'S a preview of the cover:

Can't wait to meet you back in Spring Valley!
Thank you for reading.
xoxo
Jennifer
P.S. Join my VIP Readers email list and receive a bonus scene told from Zane's POV, as well as a free copy of Saving Angel, book one in the Bestselling Divisa Series. You will also get notifications of what's new, giveaways, and new releases.

Visit here to sign up: www.jlweil.com

Don't forget to also join my Dark Divas FB Group and have some fun with me and a fabulous, fun group of readers. There is games, prizes, and lots of book love.

You can stop in and say hi to me on Facebook night and day. I pop in as often as I can: https://www.facebook.com/jenniferlweil/ I'd love to hear from you.

PART I
PREVIEW OF HUNTING ANGEL

DIVISA SERIES BOOK TWO

ENJOY THE FIRST TWO CHAPTERS OF HUNTING ANGEL, BOOK 2

Chase Winters was the bane of my existence.

Some people have death experiences and realize how precious life and love is.

Not me.

Just the opposite.

Oh, I appreciate life. I love feeling the wind in my hair, the taste of dark chocolate on my tongue, and I even came to love the country scent of Spring Valley, Illinois. What I didn't have was an epiphany about my love life.

Instead of falling head over heels in love with Chase Winters, my savior, I actually loathed him more, if that was even possible. Okay, maybe loathe was a strong word. Truthfully, I didn't know how I felt about Chase. Sometimes I saw glimpses of kindness. He could be sweet, considerate, and incredibly protective. But even so, Chase wasn't the kind of guy who was easy to love. Sure, he looked like he was sculpted by the Gods, but the second he opened his mouth the godly illusion evaporated. Mostly all I got was a selfish ass. To make matters worse, we were linked by some Grim Reaper voodoo.

Thank you, Death.

Chase has saved my life not once, not twice...shit, at this point, I've lost count. Maybe I should have shown a little more gratitude. Maybe I should have tried harder to get along with Chase a little better, especially considering that neither of us really understood this connection we have. Or maybe I should have stay as far away as possible.

I might have, if he suddenly hadn't gone from being a douchebag to someone I barely recognized. The arrogant, snarky, asshole was still there, but with me he was different. And I found that even more dangerous. It was throwing me through crazy, messed up loops. That was what he was doing lately—messing me up.

I could handle the sarcasm all day long, but it was the charm that played with my head. Since *that* night everything changed. Or maybe it was just me who changed. Mom had gotten one heck of a surprise when I saw her that night after work. I hugged her like I was afraid to let go. We had spent the rest of that night on the couch together watching our favorite movie until I'd finally fallen asleep. She had sensed how much I needed to just spend a night with her, like we used to. It was the best medicine in the world—a mother's love.

And her special chocolate milkshakes.

There really was no point in dwelling on what I couldn't change. What was done was done. I should have been focusing on what happened now, like finding out if I was still human or some genetically altered badass. Hey, it was possible. As much as I despised to admit it, Chase was *the badass*. So it was deducible that some of his awesome badass-ness could have rubbed off on me.

Oh who was I kidding? I didn't feel like a badass. It was strange—I felt different, yet I couldn't put my finger on what those changes were. When I looked in the mirror, my face looked exactly the same. Not one blasted freckle out of place. My hair was still as straight as a board and as black as spades. I hadn't gained or lost any weight. I was still only five foot three, and my tongue was just as sharp as ever—maybe sharper.

What I really needed was a distraction from my own rambling thoughts, something to fully occupy my mind. If I kept going at this rate, I would drive myself straight into the loony bin. I knew just what I needed.

No, not Chase.

Tiptoeing down the hall in my striped knee-high socks and white cotton shorts, I skipped down the stairs trying not to disturb my sleeping mother. It had been a long night. Sprawling out on the zebra print sofa, (mom was totally into animal print) I flipped the TV on, finding my favorite YouTube channel. Yes, this probably raised my geekdom levels, but I couldn't help it. I was addicted to YouTube.

I was completely immersed in the repartee between Sips and Sjin when I felt the familiar heat skirt down the back of my neck, and the tattoo now gracing my hip tingled. Every time *he* was near, the same symptoms came over me. It was both disarming and irritating.

"What are you doing?" he asked, making himself at home on the couch beside me. His long legs stretched out in front of him. Letting himself into my house whenever he felt like it, had also become a habit.

My eyes were glued to the screen. I fought the urge to look over at him, finding it more difficult than it should have been. Whenever we were in the same room, I instinctually sought him out. Our eyes would connect, the world would standstill, and then we would go on as if nothing had happened. So recently I began to challenge myself, to see how long it would take me before I caved. "What does it look like? I'm watching TV, genius. Even you should be able to figure that out." I answered, in a droll voice never taking my eyes off the tube. Try as I might to ignore his overbearing presence, I failed. Epically and continuously.

"This is not TV," he argued, remaining as difficult as always.

"It's Sips and Sjin," I added, clenching my fists. My nails dug into my palms. It was all I could do to not look at him.

I felt those silver eyes on me and shifted under his gaze. "Is that supposed to mean something to me?" His voice alone could cut straight to my heart and make it beat a million times faster.

Tossing a handful of green and red skittles into my mouth, I snickered at the banter between my two favorite gamers. "They do a play through of games and post them on YouTube with snarky humor. It's a-ma-zing," I informed, chewing on the wad of rainbow candy.

"Attractive." His weight sunk his side of the couch.

I grinned, finally giving in and meeting those smoky eyes that haunted my dreams, no matter how much I willed otherwise. "It's totally turning you on," I teased, over exaggerating my chomping. I hated that just a peek at him in ripped jeans and a black t-shirt could leave me breathless.

Joke was on me. His silver eyes flickered gold, and he shot me a devilish grin. "You're right."

Shit.

I swallowed. Uh, that totally backfired. My pulse picked up, and I could feel myself pulled toward that god-worthy body. "Whatever," I shot back weakly and returned my attention to the TV, though at this point he'd ruined it for me.

My feet were pressed against his thigh, seared by his incredible heat. He was like an inferno. "Okay. So let me get this straight. Instead of playing video games, you are now watching someone else play video games?"

I kicked him lightly in the thigh. "You got a problem with it — leave." I put on a much braver front than I felt. Truthfully, if he did leave, I knew that the moment he was gone I would miss him. Pathetic.

"God, you are lame."

That was it. I didn't even think about what I was doing, I just tossed whatever was in my hand directly at Chase's smirking mouth.

It happened to be the remote control.

I watched as his hand snatched it out of the thin air before it connected with his beautiful bad boy face. Damn his demon reflexes. "Nice try, Angel Eyes. I love it when you're feisty."

I scowled at him. "Mom is upstairs, you know."

He lifted that stupid brow with the hoop in it. Envy-worthy long lashes fanned around his twinkling eyes. "That sounds like a challenge."

"God, you are warped."

His wrist snaked out before I even saw it coming and gripped my ankle. With a quick tug he pulled me to him, and I shrieked in surprise. "You like it," he murmured, his breath tickling my skin.

Suddenly I found myself in a very precarious position, straddled over his lap. Being this close to Chase meant trouble—of the good kind. I pushed aside the butterflies of excitement and anticipation. My body knew what was about to follow the kind of look he was giving me, and it was on high alert. "If you came over for a quick tumble you'll be sadly disappointed," I said, trying to sound completely bored and uninterested.

Yet the golden gleam in his eyes said no one was fooled, least of all him. His hands spanned on either side of my hips, burning right through the flimsy white cotton of my shorts. I cursed myself for not wearing more clothes and lots of layers. No, instead I strolled around the house next to naked.

"Nothing I ever do is quick, Angel."

Every time he said my name my pulse decided to race like it was on speed. I bit my lip to keep from sighing. The last thing I needed to do was stroke his already out of control ego.

"Do you need a demonstration?" he whispered, his voice dropping to dangerous octaves.

I swallowed, entranced by his eyes. He tipped his head forward grazing his lips across mine. A blaze of heat tore through my body leaving me achy and wanting more. I knew that I should pull away while I still had opportunity, because the small window was closing quickly.

As if I had a choice.

Wrapping my arms around his neck, I watched as his eyes darken and flicker. He wasn't the only one who could use the element of surprise. I laced my fingers into his hair, loving the way his eyes changed right before me. Never losing contact, I moved in to seal our lips together, needing—

Like I weighed no more than a pound of sugar, he lifted me in the air, and dropped me down on the couch. For a split second I was stunned...then I went up in flames. Roughly pushing the hair out of my face, I glared up at him, seething. "I am going to make you regret that, Chase Winters."

He stood hovering over me with a stupid grin. "I'm looking forward to it."

I jumped off the couch, meeting him head-to-head. Okay, well, in reality it was like head-to-chest. It wasn't my fault he was so damn tall or that I was so short. Cursed genes. "I think you better leave before I give in to the urge to stab you."

He chuckled walking to the door. "There is never a dull moment with you." Pausing in the doorway, he leaned against the frame. "It's why I like you, Angel Eyes." He brushed a piece of loose hair behind my ear.

Without further ado, I slammed the door in his face. As usual, his laughter seeped through from the other side. This seemed to be our signature goodbye more and more lately. I think he liked it in some twisted way. It was as if he lived to get under my skin or under my shirt. Propped against the closed door, I closed my eyes and released a whoosh of breath I'd been holding from his touch.

"Angel," Mom called from upstairs.

Ugh. I had woken up sleeping beauty with my outburst. "Sorry, mom," I hollered back.

Hello Monday morning, you suck. That was my first thought of the day—lovely wasn't it? Lying in my bed, I stared at the ceiling. Today there would be many firsts for me.

First day back to school since my...*accident.* Is that what I should refer to it as? An accident?

First time I would see Brandy since she lured me into a trap. In her defense she had been compelled, so I couldn't really hold it against her. Chase on the other hand, had absolutely no qualms about holding her entirely responsible. Nothing in his thought process made any sense to me. Or maybe that was just guys in general.

First time I would be leaving the confines and security of my house. I would have to be a fool and an idiot after all I went through to not be nervous and cautious about the creepy and scary as shit things that are out there. They weren't just stuff made up in nightmares and horror films.

Rolling out of bed, I stood in front of the mirror and pulled up my t-shirt. There it was—the black swirly design. A constant reminder of *that* night, the night I became something more than human. It had been a week since that hellish night—a week of me skipping school. Mom thought I had come down with some kind of extreme illness. I told her I caught it from Chase, which in a funny way was the truth.

The intricate swirls were no longer red or caused me pain, but the mark did sometimes tingle or get warm. Tracing the tribal lines with my finger, I thought about Chase and what he had done to save me. I still didn't fully understand what he had sacrificed other than tying our souls together forever.

Forever.

It sounded so definite. Forever with Chase. I should have been horrified by the idea not...

Thrilled.

Eager.

Elated.

Huffing at my reflection, I pulled down my shirt and went to my closet. School waited whether I was ready or not. I'll admit there was some apprehension coiling in my belly. Tossing on a pair of jeans and a cardigan, I raced downstairs.

Heading into the kitchen, I went to grab myself a bowl of Lucky Charms. I could use a little luck of the Irish. There was a pink note on the granite counter that captured my attention. A small box sat under the note. It was from Mom.

Angel,

I love you dearly, but I swear if you drop this phone in the toilet, run it over with your car, or any other excuse you can come up with, it will be the last time you use a phone. Got it? I'm pretty sure the guy at the phone company thinks I eat cell phones for dinner. Please be more careful.

Love, Mom

P.S. Speaking of dinner, I made extras tonight for Chase.

Good Lord. Now my mom was cooking him dinner. He even had her wrapped around his finger. I would deal with that later, but right now I grinned as I tore open the box to my new iPhone.

Hell yeah.

The worse part of getting a new phone was that I had to input all my contacts again, which I guess wasn't as bad as it seemed. I mean, I live in Spring Valley. There really weren't that many people to add. Glancing at the clock, I realized my glee was to be short lived. If I didn't hurry my tushie, I was going to be late for school. Slipping my new kickass phone into my backpack, I threw down a bowl of leprechaun cereal just before a car horn beeped outside my house.

CHAPTER 2

The horn beeped again two seconds later. "Hold your boxers on," I mumbled. He could be so intolerable. Why had I agreed to ride with Chase and Lexi to school this morning?

Oh yeah, that's right. He hadn't given me a choice. Chase had gone all macho and bossy insisting that we ride to and from school together, for my safety of course.

What a bunch of baloney.

Grabbing my bag from the corner, I locked the front door behind me. I don't know why I bothered. There wasn't a lock Chase couldn't get around. It was on his long list of skills. There, in my driveway was a shiny, brand-spanking new, silver Audi. The color reminded me of his eyes. I was starting to think that Chase went through vehicles as much as normal people change their sheets. It was insane—and costly.

Plopping into the passenger seat, I smiled at Lexi in the back. "What happened to the bike? Don't tell me you totaled it already."

He gave me a disarming grin, ignoring my barb. "It's been retired for the season. You like?"

I shrugged. "If you're into flashy. Not my style." I was trying hard not to be impressed. It was a very attractive and sleek car—sort of like its owner.

"I'm flashy, and I'm your style," he said cockily.

Lexi snickered from the backseat.

Laying my head on the back of the seat, I groaned.

"Better buckle up. This baby has quite the pickup."

"Fabulous," I muttered under my breath, clicking the seatbelt securely in place. Just what he needed…another ultra-fast car to kill me in. Given that I could be killed—again.

We arrived at school in record time, which was a good thing, because we were running late. The bell rang just as we were walking through the parking lot. Hall High looked exactly the same as the last time I'd been here. I shuddered, not realizing how being here again was going to affect me. This school was definitely filled with unpleasant memories. Somehow I always ended up fighting for my life.

Chase was immediately at my side. "Hey, you okay? Your face just lost ten shades of color."

I nodded, unable to speak. My throat had closed up on me as I mechanically put one foot in front of the other.

Nodding for Lexi to go on ahead of us, he put a hand on my shoulder, halting my movements, and turned me toward him. "Angel, look at me." With his thumb, he titled my chin up, staring into my face. "Nothing is going to happen to you. Not while I'm here. I promise."

I wasn't convinced. "You can't be sure of that. What about when I'm alone?" Yes, I was totally acting like a frightened, needy baby, but that was exactly how I felt. No matter what I do or where I turn, trouble found me. I was like a heat seeking missile for misfortune. To make matters worse, I was now marked. There wasn't a safe corner for me to hide in.

"You won't be alone."

I gave him a funny look. "What? Are you going to follow me into the girl's bathroom?"

He smirked as if the idea held promise. "If I have to."

The big jerk probably would and enjoy it too. "Be serious, Chase."

His hands ran down my arms leaving behind tendrils of warmth. "I am actually. Look, last week Lexi and I sort of talked with administration. We rearranged our schedules so that one of us will be in your classes."

Oh goodie. I had babysitters.

By talking, he really meant they had used compulsion. I took a deep breath. Looks like I was going to be spending a whole lot more time with Chase than I ever could have imagined. If I thought one class was bad...what were multiple classes going to be like? A part of me knew I should have been outraged, not relieved, yet I couldn't rationalize anything *normal* anymore.

"Come on. We need to get to class before we're late. I wouldn't want us to spend your first day back in detention. I have plans after school."

Plans? I ignored the tiny flutter of panic that sprinted across my heart. If he was going out after school why should I care? It was not like he had to check in with me or anything. He was a free agent and able to come and go as he pleased.

Then why did I feel this irrational beating against my ribs at the thought of being away from him? It made no sense. It was not like we were with each other twenty-four seven. He lived next door for God's sake.

I was shocked how easy it was to get back into the swing of things. It helped that Chase had made sure I didn't have any homework to make-up. I am sure that this applied as cheating, but in this case I was willing to let it slide. Though I think he was using his mind-altering talents a little too freely. I was going to have to have a talk with him before it started to get out of hand.

In-between classes, Lexi (my assigned shadow for the period) and I were at my locker when I heard a voice that made me cringe and stew with distaste. I felt a foul taste in my mouth like coppery blood and battery acid. Yeah, it was that bad.

"Oh. My. God. You've got to be kidding me." Glancing over my shoulder, I found Sierra glaring at me with hate. "It's true."

I scanned the halls looking for the source of Sierra's freak-out, even though I knew she was talking about me. "What the hell is she spazzing about?" I asked Lexi beside me. I figured that the other Divisa had been brought up to speed about what went down that night. Hayden had been there, he must have told them what happened. So what was Sierra's deal? Maybe she had a hard time believing it, or maybe she was just pissed off that I hadn't died so she could have Chase to herself. Sorry to disappoint.

"I can't believe it. I just can't believe it," she went on and on like a broken record. Her screeching voice was making my ears bleed.

So much for lying low and not causing a scene on my first day back, I should have known that it would be Sierra who was the hiccup in my otherwise normal day. "Why's that so hard to believe," I spat, crossing my arms. It was no secret Sierra and I hated each other's guts, though it was probably not the smartest idea to bait her. She was part demon after all, more to the point—she was a bitch.

"I get that he saved you, is *always* saving you," she dragged out overdramatically.

I clenched my jaw.

"But this," she threw her hands in the air making her red locks fly with the exaggerated movements. "This is too far. She reeks of him."

"Sierra," Lexi warned low. "If Chase finds out about this…" Lexi's words implied that he wouldn't be happy.

She smiled smugly at me. "At least he hasn't completed the bond. One out of three, I guess that's a small consolation."

I wanted to slap that superior grin off her gorgeous face. Forget that I had no idea what she was talking about.

What the hell was going on? What did she mean I reeked of him?

Before I could demand answers, a rush of warmth spread through me, and my tramp stamp started to tingle. I didn't even need to turn around to know who stood behind me. He was like a looming force of steel.

"Is there a problem?" he asked Sierra in a condescending tone.

She glared at him over my head with tiny spears of disgust, and then promptly turned on her Dior heels and stomped gracefully down the hall. I watched in a haze of confusion and animosity as her painted on jeans sauntered away.

Hello Hall High…I'm back for your amusement. Step right up as we watch Sierra make mincemeat out of me. *Ugh.* Sometimes being a teenager sucked. Being an altered teenager bound to a half-demon was proving to be cumbersome.

Chem class proved to be even more entertaining, if that was possible. Chase assumed his bodyguard duty behind me, causing the temperature in the room to rise by about a hundred degrees. Pulling out my notebook, I heard my name whispered to my right. I glanced sideways to find Brody, the football jock, smiling at me.

His chocolate eyes were bright with excitement. "Hey, I'm glad to see you are back. We really missed you around here."

I blinked. In school this size it was impossible to not be missed. "Thanks, I think."

His boy-next-door-grin widened. "Anytime. This class just isn't the same without your pretty face."

I got the feeling that he was being overly friendly, almost as if he was into me. Not that long ago he sort of asked me to homecoming, and that hadn't ended well. I just assumed that had been the end of it. I must be the most clueless girl in the school. "I'm sure anything beats Mr. Edginton's monotone lectures," I replied, trying to downplay what I thought was a come on.

Chase shifted in seat, leaning forward and making his presence known. I don't know how anyone could forget he was in a room. Try as I might, I never could. Brody's eyes darted to Chase warily and then back to me. He cleared his throat, and I knew from the shuffle of his feet under the desk what he was going to ask before he said it. "Maybe we could, I don't know, hang out sometime."

Oh boy. He was totally nervous. And I was dumbfounded. The day wasn't even half over and this was like the third time a guy had suggested that we *hangout*. For real. The first one I figured no big deal. The second one I thought coincidence, but a third one? This had to be a joke. I most definitely was not that popular, even in a school this small.

It was on the tip of my tongue to tell him to bite me, yet... Chase leaned back into his seat and snickered. Not just any kind of snicker, the kind that made me what to make him crazy, insanely, jealous. Served him right. "Sure," I found myself answering.

Truthfully though, I knew that when the time came, I would find an excuse why I couldn't go. It probably would have been easier had I been up front with him, but I was too nice and afraid to hurt his feelings—again.

Class started shortly after that, and I was listening intently to Mr. Edgington's lecture, hanging on his every word. Okay, that was a total lie. What I was really doing was trying to pretend that Brody wasn't winking and air blowing kisses at me from the next aisle over. Uh, maybe the air-kissing was going too far, but still, what the hell? I was also trying to ignore the rapid tapping of Chase's pencil on the desktop. Apparently, I wasn't the only one who had noticed Brody's cheesy attention.

Boys could be so oblivious.

Did Brody actually think that was the kind of attention I wanted when I'd said yes? He had to be out of his mind, or more likely drunk, to try and hit on me in front of Chase. Everyone knew that we sort of had a thing going on even if *I* didn't know what exactly that thing *was*. I was pretty sure Chase was going to choke-slam him after class if the growl that came from behind was any indictor of what Chase thought of Brody's behavior.

I slumped lower in my seat, trying to make myself as small as possible. I was so ready for this day to end.

After school, Chase dropped Lexi and me at home, and then went off to do something that apparently was none of our business. I huffed and tried to pretend my heart didn't tighten as I watched him drive away. Whatever—it was fine by me, so I stuck out my chin. I had a few questions for Travis and Lexi, plus it would give Travis and me some time to gush over the upcoming release of Black Ops II. Hell yes. The video game of all video games—the newest Call of Duty. I'd been counting down the days since I pre-ordered a copy, seemingly eons ago. Travis was the only one who I could talk to, the only one who really understood.

I walked into their house after Lexi and found Travis already assuming his usual position on the couch. Devin was at work, so it was just us. I sat beside Travis. He grunted an inaudible hello, never losing concentration from the game he was absorbed with. I totally sympathized and just reclined into the couch.

"Travis, you need to get a life," Lexi announced, clearly annoyed with her brother. He ignored her. "You are such a TV hog," she whined, stretching out on the chaise.

"Sshhh. You are going to get me killed," he shot back.

Lexi pouted and grabbed the newest Victoria Secret magazine that had just come in the mail.

I should probably have intervened before things took a turn for the worst. "Have you guys noticed anything different about me? Something a normal person wouldn't pick up on?" The question had been rolling in my head since seeing Sierra.

"Yeah. You stink of Chase," Travis answered without peeling his eyes from the game.

"Funny, but I'm being totally serious here."

"So was I," he answered.

Lexi nodded her head. "No, it's true. You give off this scent that screams you belong to another half-demon."

"What do you mean scent?" I did not like where this was going at all. Not. One. Single. Bit. I didn't want to smell like Chase.

Travis dropped the remote on the table forgetting the game for a moment, a sign that this was going to be a solemn discussion. "I can see the little wheels working in your head. It's not like you think. You don't physically smell like Chase."

"Thank God," I sighed.

"Well, don't be relieved just yet. You do give of this vibe or odor that states you belong to another one of us, a half-demon. It's a way of letting others know not to mess with you—a hands-off kind of policy. Those who know Chase will recognize the signature as his. It also makes you a target for all the nasties."

"And how long have I had this *scent*?"

Lexi pulled her knees up. "Since that night."

Meaning, since the night my life changed forever. Since the night I died and Chase bartered for my soul. Since the night we became linked. "Figures. And before that, I didn't have a *scent*?"

"Nope," Travis grinned wickedly. "You were fair game then."

"And now I'm not fair game?"

"You got it toots. There isn't a Divisa around who would risk Chase's wrath by touching you. They would have to have a death wish."

I looked at Lexi for confirmation that Travis wasn't just pulling my leg. She nodded sending her blonde ponytail swishing with the movement. "Yep. You are like, sprayed with Divisa repellant."

I slumped against the back of the couch. "Great. I stink."

Travis gave me a lopsided grin, throwing an arm around my shoulder. "You might smell like crap, but Lex and I still tolerate you."

Lexi snickered from her chaise lounge.

"Thanks," I mumbled dryly. "You better not get too close, or you might wind up dead," I added snarky. I couldn't help it, I was feeling snarky.

He removed his arm slowly, a playful gleam sparkling in his turquoise eyes. "You're probably right. This face is just too damn good-looking to withstand a thrashing from Chase."

I snorted. Like that had ever stopped the two of them from going at each other like two cage fighters, if anything, he was probably looking forward to good fight with Chase.

I stayed a little while longer before hiking the short distance to my house. I had most definitely not been waiting around to see if Chase would show up—which he hadn't. Not that I cared.

There I go lying to myself, again. Maybe mentally I didn't give a monkey's butt what Chase was up to, but this link we had…um, it had a mind of its own. And it was growing more anxious by the second.

As I got ready for bed I caught myself several times picking up my new phone to call him. Since I got home, I'd spent the rest of the night messing around with all the options and adding a gazillion apps to my iPhone. It could pretty much do everything except pee for me, and I was sure there would be an app for that soon. I had customized the crap out of it, including programming Chase under Douchebag. I had quite a giggle over my ingenious.

Curled up under the covers, sleep evaded me until the moment I heard the crunching of his tires next door. Then a serene calmness overcame me, and I promptly fell to sleep.

Figures. Stupid bond. I hope he suffered miserably.

Want to continue reading Chase & Angel's story?
Grab your next Chase fix in *HUNTING ANGEL* the second book in the Divisa Series!

Here's a preview of the cover :

Can't wait to meet you back in Spring Valley!
Thank you for reading.
xoxo
Jennifer
P.S. Join my VIP Readers email list and receive a bonus scene told from Zane's POV, as well as a free copy of Saving Angel, book one in

the Bestselling Divisa Series. You will also get notifications of what's new, giveaways, and new releases.

Visit here to sign up: www.jlweil.com

Don't forget to also join my Dark Divas FB Group and have some fun with me and a fabulous, fun group of readers. There is games, prizes, and lots of book love.

You can stop in and say hi to me on Facebook night and day. I pop in as often as I can: https://www.facebook.com/jenniferlweil/ I'd love to hear from you.

THE DIVISA SERIES

(Full series completed – Teen Paranormal Romance)

Losing Emma: A Divisa novella

Saving Angel

Hunting Angel

Breaking Emma: A Divisa novella

Chasing Angel

Loving Angel

Redeeming Angel

LUMINESCENCE TRILOGY

(Full series completed – Teen Paranormal Romance)

Luminescence

Amethyst Tears

Moondust

Darkmist – A Luminescence novella

RAVEN SERIES

(Full series completed – Teen Paranormal Romance)

White Raven

Black Crow

Soul Symmetry

BEAUTY NEVER DIES CHRONICLES

(Teen Dystopian Romance)

Slumber

Entangled

Forsaken

NINE TAILS SERIES

(Teen Paranormal Romance)

First Shift

Storm Shift

Flame Shift

Time Shift

SINGLE NOVELS

Starbound

(Teen Paranormal Romance)

Dark Souls

(Runes KindleWorld Novella)

Casting Dreams

(New Adult Paranormal Romance

Ancient Tides

(New Adult Paranormal Romance

For an updated list of my books, please visit my website: www.jlweil.com

Join my VIP email list and I'll personally send you an email reminder as soon as my next book is out! Click here to sign up: www.jlweil.com

ABOUT THE AUTHOR

USA TODAY Bestselling author J.L. Weil lives in Illinois where she writes Teen & New Adult Paranormal Romances about spunky, smart mouth girls who always wind up in dire situations. For every sassy girl, there is an equally mouthwatering, overprotective guy. Of course, there is lots of kissing. And stuff.

An admitted addict to Love Pink clothes, raspberry mochas from Starbucks, and Jensen Ackles. She loves gushing about books and Supernatural with her readers.

Stalk Me Online
www.jlweil.com
jenniferlweil@gmail.com

Made in United States
North Haven, CT
01 November 2023

43482974R00139